Anthropology

A Science Fiction Anthology

Finley J E Clayton

For Mum, read the foreword...

Contents

Part 1: Anthropocene

The Sneeze   6

Revolution   8

Landing Site   12

Bronze Age Collapse   20

Socratic Dystopia   33

Caesar's Flying Column   52

The Connecticut Yankee   64

Vitruvian Man   73

Treaty of Ypres   79

Slash and Burn   83

A Pitch to Boeing   86

Part 2: The Discreditable Future

The Children Can't Hop Anymore   96

The Algorithm   98

Road Resident   127

One Child Army   134

Neo-Imperium   155

A Century of Martian Excavations 158

Orbital Stew 208

First Contact 210

The Great BBQ 216

Conscientious Objections 220

Electric Theatre 246

Progrom 283

Conference Call 285

Digital Puritans 289

Asimov's Stack of Paper, a foreword to Anthropocene

When Isaac Asimov imagined his future galaxy, set 50,000 years ahead of us with its own rich and logical history, he imagined it all revolving about the capital planet of Trantor. Trantor, in his foundation series, is the capital of the Empire and home to 40,000,000,000 souls, all pushing bits of paper to keep the Galactic Empire in order. With underground tunnels connecting the administrative buildings what he describes is a planetary computer, just running on humans. Many of the leaders in his books are shown in relation to their paper stacks, some neglecting the tasks of leadership as they pile up, or others neatly organising their work in a characterisation of their efficiency. But not 20 years after he published, it was an unrealistic projection of the future. Computers made bits of paper and the people who push them obsolete. I'd imagine he knew this, that in 100 years everything would change, then again and again and again until the world was incomprehensibly unrecognisable to him. So why did he hide his characters behind improvements of 1950's technologies, when he possessed a special mind capable envisioning a perfectly realistic future world?

Because we like to read about the familiar. But it was slightly more than that, it's about not alienating an audience. That is not to say that any given author who can imagine the realistic likelihoods of a given future is preaching to a mass of idiots. The truth is that with the same information, reasonably smart people (most of us in the educated world) will come to, or at least understand similar forecasts. For example, we can make a pencil float on a desk by manipulating waves, therefore in a thousand years this will probably form a more widespread function. So in my book, I have a door open for my character using such a manor. But then why not hold open his pockets the same way? Or even make all his clothes out of waves holding his bits in place and manipulating a dye to depict the perfect fashion of the day covering his modesty? This would be the likely eventual outcome of wave manipulation technology. However, it is so different to our current lives, that it requires a tiresome amount of imagination to constantly place yourself in a world with all these tweaks. This occurs to an Nth degree, when you apply this to every possible technology that exists today, or could exist in a future world you create. It becomes a thought exercise instead of entertainment.

In most sci-fi universes, the scene is not an accurate prediction of the future, rather a lick of futuristic paint over the world we already live in. I am not an academic futurist, I just have occasional ideas about what the future could include and put them in my fiction to save them from serious criticism. The purpose of this anthology is not to accurately predict the future, but to tell stories that sometime rely on an abstract or futuristic idea.

I am new to science fiction, both as a consumer and an author. I have taken my inspiration from a wide range of sources, from academic futurist literature to throw away drunk conversations. On a daily basis I consume a great number or articles, YouTube videos and conservations relating to the concepts in this book, and where possible I will try to credit my inspirations in the notes of this book. If you find yourself reading my book and think 'hey, I'm sure I've heard this theme before' or 'that argument came from person X!', then you're probably right. Although to my pride a surprising number of the stories in this anthology (at least to my knowledge) are entirely of my creation from theme, to technology to arch, a great number are not. I'm not ashamed of this in the slightest, and will do my best in the notes to honestly record my inspirations and sources of each story, so that whoever conceived the idea may receive the credit due.

With the (shamefully self-) publication of this book a huge thank you is also owed to my friend Mary Taylor Lewis. Mary you were the first to read this cover to cover and that means a lot to me. Additionally your extensive and honest advise on how I ought to revise my stories and encouragement to even publish have been invaluable. I'd promise to make the next one less grim, but as you've already read the sequel you'll know that's a lie. Thank you for your encouragement and tips, and here's to making the third part less grim, though I should warn you it's currently called *Dark Age*…

A big thank you is also owed to Holly Pitkin for the wonderful cover art. I don't know where else I'd be able to find an artist willing to draw a picture of an astronaut being penetrated so hard by a rocket that they reached escape velocity.

As always I want to thank my eternal rock, Flo. Flo you've let me slunk off for countless hours alone with my computer where many other girlfriend's wouldn't. You've listened to me chatting shit as we slipped into sleep, encouraged my art with your own and always been supportive of what I want to do. Thank you for standing tall (as you can) with me when things are good, catching me when I fall and being there when I can't get up.

Now this bit is for you Mum. Although I have now decided to name this the far more marketable 'Anthropocene', that is not the true name of this collection of stories. For a while I codenamed this loose project 'Rocket Donkey', a way to conceal the true name 'The Rocket Up the Arse Anthology'. You'll remember in February of 2018 when I missed a vital deadline for university, you and Dad were understandably disappointed in me (as I was of myself) and you said I needed a 'rocket up the arse'. I agreed completely, and even wrote down an early version of this forward that same evening. This collection of stories is the rocket up my arse. It has focussed me, allowed me to realise my goals and who I am and caused me to develop further as a writer in a few months than I had in all my previous life. Thank you for being supportive of my work when it's good, harsh when I'm stagnant and always loving as my mother. So this anthology is for you Mum, for all the support, the carrots and the sticks throughout my life that have guided me to where I am now. Most of all, thank you for launching a rocket up my arse, lets see how far I fly.

Back to the reader, I hope you enjoy my stories as much as I enjoyed writing them, and that they spark in some of you that same creative inspiration my sources did in me. Keep always in mind that this is a loose and fictional projection of the future of our solar system. I hope you enjoy my lick of paint.

Finley J E Clayton

Part 1: Anthropocene

The Sneeze

3,000,000,000 B.C, Earth

The two aliens stepped hopefully out of their landing craft, surveying the potential real estate. One looked about happily at the prospects and the other clung to its arm lovingly. Perhaps they would make a home here. The mountains were black, the air was ashy, the heavy bombardment of asteroids comforted the creatures and the lack of a pesky ozone layer allowed for plenty of ultra violet light to sterilise their days. Not that they seemed to need sterilisation, the surface rocks bubbled temperately as magma, glowing and pleasantly reforming again and again over themselves. A third alien, a real estate agent stepped down off the ramp.

'I can see you love it already! Great place to start a hive am I right? Let me give you the basics. It's the third planet out from this star, which I know sounds a little far out but as you can see it's lovely and warm here. It has a moon too, far bigger in ratio to the planet than you'll find anywhere else for such a good price, and isn't it pretty to look at? As you can feel the gravity is a little light, but oh how your hivelings will leap about the place! So, what do you say?'

'It's lovely!' said one of the couple. 'But so far out from the star, I'm worried about long term cool down, it's already a little chilly here for my liking, and the dust, it's a little…' the alien sneezed violently. 'Well you see what I mean… I don't know sweetness, what do you think?'

'That if it's not perfect it's not for us', the alien hugged its partner and nodded to the real estate alien to take them for their next viewing.

Wriggling in the boiling rock behind them were a few microbes in the alien's snot. Of course they perished, all but the toughest ones, which had to reduce themselves to the size of a single cell, and linger, for a very long time… Eventually they multiplied once more, the planet grew water oceans and the cells became fish, the fish walked onto the land and the land inherited a wealth of creatures big and small, animal and anthropic.

Revolution

10,000 B.C, Eurasia

'Ooga!' hissed Booga from the bushes. 'Oi! Ooga!' the hairy human looked up this time, catching his thumb between the two flints he was knapping and uttering a long since forgotten swear word. 'Ooh, sorry mate... Put the bloody flints down and get over here, I have something to show you!'

'Ooh is it berries?'

'No, it isn't berries'

'A deer?!'

'It isn't a deer'

'Oh shit it's a lion isn't it?' Ooga turned back into the clearing, searching the scorched ground for something to hide under. A log? An animal hide? That would be appropriate.

'No Ooga, it isn't a lion, just come with me!' Booga barked, now losing his patience.

The two cavemen, horrifically misnamed as neither had either the desire or bravery to set foot in the dark and rocky inconvenience of the subterranean world, walked through the thicket of the forest. They were hunter-gatherers, the chic new name modern man had coined to discern how exactly he was different in any way than the other animals of the forest. It was a late Mesolithic media spin, a lick of paint over the human form, not to be mistaken for the actual red ochre paint over their human forms (about the only thing Ooga or Booga wore).

Humanity had gotten all high and mighty of recent. It all began a few millennial decades earlier, when some wise cracking super ape thought it would be funny to draw an abusive and racially charged picture of his boss on a cave wall. It took off, the apes started drawing things. It started off simple enough, a way to express and communicate, but it got darker. Anti-Neanderthal propaganda emerged, plastered on cave entrances, dividing the two peoples. That was before the Neanderthals disappeared. Completely off the face of the earth! Right after the humans had that argument with them. Booga often wondered what became of those furry friends of his...

In hindsight they began calling it a cognitive revolution, fancy name for some scratches on rocks, but the humans took to it. The Palaeolithic was declared obsolete. They were to move into a new age, the Mesolithic. One defined by the betterment of the species, new ideas and more importantly newer names for them. Ooga fancied himself a tribal inventor of sorts, knapping all sorts of weird shapes into rocks, hoping something useful would tumble out into his palm. Creatively speaking he was amidst a severe dry patch, having produced little more than sharp flakes of recent.

Booga lead Ooga away from the clearing where the band had settled for the night, out through the woods and to its edge, where wide fields of grass opened out to the horizon. It was an often ignored place. Sure, it had its herds, but it was harder to sneak up on them, harder to divide them between the trees and catch up for the almighty butchery. Then something most strange emerged.

'What's this?' asked Ooga.

'Well this is what I came to show you'

'Is that a hunting cabin?'

'Of sorts yes. Just let me speak will you? So I've made this little invention, it's a new way of getting food. Instead of gathering and hunting, I call it growing and killing'

'So you're a grower killer?'

'Okay, I'll work on the name… But anyway, you heard of those fences they were using up in Denmark? To trap herds as they migrated. Okay good, because they're going to be very important. I found this plant thing, grows and you can eat it. Instead of walking around looking for lots of it to eat, I simply put lots of it in one place and when it's ready I'll harvest it. And here, between some of those fences, I've captured some goats. Turns out you can milk them'

'How did you find that out?'

'Trial and error'

'Hmm'

'Anyway, when I feel like meat, I simply kill it and butcher it, no chasing. Smart right?'

'You mean you'll live with them, feed them, watch them grow up then kill and eat them?'

10

'Yes'

'That's a bit psychopathic Booga! But I like the sentiment' Ooga stepped over a fence, walked into the field and took up a vegetable ripely sitting on the churned surface, then set to gnawing at it. 'But what if everyone else finds out? Like decides they want to eat the food you put here?'

'They can't'

'Why not?'

'Because its mine'

'What?'

'Like this land and the stuff on it, it's only for my use. Since I put the fence up'

'But the world is shared, and the fence comes from wood which came from the forest which, we share!'

'Yeah about that, I thought maybe if we don't. Like, everyone can put up their own fences and then those bits will be theirs'

'Well why is this bit yours?'

'Because I'm here now'

'What if you weren't?'

'Well… Well I hadn't thought about that…' Booga scratched his chin, thinking for a solution. At that moment Ooga brought an adze down through his skull, rolled the body outside the fence and smiled. Proud to be the world's first farmer.

Landing Site

2560 B.C, Giza

The sun rippled with the curvature of the saucer's dome as the craft descended. It was a hot, yellow tinted sun, the waves of which more than resembled the sand dunes sprawling themselves wide across the distance. Not like the ground underneath however. No, that was green, or otherwise dark and rich with fertility. The alien officer looked through the curved dome, squinting his hjasdim under the light of the sun.

The Nile was like a root through the dessert, gently ushering the fertile alluvial soils along its river beds. Civilisation grew from it, like the leaves from a branch, dark and different against the light of the dessert sky. The alien smiled, for it was more than a fertile slip in the dry desserts. The ground would be lush and green without interference. The Nile would still roll the life giving mud, flood at appointed times and flow without prompt. The alien smiled because of the buildings in between.

The patches of fertile land took on less natural shapes. They were manged. They were lived in. There were humans here.

'They're still here' he said fondly to the pilot.

'What did you expect?' he asked in reply.

'I don't know, I was just…'

'Worried'

'Yeah, I like the old things' he reasoned. The observation team of which the two aliens were a part had been assigned to the Earth system for a few months now. Though Earth and some of the moons around the gas giants were the only bodies showing reasonable signs of life, they had to fly elsewhere, just to check. The aliens had been posted to Mars, to see if life had returned. It hadn't, and so they had promptly returned to their preferred planet.

Being on live observation had been a long and boring game, billions of years of cataloguing slight improvements to the bacterial slime on the planet below. Sure, there was a biological explosion every now and then, producing all sorts of weird creatures. But they were stuck in a billion year survival loop. It left the aliens with no one to talk to, very little to do. For all their apparent intricacies, all the over-evolved slime balls walking, swimming, flying or otherwise traversing the face of Earth stuck to a very limited list of activities. Primarily eating, sleeping, fucking, birthing and dying.

The stagnation, as they'd call it in their history book, had become so bad that they'd had to… Accelerate, things. Sometimes one had to break the rules, many hundreds of them in fact, to properly oversee life. The creatures of Earth were stuck. Stuck! The conditions were simply too fair, nature too kind and thus selecting too many of the same genes to pass onto the next generation. Evolution happened, sure, but no intelligence! Any organism could learn to fight, run or swim its way out of a survival situation, but that produced nothing of long term use. What the aliens were after was intelligence, the weaker things that consequently had to think their way out of unpleasant situations. So they nudged an asteroid into the surface of the earth to speed things up and badabing badabomb within 55 million years they had the beginnings of a half decent intelligence.

Back home the two aliens were total losers. Why would too successful Omithors volunteer to exile themselves to the wrong side of the galaxy to watch over some bacteria? But when the humans came about, boy did those two losers start to feel godly! They'd swoop below the clouds to watch how things were going, even the slightest glimpse of them would breed three different religions. It was fantastic. They watched as the spears became sharper and longer, then as the emerging humans used them to stab everything in sight. They stabbed the animals, each other and eventually, the ground!

That was the real breakthrough, as stabbing the ground revealed agriculture. Why wait for the berries to be in season when you could plant something better? From there it was another explosion, not of species but civilisations. They'd start around rivers and in fertile basins. Tribal farmsteads would unite and in the best cases, there would be states.

The Aliens had to pick one to champion them, and decided to go with the Egyptians. They'd spoken with their leader, given them advanced mathematics and tools then as protocol dictated, left for a few hundred years to see what they would do with it. If they worked together on megalithic projects, then it was a success. They had the group work gene and could thus be admitted into the divine council of intergalactic civilisations. If however they entered a dark age and forgot it, well then it was back to the drawing board.

'They did it!' said the alien proudly looking out of the window. It looked down over the stones, dragged for miles by slaves, they could figure that one out later, and wrought into a cacophony of wonderful shapes.

'Bit messy isn't it?' asked the other Alien.

'What do you mean?'

'Well, there's those dog headed people, that's a bit of a mess' it pointed at an enormous statue, human up to the neck then otherwise canine.

'Ah… No, it's imaginative!'

'No it isn't! They just took two things they already had and spliced them together. That isn't imagination, that's reorganisation' it corrected.

'Fine, but look at those! Those triangular things! What do you reckon they are?'

'Bloody hell, they're pretty good actually. Are you sure we didn't help them with those?'

'Positive'

'What are they for?'

'Let's find out' the alien swooped the craft down to land at the river's edge. A shocked farmer looked up from his work, where he had been poking the squishy soil with a stick. The farmer didn't speak Alien, then as they attempted to translate it transpired that he also did not speak Egyptian. The confused man ran off down the river and fetched a passing group of officials on horseback. Their arrival was announced by the gold glint of their kopeshes, radiant light slicing through the bushes. The horsemen pulled up.

'Greetings!' said the Alien officer. 'We have returned!'

'You have the pharaohs' hospitality' said the Egyptian, bowing low. 'We have used the technology you have given us to craft you a landing pad!' he announced. The Alien Officer tried to contain his joy. This was perfect. Not only had they cooperated and not annihilated themselves, but had remembered the aliens to which they owed their success and constructed a monument of practical use!

'Brilliant!' replied the Alien Officer. 'Where is it?' The Egyptian drew his kopesh and pointed over the bushes, where three triangular objects loomed over the horizon.

'Oh yes' said the Pilot. 'We were going to ask. What are those?'

'Isn't it obvious?' boomed the Egyptian.

'No' said both aliens at once.

'It's a landing site for your flying saucer' he grinned widely, genuinely pleased with what his culture had to offer.

'A landing site?' asked the officer. 'Which bit are we supposed to land on? Do they point to a landing site or?'

'No, you land right on top of them'

'Right on top of a pyramid. On the point?' The Alien Officer now felt like he was talking to a child.

16

'Exactly'

'Ah...' He looked at the pilot, then with their best impression of a friendly expression they took off.

'I can't land on that' said the pilot. 'Are they fucking mad?'

'No, just a little underdeveloped. Look, this is politically sensitive. We're about to welcome these people into a galactic civilisation. Should we really start by insulting their gift? At least try to land on it'

'But it's triangular and pointy. Who on earth would think it was an appropriate place to land anything? Let alone a literal saucer? I mean have they ever managed to safely toss a plate onto the tip of a spear? Of course they haven't, because it's a terrible fucking idea!' protested the pilot.

'Look, just do it!' ordered the Officer. They nervously began shifting the saucer toward the Pyramid, hovering briefly to decide which one they were supposed to land on. As the ship came closer and closer to the hypothesised landing site, the success of the operation slipped deeper and deeper into unlikely hood. After a minute of nervous aerial back and forth, the two aliens found themselves looking down through the floor screen at the spear sharp tip of the white glistening monument.

'Oh my god it's a bit high isn't it?'

'You're a pilot damn it, land!' shouted the officer. They paused, looking down at the expectant faces of the Egyptians below them, who had gathered in an excited mass. 'Fuck, they're so proud of themselves' mumbled the

Officer. 'Look, an intergalactic union between species relies on this single moment. If we spurn their... Landing site,' it hesitated to use the word. 'Then we'll be setting our worlds off to a bad start. We have no option but to-'

The Pilot pulled gently down with the joystick trying to set the saucer down atop the pyramid. As the final millimetres closed a thousand lines of inquiry opened. How would they balance the saucer on top of the pyramid? Why did the Egyptians build such a thing? If they landed, how would they get down? The last millimetre closed. The hardened stone tip of the monument contacted with the underside of the space ship's hull. It pierced.

In an instant the ship lost power and began toppling fatally down the steep sides of the monument. The crowd below gasped as they watched their gods tumble from heaven, then winced as the clearing dust brought the crashed wreck into focus. They'd done it. With all their maths and hard work, they'd over complicated the landing pad to impress the gods. And now they were dead! They would be the embarrassment of all mankind. Mankind could not know.

The Pharaoh had everyone in attendance killed, last of all himself. They bore complicated and trapped tunnels and chambers into the failed landing pad, then piled the shards of the space ship and all the bodies inside, then sealed it forever. That ought to have done it. The pyramids were after all clearly a bizarre megalithic monument. Meant to show off the engineering skill of Egypt, to use the logically stable shape of a pyramid to climb as high into the heavens as possible. The enormous blocks would be presumed not to have been moved with alien tractor beams, but slaves. You could do anything with enough slaves these days! Looking at the shape of them in his final moments the Pharaoh decided that his terrible secret was safe. Who on earth would think that the Pyramids were an alien landing site?

Bronze Age Collapse

1200 B.C, Mycenae

The Mycenaean Merchant looked out through the wide porch of his villa, down the cliff stones sun bleached nearly white, to the deep blue of the Mediterranean. Far off a ship dipped front first timidly over the horizon, one of his, bound for North Africa where it would trade the wares of Greece for the exotic offerings of the east. Slaves? Spices? Something new? He wondered for a moment after his ship, as it dipped front first over the apparent curve of the horizon. He wondered of the wider world, of all the horizons to dip over. If they ever became so steep that one could fall off them. If so, where would one land? More interestingly, if they do not eventually dip to the traveller's restriction, where do they go?

Antikytherus coughed, snapping the attentions of the Merchant back to the cool of his porch. It was aimed at the sea, to catch all the cool it could, what little was blown in off the sea on those hot summer days. Perhaps the ship now gone behind the horizon would bring back cool, and he could trade it for all the gold of Greece. That would be wonderful.

'My apologies Antikytherus!' Said the Merchant. 'I always watch to see my ships safe over the horizon. Something new you say?'

'Yes, my latest invention'

'Go on then! Let's see this triumph of yours'

'Well it is no triumph, rather a taste of the true glory to come, it's the beginning of something' the inventor fumbled at a bag tied tightly around his waist, more than a little reminiscent of a babe feeding at its mother's breast. He pulled a tab, untied a string and opened the bag, then with the utmost delicacy removed what appeared to be little more than a bronze plate. He removed a section of thick cloth and unrolled it onto the table, then with unbroken care set the thing down upon the fabric. Intrigued, the Merchant took a step closer.

Stooping his head over the plate and screwing up the edges of his eyes he begun to focus on the details. The plate was overall circular, thick more like a stack of ten plates at least. The outer rim was flat bronze, polished to a near silver finish. Antikytherus watched the merchant with the same intensity as the Merchant beheld the plate, then when he saw sure he was done observing the outside of the plate, he opened it! A little switch, so small and fine as it had evaded the Merchant's observation was flicked and the plate opened up, revealing smaller and serrated circles, laid over and in each other. Antikytherus began to turn something, a little lever that set the entire device into motion, bits of bronze rolling over themselves like the clouds of a tempest. After a while he stopped, closed the hatch and flipped the device over, revealing the underside. The underside was the same as the top, but with little windows displaying numerals and letters. On their own they ticked over, clicking and eventually settling on a figure. Antikytherus allowed the Merchant to squint over it for a minute or two before putting him out of his misery.

'It's a calculation of the date exactly four years from now'

'Oh…' he sounded deflated. 'Well it's not the date that concerns me Antikytherus, it's the device itself. Why I've never seen bronze wrought so beautifully, how did you cast such small pieces so precisely that they move both as one and their own?'

'Simple craftsmanship sir' he said humbly.

'So the date. What's the importance?'

'Well there isn't one. I simply set this machine to calculate it, the importance is that it did it. See here, when I open up the back, by moving these switches and these values I can ask the device to calculate certain numerical problems, which by precise moving of the inner cogs it does'

'It lives?!'

'No sir, but it certainly thinks'

'Metal that thinks…' he pondered it for a moment. 'Why young man, you have certainly earned my investment, but I am left wondering why you need it? You have after-all already created, this…'

'Computer'

'Computer, yes. What could you possibly need my money for?'

'This' he tapped the computer 'is simply a proof of concept. Proof that metal can be engineered to perform mathematics. What I seek your investment for is something far greater, a true thought machine. One where you can enter your thoughts as though you were writing, then have them stored in the machine where other people can access and modify them. I hope to create a library that all the greatest minds can contribute to, where human knowledge can excel beyond all else'

'But how?'

'I will be working on the principle of the abacus. What I need your patronage for is to allow me to dedicate myself to this task, for years if I must, until I have created a true thinking machine'

'And once you begin selling this machine?'

'I will give you a quarter of my earnings, on top of a complete return on your investment'

'It seems we have a deal young Antikytherus. Go, take as much gold as you need and go, don't come back until you have completed your most glorious task!'

*

Ten years passed before the inventor returned. Ten winters, each in which the Merchant worried with growing pessimism that he'd been swindled, taken for a ride, or rather that the inventor had taken a ride with his money. As the uncertainty of time passed over his memories he began to question the device he'd seen so long ago. He remembered the cogs, the glint of the bronze in the summer orange sun. Did it move? Sure, things could move, nothing new. A chariot's wheel, an archer's bow, the curtains that fluttered on the edge of his porch. Locomotion was hardly an invention, and if it was to be considered as such then the credit surely laid upon the work of Zeus or some other sky fatherly deity!

The invention that captured his mind so intensely that all logic fought to rebrand the memory imagination, was the calculation, or whatever produced it. Had it really thought? That little plate? A small appliance of critical thinking would suggest that it was more likely the inventor had played a trick, some illusive sleight of hand at just the right moment. Some distraction, perfectly timed twitching of the shiny shiny plate. Downright idiotic to fall for such a trick! But what if it wasn't?

Ten years and the free time bought by the Merchant's various income streams provided a lot of time to speculate on that. On the periodical peaks of his rising and falling expectation for that device and its future he got to wondering what one could do with such a think? For one the precision of the cogs proved the inventor, Antikytherus, had a knack for machinery like no other. He'd put any cart maker on the Aegean to shame. He was clearly capable of applying more precision to movement, and could therefore make intricate moving vessels. Like carts, but with the legs of an ox, the legs of a man or the wings of a bird! And the thinking, why he could mount this inside these vessels. A mind, almost human, but free of the awkwardness of the bipedal body. They could have wheels or wings, there would be no limit.

Sure, the thinking task Antikytherus had demonstrated so long ago was simple. But did not men start off the same way? Gargling and shitting themselves for years on end, rolling around uselessly hoping something smarter would have the kindness to intervene and make sure they didn't freeze, starve or otherwise die? And out of that immense stupidity did not the greatest minds of the thinker arise? Perhaps it was a long way off, but eventually, the Merchant decided, the thinking machines would become wise. He could talk with them, if Antikytherus could invent some means of them vocalising. Mount a harp to the device? Use the notes to spell out words? It could work...

The Merchant thought some more on intelligent design, began wondering where he and everyone else came from. Promethean tinkering or cosmic accident? Perhaps humans were just the thinking machines of whoever came before got out of hand. Will Antikytherus' plates replace us? Despite the summer heat he shivered a little when that thought came into his mind. He tried to push it out with optimism. Perhaps he would become one of the machines, his mind placed in immortal metal, he could live forever, ascend mount Olympus and join the rest of the immortals. He dared not apply critical thinking however to this fantasy, recalling what typically happened to the wild life when men like him decided to make a new pasture.

Then one day a ship poked up over the horizon, not one of his, but headed straight for him. The Merchant expected that if young Antikytherus returned it would be with a retinue of machines, thinking and moving for him. Admittedly in the passing of ten of each season he had become a little carried away with his ideas of how to apply the new technology. When at last the young man, a little less young, returned it was on a simple bark, and he hopped out splashing down in the light surf like any other man.

'Antikytherus!' announced the Merchant, booming from the shore with his arms spread in sweaty embrace. 'Oh how I've wondered after you, come, come! We must welcome you, why if you'd sent word ahead I'd have arranged a symposium. Pray, what word do you bring? And who are these fine gentlemen at your side?'

'Hello to you too old friend. These are the Sea People'

'Sea People?!' the Merchant was aghast. He'd heard terribly vague yet somehow terrible tidings about such men. Little snippets making their way onto the open roads from burnt cities. A new people, a conquering people, bearing new arms, armour and prowess. New metal even! Iron, the Merchant had held some. Ugly stuff in the glow of bronze, but apparently superior in certain respects. Mixed with coal it could bend like a bow arm, retain an edge and all this in a longer, lighter package than any of its bronze counterparts.

'Hah!' Antikytherus was amused. 'Oh don't worry, they're just tradesmen. You know how people are when foreigners workers come in, like to exaggerate. No these are my affiliates'

'Affiliates?' he thought for a moment. 'Ah! Then you come bearing news of your device. Have you wrought it in iron, iron bought from these Sea People? Tell me, what benefits can one gain by using iron in lieu of bronze'

'None' he said, disarmingly and with a smile. 'No it's far less malleable than bronze, see I need something soft, that I can cast, cut out with precision. These fellows just use iron tools for installation is all'

'Installation?'

'Yes, of my device, let me show you the returns of your investment'

*

The two men left the boat and the Sea People in their wake, walking up the white rocks of the cliff face. The summer heat radiated off them, like warm breath from the very alive stone on which the Merchant's villa sat. Behind them the Sea People were already at work, hammering something into the side of and up the cliffs. The Merchant looked with mild worry, only slightly over come by his intrigue at whatever device Antikytherus had wrapped up in his arms.

They walked into the porch, where Antikytherus immediately set to ordering the slaves about. 'I'll need a large table, take the fruit off and put it in the breeziest part of the room. You. Go fetch a chair that will fit under the table and you go help my men with their equipment' when he was done ordering everyone around he set the cloth package down and unwrapped it. Inside was a small square plate, on which little tablets displaying the alphabet were arranged. The entire device hummed gold, polished to a mirror in which the Merchant saw distorted the lines of his face as he examined the panel.

'The tablets, they're remarkable, but out of order' he said at last.

'Yes, I had a linguist in Egypt with a good knowledge of our tongue analyse the alphabet and the distribution of its characters within common communication. Here I have arranged them in a manner that they will compliment your typing'

'My typing?'

'Ah, sorry yes... Years of work produce a dialect of terminologies! Typing is like writing, but instead of using papyrus and ink, you press these tablets. When you press them the corresponding letter displayed upon their surface will be recorded. Press them in the order in which you would write and you can form words, sentences and books'

'This produces books? Why that is wonderful! Every man will be able to record his innermost thought without worry at expenditure of papyrus! You must remind me to sell my papyrus stock before this device hits the market...'

'It can produce books, but there is a far greater use. Allow me to show you'

At that precise moment to Sea People huffed into the porch before heaving an enormous box down upon the table. The legs creaked a moment, then settled. Antikytherus removed the cloth concealing the device, then slotted it into the tablet board. 'This is the page if you will. I'll demonstrate...' he tapped a few keys at random, each in turn popping up on long arms into a viewing area, semi circular and reminiscent of the stage. The Merchant inhaled preceding his praise of the device, before Antikytherus raised a finger of pause for more. 'Now if we slot this page into this pipe we will connect to the Mediterranean Net' the Sea People moved forward, connecting the device to a pipe they'd run from the shore to the villa.

'This is where my affiliation with the Sea People comes in. If one were to connect this book making device

28

to another they could via these pipes exchange words and thoughts. I created this machine within a week of your investment. The past 10 years have been spent making more, distributing them and connecting them. The Sea People are a simple race of seafarers, nothing ominous about them. They hail from an island nation named Atlantis, where I have constructed my server. The server is named such because it serves all the machines like this one, relaying their messages from one to the other. It is an enormous machine, where out of metal I have constructed a path of gates through which information can flow, be adjusted and exchanged. What a man types in Egypt will go through his pipe, to the server via underwater pipes. There my server will convert his language into yours, before sending it via pipe to your page to be displayed as text here' he finished pointing at the characters on screen.

'Today is the agreed launch date for these devices, where my men on Atlantis will open the gates allowing words to flow between machines. At present there are fewer than 10 users including yourself, but I hope to expand the operation inland to reach the masses. In the machinery of the server I have created if you will a place, called the auditorium, a chat room where you can discuss with the other users. Shall we try it out?' With nervous excitement the Merchant nodded, flexing his hands and placing them upon the writing tablet. 'I've taken the liberty of naming your device Mycenae_500, the other users have named their own'

There was a click of metal locomotion from the pipe, which flowed into the Merchant's. After a second characters on long arms elevated themselves in the air, reading: AUDITORIUM.ATLANTIS. He placed his hands and began to type.

Mycenae_500: Hello? Anyone there?

EgyptianPIMP900: Yo, what up?

Mycenae_500: I'm from Mycenae, it's a pleasure to make your acquaintance. To think, how with the marvel of Antikytherus's invention two minds separated by ocean and immeasurable distance may exchange thoughts, words and good will. I...

EgyptianPIMP900: How big is ur pyramid?

Mycenae_500: I live in a villa actually, but I find it very interesting and productive to learn about the dwellings in which you...

EgyptianPIMP900: Lol pyramid's is better!!!!

Mycenae_500: And I respectfully think that...

Fraktin: Oi oi Hittites in tha house!

EgytianPIMP900: Yo wtf m8? I saw u movin up on my territory the other week

Fraktin: Yeah well you killed my scouts

EgyptianPIMP900: And they died like lil bitches

Fraktin: Fuck u. Oi Graeco boi, you in with this triangle dwelling dweeb?

Mycenae_500: I believe this is a place where we are all "in" with one and other. Do you not see we are now one by the magic of...

EgyptianPIMP900: I AM A LITERAL GOD

Fraktin: Keep telling urself that. You're a tard with a funny hat and a weird shaped house

EgyptianPIMP900: Hey I don't live in the Great Pyramids, they're our tombs

Fraktin: Same thing innit? What with your dead social life

EgyptianPIMP900: I'll put you in a fucking tomb

Fraktin: Like to see u try. Gay boi

Mycenae_500: Now there's no need for!

Fraktin: Grapes are shit and so's goat's milk. U is a joke Greekie. EGYPT IS HITTITE #removepyramid

EgyptianPIMP900: 1v1 me prick, I'm getting my Kopesh

Fraktin: Ooh I'm so scared! Dipshit. I'm coming 4 u next Mycenae lol

MesopotamiaMilitaryServices.LTD: *Started a bid for "Military Service"*

EgyptianPIMP900: WTF? Snake!

Fraktin: I'll let u keep Egypt if u ice this pussy

MesopotamiaMilitaryServices.LTD: *Has accepted your offer*

EgyptianPIMP900: brb, rebellion.

Fraktin: I'm gonna flatten his hook nose

Mycenae_500: Brothers! Please! Stop this madness. Do you not see what we have here? Antikytherus has blessed the world with his communication machines. He has enabled mortal men to talk freely to one and other, regardless of distance, language or creed. This net which he has thrown over us should unite us as one, not inspire hate for men you've never met. Let us use this wonderful forum to hold debate and celebrate our differences, not widen them. Shall we start over? Use this internet between us as a way to connect and a tool of love?

EgyptianPIMP900: Lol gay

    The Merchant stood up, throwing the writing tablet across his porch, roaring to his servants. 'Get my fucking sword, we're going to Egypt! I'm going to make what we did to troy look like a fucking day spa'

Socratic Dystopia

399 B.C. Athens

Socrates walked away clear of the venue. It would take a lot of polishing to turn this into a respectable dialogue. The names were in position, Plato and Socrates, topic in place, food, and the arguments had been laid out for all the world too hear. Through the streets of Athens men of influence weaved their ways back to their villas, under the sun hot canvases of the market stalls, each flogging their wares. Elixirs of health, magic potions and other snake oil nonsense.

More markets than not were selling not the magic cures to all ailments, rather the causes. Food, decadent food was strewn in abundance. Bits of lamb going off under the sun, the flies feasting before any of the buyers and the milk souring in the casks around. Socrates hoped that enlightened by his points, a few more of those men of influence would pass these stalls with a little more thought. That his words might have inspired change, a better Athens, a better Greece and a better world.

Diets were the newest fad in Athens, hippy gurus preaching from behind every pillar about humours this and humus that. Though not as invested as some of the movement's more passionate members, Socrates too had become interested in the correlation between diet and health. But he was not a man of fads, rather facts, and so began extensively researching the topic. After a while, he had dived so far into the issue that he was beyond the surface problem of human health, and instead exploring the deep societal repercussions of the Greek palate!

He knew the truth, and it felt like *only* he knew it. Everyone else had to find out. They deserved it, knowledge was their right! But what had happened when he had bent down to the people of Greece with his illuminating flame? Why they'd treated him as the ancients had Prometheus. He had illuminated and they had scorned. It made him sad to see the way things were going, the proud men who once unseated the Trojans with cunning and bravery succumbing to their bellies. There was no amount of loose robes that could conceal the growing rolls at men's sides, Athens was getting a little chubby…

And why shouldn't they? The Peloponnesian wars were after all done and dusted. Not done particularly well, but done at least. Many of the fat men in the streets beside him had been skinny and muscular once. Side by side in the phalanx. Why, how Socrates missed the regimented day to day of the hoplite's existence. There was no freedom, a near spartan existence, but in a way things were simpler and he was happier back then. Back when someone told him where to go, what to do and how. They'd eaten whatever they had and marched it off. Why he'd never felt so healthy as he did back in those glorious days.

He looked around the street at all the aging hoplites, bigger than they'd ever been in uniform. When food was scarce they had been happy, thinking from one moment to the next. But now they had their pensions, their own slaves and as more than they could ever consume, though they tried their best. Of course Socrates was not advocating fasting. That fad would likely fade as soon as its proponents became so mad with hunger that they ate each other. Socrates was promoting something far more radical.

But Plato had been so smooth, greased by the establishment at his side. It was always easier to defend what was rather than to affect change. Socrates had tried his best, but the crowd was not his, nor was the floor, Plato interrupting again and again. If only he could lay out his opinions without interruption... No. An impossibility.

He passed an amphitheatre, masked men in dresses beckoning him in to see some comedy or tragedy. He thought about it for a moment, the distraction was certainly appealing. He could sit down and lose himself for a while in the fictionalised dramas of Thebes, transport his mind to a place where he had not lost. But he couldn't! He had work to do. A city to restore. A people to improve.

Socrates turned swirling his robes away from the theatre and continued down the street. He had to get home, away from the businesses and the beating of the sun to a shady spot where he could think. He needed to indulge in his own thoughts for a few moments, revisit his arguments and reform them. He was going to hand Plato his arse on a platter. His hurried return home brought him past many more market stands, selling dinted bits of iron recovered from the battlefield. Broken swords, rusty helmets and half bits of shields, pitching junk as if it was a relic. Relics of what? For Athens the war was best forgotten. He thought the vendors ought to melt them down, make new swords. A tool was only as valuable as it was useful, and once in defeat the tools of war were damaged beyond repair, they became utterly useless. Nothing. Who would ever want an old broken tool?

*

Socrates entered the breezy open parlour of his villa. There was nothing like stone to soak up the heat. He slipped off his sandals and let the heat sink down and out of his body into the floor. It was glorious. He shut his eyes and angled his nostrils up to catch a little of the salty sea breeze. For a moment he was at peace, before a violent shuffling disturbed the quiet. In an instant he was able to identify the irregular footsteps as belonging to his lame limping slave Crito.

'Alright Soc?' he asked.

'Please don't call me that' responded Socrates, opening his eyes. Helen was there too, aged about 11 or 12, her father thrust her again and again onto the property hoping Socrates might take her on as a student. 'Oh, hello Helen' he said amiably as he could.

'Hi' she said, awkwardly looking down. She was as unhappy about her being there as he was.

'Owd it go?' asked Crito, grinning. It was like he already knew and was revelling in his master's defeat, but Socrates comforted himself with the reminder that Crito didn't know anything.

'Poorly' replied Socrates. 'Plato-'

'Kept interrupting you didn't he?' burst out Helen. Socrates turned his eyes on her.

'You were there?' he asked.

'Yeah' she replied, all boldness sinking with her eyes back into the floor. 'Dad wants me to go to all of them. Says-'

'That my public appearances are free lessons. Yes. He's said it many times, loudly and near to me...' he paused to regain his composure. 'A wise man. We should all listen a little more. What did you think of the bits Plato and the crowd didn't shout over?' he asked.

'They were...' she spoke slowly, mouth clearly outpacing her brain as she scratched for the politically correct way to phrase it.

'Unorthodox' he said, rescuing her.

'Wait, what was this talking thing about?' asked Crito.

'Dialogue' corrected Socrates. 'I was engaging in a dialogue with Plato on the merits of diet upon health' he said tiredly. Having been present at many of Socrates' practise runs in the parlour, Crito ought to have known this.

'Okay, what's he saying?' asked the slave.

'That the food we're eating is fine for us'

'Isn't it?'

'Well we are fat and dying of fatness, so I'd say no'

'Oh'

'And I say that this could be remedied if we did not consume the products of other animals'

'Sounds like another fad to me' said Crito.

'Perhaps' admitted Socrates. 'I argued that eating the product of another animal exposes us to health risks. That it is impossible not to also consume their diseases and imbalance our humours. But it goes beyond health, I looked at land use, sustainability and-'

'I liked the bit on the apocalypse!' blurted out Helen.

'What bit on the apocalypse?' asked Socrates. Wondering if she had really been there.

'Umm, with the doctor and the lawyers and the constant fighting and dying. That bit was interesting. What would that world be like?' He paused and looked at her.

'That was a throw away comment, a meaningless speculation' he said in his loftiest voice. She looked disappointed. He paused again, thinking about it, trying to remember exactly what he had said. He highlighted the poor health of those consuming animal products and the strain it put upon Athens. In light of his he also assessed the land usage required to rear animals. To produce the same amount of meat as of equally filling vegetables, many times more land needed to be used, and in the days following Athens' defeat this was a scarce resource. He therefore joked that if they continued to eat meat, Athens would become full of doctors and lawyers, fixing the poor health and settling disputes over the limited land.

He turned from Helen and Crito, who gaped at him, wondering how he might expand on this idea. It was absurd that the hypothetical had engaged them so much more than the here and now. As a man of facts he thought that people wanted to hear about things that were already effecting them. Surely they were of the most importance?

'This idea interested you? Even though it was a fiction?' he asked the girl.

'Yes, I'd like to hear more if-'. He stopped listening. Admittedly fictionalising his points in a narrative was not his style. Allegory was the closest route he was willing to follow. But, if he had to cloak his point in fiction for it to be heard, the surely that was better than no one listening at all? He began to think of the truths concealed in the Odyssey and the other epics. For thousands of years of retellings they had been disgracefully embellished. They were full of mythical creatures, gods on the battlefields and magical bags of wind. But between the fictions laid the fundamental truths. A timeless tale of marital strain, of war, of the bond between soldiers in war. Perhaps he could do the same. Make his own entry into history…

He'd lost the debate with Plato, but history was written by the victors. Or did they write themselves into it? Could Socrates become the victor if he constructed a future where he was right?

*

Socrates finished his narration. It was done. His epic. His dystopic vision of humanity's far future. He fell back into a couch, a little breathless from his own performance. He'd thought of most of the story before he began speaking, but conjured many of its characters, events and features as he dictated it to Crito. Crito had been scratching his words in ink across the velum, stretched skin, writing up down, flipping it over and filling the words right out to the irregular margins. Velum was expensive and crude, he didn't have access to Egyptian papyrus like the publishers, but he could let them worry about that. As a manuscript, it would do. He walked over to Crito, who was watching the uncontrollable twitched of his writing hand.

'Give me that' he said, taking the thick stack and inspecting it. He looked at the ink, blotchy and illegible across the page. 'Crito what the fuck is this?' asked Socrates. Crito stood up slowly, then sincerely looked at the page to see what his master meant.

'What?' he asked, unable to identify the problem.

'It's barely legible!' shouted Socrates. 'My epic is barely legible! There aren't even any spaces! What the fuck is that about?' Crito looked again at the characters, scrunched close together without space nor punctuation to divide the long text.

'You said to save space…' reasoned the slave.

'Not by missing spaces. Or punctuation. How are people meant to know where to pause?'

'Maybe it's an exciting romp without need for pause' replied the slave smarmily.

'Thank you' said Socrates. 'But also fuck you. We've just spent a week dictating and writing a barely legible manuscript… I suppose it will do for-' his eyes snapped up from the page.

'What now?'

'You've simplified the language'

'Have I?'

'The final words Crito. They should read "and so Hela looked down upon the corpse strewn field of death. Plate for the crows, the defiant youth of Athens reduced to rot between the blades of grass, their swords perishing in rust beside them, breastplates dented in like the caved ribs of their broken chests, her love among them"'

'What did I write again?'

'The battle was over and there were lots of bodies' read Socrates from the final page.

'You spoke so fast! I couldn't get it all down! And my arm was hurting…'

'You didn't seem to get very much down at all'

'Isn't it aimed at teens anyway? Simple language is good for them right?'

'They're teenagers not retards Crito. But I suppose a certain simplicity might work' he huffed and began packing the manuscript into his satchel. 'Come on, we're off to the publishers'

*

The publishing agent leaned back in his chair, lazily regarding Socrates. 'So, gimme a synopsis. Nothing too big. Snappy, the kind of thing we can shout out into the street to get the kids to give up the silver. Tell me why this book'll sell'

'Well…' started Socrates. 'The idea came from an apparent interest in a speculative comment I made during the course of my debate with Plato'

'Speculative what? Who from?' asked the man sharply.

'A teenage girl I interviewed' he embellished.

'Ha! Strike one, teenage girls do not consume fiction and never will. Please don't tell me you based the epic on that assumption? Hades… Just gimme the summary'

'Well as I said my narrative sprouts from the debate between myself and Plato on the use of animal products. I said in this discourse that owing to the health complications of meat consumption and the land it takes up, Athens will be full one day of doctors and lawyers constantly trying to fix our health and legal battles over the limited land. This idea appeared to interest certain people, therefore I decided to run with it'

'Set in the future?'

'Yes'

'Can you do that?'

'I did'

'Strange… Carry on'

'It's a dystopic novel. Athens is in a sorry way, the lawyers and the doctors run everything, suppress anyone that disagrees with them and as a result everyone's poor and killing each other. This elite serves itself and everyone serves under them. People are too busy dying and killing each other to do anything about this. Things descend into decadence, until Greece is conquered. The next Thermopylae, but this time we're too weak to fight back, so we lose'

'Against Persians? Laughable'

'No, not Persians this time. Something more terrifying and savage. A steppe peoples, horse archers and stuff, real visual potential if you wanted to sell merch vases of the stuff. Anyway these barbarians inherit Greece and all its ideas, including the whole doctors and lawyers conundrum. The fall is so bad that the barbarians take thousands of years to relearn everything we know now and effectively get back to this point'

'Okay?'

'That's the backstory. The real story begins in the dystopia in a few thousand years, when the barbarians have relearnt everything lost in the fall. But they're still sick with in fighting, land is scarce. Things are a little worse than now. the It's so scarce that the barbarians have made their own grain colonies, like ours in the Black Sea. But off west somewhere'

'preposterous!'

'Just run with it. So in this dystopia as you know, everyone is sick, living short lives in debt to the elite who want to keep them down. They never fully recovered from the fall, they reduce our knowledge and our gods, the descendants of the barbarians are too stupid and so only worship one God. They reduce all systems of government and belief into one. This brings the doctors and the lawyers into conflict with each other. What's worse, is more barbarians are coming out of the east again, it's looking like the whole rise and fall of civilisation thing is cyclical, and that this is a vital point in time to stop the next fall. So our protagonist, a teenage girl called Hela, challenges the system. Her and her underdog band of teens has to topple this evil government before it is toppled by chaos. They are exiled and have to start their own society. It turns out to be a utopia of the youthful. Vegetable gardens and green in every direction, they're healthy, happy and don't need to fight over land. But Athens collapses, and the barbarians are coming for them next. So the band of teens militarises and stands alone against the combined forces of evil' the agent looked blankly at him.

'That's it?'

'Yes?' said Socrates.

'Come on. Look out of the window. Do you see it? It's white and painted pillars where once there was dirt? Can you imagine the civilisation that produced this falling to glorified horse archers? Barbarians even being able to comprehend our learnings? Organising themselves? You know the reason they're barbarians is their complete inability to unify. This god thing too. Impossible to publish. First problem is which god do you pick? Zeus? Zoroaster? Mithras? Don't tell me that you've thought of inventing a new one, you can't just make up a new god. If we pick Zeus you offend the cult of Athena, vice versa likewise. You were a hoplite, you know that teenagers leading a military campaign against an organised government would fail.

That's a stupid story idea and you know it. Beyond all the notions of implausibility, who'd read it?'

'As I said, teenagers' he smiled.

'Get out' said the agent, already glancing over his shoulder to find a slave. 'And someone get me a gyros, I'm starving!' he looked back to Socrates, still sat hopefully in his seat. 'If you want to publish it, you'll have to do so yourself'

'Fine. I will'

*

Socrates had decided to establish his own publishing house. One free of the requirements of the strict establishments. He'd be beholden to no one but himself. No one to censor his ideas. No one to interrupt him. If he offended the cult of Zeus or Mithras then that was his problem and his alone. Socrates realised in his meeting with the agent that he had no hope of appealing his argument to the old and established. They'd grown up with certain notions, ideas which now formed an inseparable part of themselves. They couldn't be blamed for not listening. But the youth, if Socrates could craft convincing enough of a world as to engage the youth. Why them through ekphrasis he could earn their sympathy. He would not speak to them in his own voice, but the voice of his characters. He wasn't going to ask them to listen to a barmy old man in a robe, he'd ask them to listen to dazzlingly handsome and beautiful teens of their own age. His words would flow in their language, and perhaps by his hypothetical device real world change could be initiated!

It had snowballed of course. Socrates merely wished in his dialogue with Plato to explain that plant-based diets were more healthy and efficient, it was supplementary to his argument. His *Dystopia* was an exaggeration, and a deliberate one at that. People wouldn't listen to him when he was being moderate. People tended to downsize the beliefs of others. A moderate belief therefore downsized to nothing. If he wanted his suggestions to be heeded, he'd have to supersize them. Blow up his narrative to the size of an invented world, thousands of years in the future and grand in scope. His characters would have to be characters of what a real person was and the situations twice as mad as anything in real life.

What had begun as a reluctant project now burst from Socrates' every fibre. He couldn't wait to publish his *Dystopia*. First in establishing his publishing house, was the purchase of a house. Followed by slaves, ink and papyrus. All were reasonably easily obtained. Socrates entered the square, where he bought a nearby plot of land. That was the benefit of the economic state of Athens, everything was cheap. Most of all, slaves.

The Peloponnesian wars had made slaves of many free men cowardly enough to surrender. The Spartans now were selling the men of Athens back to the city, one shipment at a time. 'Hey Socrates!' came one merry voice from a line of chained men.

'Oh, hey Mik, how're you doing these days? I haven't seen you since…'

'I surrendered, yeah, long time. I've been alright. Passed around a few masters. Some good, some bad. The last one really liked me…' he paused and rubbed his behind. 'But hey ho, back in Athens so it isn't too bad. What're you doing?'

'I'm buying slaves' said Socrates amiably.

'Ah, neat'

'Yeah, I'm setting up a publishing house. I'm tired of sales obsessed idiots redacting my best arguments. Do you know how many of this lot's literate?' Mik looked back.

'Most of us really. Going cheap too. Go on Soc, it'd be great to be working together again!' he tried to clap his comrade on the back, but the chain cut him short. Socrates paused and pondered for a while, then withdrawing a bag of silver hailed the slaver. A short slaver walked over, introduced himself as Asclepius and bartered for payment. After a few angry minutes and the promise of an extra chicken on top of the silver, the slaves were his.

*

Socrates looked proudly over his printers. A block shaped arrangement of about twenty men, transcribing his epic as fast as they could. He had men working on the same page, a chain of assembly now working at terrifying speeds. Socrates had done it. Self-publishing wasn't so terrifying after all...

He awoke the next morning to a terrible drone. A high pitched wining, less like the siren songs to lure a man into the rocks, more the kind that made a man deliberately aim his ship straight for the sharpest one. He sat up groggily. As wakefulness returned his ear began to isolate parts of the vile symphony. After a few more moments of examination, he was able to make out a variety of annoyingly screeching sources of the noise. Voices. It was a crowd.

'Crito!' he called out for his slave. 'Crito get my spear. What the fuck is going on?' a few moments later Crito entered, spear in hand. 'Crito what the hades is going on out there?'

'Crowd' answered his slave.

'Yes. Yes Crito. I see that. What I mean is why are they both screaming and stationary outside of my fucking house?'

'Dystopia'

'Sure seems like it'

'No, your *Dystopia*'

'What?'

'It was an overnight success!'

'Is that really a thing? I thought that was just something oracles said to advertise their tomes?' Socrates began standing up and walking to the window. He parted the curtains and looked out on the screaming crowd.

'How did they read it so quickly?'

'Simplified language. They're really into the story'

'Why are they here?'

'They want a sequel'

'A sequel? Nearly everyone dies. It wouldn't be a sequel it would be a different story!'

'Ah yes. They've got a theory about that'

'A theory about my epic?'

'Yeah, that most of the main characters didn't actually die. It's their own interpretation of it, there are like five different ones'

'But they can't do that! It's my fucking story!'

'Not anymore. They're writing fan fictions too'

'Should I ask?'

'Their own stories with your characters. They've added bits to your story'

'Fuck' said Socrates. He had gone too far, he'd speculated. By doing so, writing was no longer subject to what was, but what could be. He had well and truly opened pandoras box here. 'Okay…' he said slowly. 'I'm going to go and reason with them' he began standing up. Crito offered him the spear, which he slapped away, before walking to the edge of the villa and onto the street side.

The fields surrounding his home were full of screaming tweens, boys and girls out in droves in celebration of his dystopic fantasy. Who'd have known an underdog story could do so well? They were waving to get his attention, screaming not only his name, but his characters names, holding up mosaics they'd made depicting them, sometimes in sexual embrace with one and other. 'Wait? Why are Haemon and Theba fucking each other?!' he shouted at one tween holding aloft her pornographic mosaic of two prominent characters. 'No! They're related! Destroy that mosaic immediately!'

'We ship them!' shouted back the crowd as one.

'What does that even mean?!' he screamed back. 'They're my characters!'

'We love you Socrates!' shouted another. Before the crowd began chanted 'sequel' again and again.

'But they all die at the end' he responded.

'Spoiler!' shouted a tween from the back.

'I have a theory about how they survive, when the armies of-' shouted another, before their reasoning was drowned out by a hundred other theories blurting out at the same time. From the mass, stepped forward Helen.

'Hi Socrates' she said nervously. 'Big fan-'

'Helen. Fuck off' he responded.

'I… Um, represent the community' she said.

'What community?'

'The *Dystopic* fan community' she replied.

'The name's appropriate. What do you want?' he asked. She thrust forward a stack of papyrus, smiling and meeting his eyes.

'Will you sign it for me?' she asked.

'Put my name to it? No. What else?'

'Sequel'

'No'

'We were prepared for this' she said coolly. 'If you don't write a sequel, we'll start killing ourselves' she said confidently.

'Do it' replied Socrates, earnestly. He looked across the crowd. The sequel deranged tweens. They were mad with and for his story. What had he done? He just wanted to promote vegetarianism, yet had inadvertently assembled an active cult. They were writing fan fictions faster than he could discredit them. Diving deeper and deeper into the fictional pit he had made. Socrates had been trying to purify people's diets, but realised with horror that he had corrupted the youth of Athens.

He turned away from the screaming tweenagers and walked into his villa. He realised that he too had become lost in his narrative, not properly thought out the consequences of publishing such trash. He rubbed his temples, bringing himself back to the real world. 'Crito!' he shouted. 'We owe a cock to Asclepius. Also get my hemlock'.

Caesar's Flying Column

15th March 44 B.C, Roman Republic

It was a warm, orange bathed March day. The fifteenth of the month. The sun rose gently over the hills and aqueducts, and a warming glow crept up the flaking paint and marble of a hundred columns. Another day in the Roman Republic, at it's very beating heart, for which to some the world seemed to turn in obedience. Another day, and another gentle sweep of the solar rays across the earth, brushed the winter a little further away, and hailed the coming summer. Farmers already busied themselves in the olive topped hill sides, picking diligently in their groves, vineyards too were ripening, ready for plucking ahead of the symposium onslaught the warm weather would bring. Soldiers sharpened their gladius, straightened their pila tips and fitted their mail for another campaigning season. Men and women of every class and kind, high, low, plebs, slaves and senators, all rose a little easier than the day before. Slowly at first, but quickly now, everyone began to go about their business, fulfilling their duties to the Republic.

Among these people, were a small gaggle of Senators, rushing to hear the latest announcement of their dictator. Leading them, running messily in their togas, were Marcus Junius Brutus and Gaius Cassius Longinus. Hot on their heels, with his bronze breast plate of hammered abs and pecks, around which pinkish fat bulged, was Mark Antony. Mark was always wildly unwelcome among the senators. A military man, a speaker not a listener, a glutton, a male harlot and barely short of barbarianism never to be found out of military dress. Worst of all, Caesar loved him.

He was the prodigal general, not for his thoughts or strength, but how easily Caesar could mould them at will, and with him present not a word could be slipped in by anyone else. So, as one flappy, white sheeted gaggle, the senators ran, ran to Caesar and his impending announcement. Brutus said he expected it would regard where they'd campaign this summer, and at this the senators placed their bets. 100 Denarii each. Cassius expected it would be Gaul again, another bloody rebrand, Brutus had his silver on Germania and the rest had made various absurd suggestions as Thrace, Britain and the devoid Arabian interior.

Huffing and puffing, they made it to the wide arches of the Theatre of Pompey, and barely in time slammed shut the door with that pest Antony on the correct side. His pestilence upon the Senators, an insectoid rotting of the eardrum with his every misspoken word, had grown so severe that they had taken ex-gladiators into their employment, for the soul purpose of barring doors against him. Today they did their bit. Muscular and grunting, taut against the door as one, flesh against wood, bound by a soft curve of marble, as all the doorways were. Caesar waited for them, draped in white and red rimmed robes, a golden casting of loreals upon his head, holding forward his pathetic scape over. He was shamefully bald and no crown of gold or jewels could hide it. Every man knew this. All the same, as though it were a triumph day, he had diligently waxed forward his long neck hair, and set carefully atop the awkward arrangement his gold crown, little more than a glorified hairpin. In the early morning orange, he stood bathing, taking in the sky with a new fascination for its warmth. Gazing up as he never had before, as he once had on foreign hills.

'Caesar!' hailed Brutus, with a familiar pat on the back. 'Pray, why do you glance up like a dotard?' he laughed. Caesar turned to him wisely smiling.

'Soon you will know Brutus, old friend. Tell me, have you brought your most influential comrades of the Senate as I asked?'

'I certainly have'

'But where is Mark? Why I hate to miss the poor fellow, he'd ever so interested in politics these days and it's quite endearing to hear him try. I'll make a proper Roman of him yet!'

'Oh Antony?' said Brutus, the Senators at his back coughed together to hide the banging of the door. 'Well we looked for him in his quarters, but he wasn't to be found…'

'Ah, a shame, but there'll be no hinderance. Come at once, come all of you, I have a most radical announcement'

From here Caesar led the men through the temple. It was a temple only in technicality, frequented most infrequently for that purpose. Yet as a theatre, a place of entertainment, acting, bloodletting and debauchery, it brought torrents of men and bore all the tide of Rome it could take. White, sun bleached and polished patches of marble peaked out where the paint was too well worn, over a decade by a thousand brushing hands. Some but the soft glide of a lady's fingertip, others the hard scrape of a drunk glutton steadying himself against the pillars. A thousand,

thousand hands bleached and polished the walls in focus spots. They had a human character to them. The theatre was not old, but was well used and well loved by the citizens of Rome. It was a site for drama and tragedy, for comedy and entertainment. A place where the masses and the important few converged as one, in the single joy of Roman civilisation. He led them to a viewing balcony, built around a small and marble fighting pit dug into the ground. This was not a place for plebs, a micro colosseum within the theatre complex if you will, a more exclusive and intimate place to view beasts and animals hack at one and other. Blood still congealed in the sand from the night before. This was not an unusual sight to any of the men, it was a comfortably familiar staple of their society, a bloody smell of home.

What was however very peculiar, was the column in the centre of the pit. 'Oh, that's it' the senator's mumbled as one. The Column was polished like a looking panel, to a reflective point that lit orange in the now dying light of the morning as it gave way to clearer day skies. The image of the fighting pit around it was broken and warped on its surface into a tangle of unfollowable and shifting lines, that curved with the roundness of the Column and rippled like Damascus silk. The Column, was of an immense height, about 100 feet tall, and it thickened at its middle, before thinning to a single, Pilum sharp point at its top. The top, twinkled brightly under the convulsions of the sun and the clouds underneath, darting about the room like an observant eye, erratic as reflective water and thrice as beautiful. About three-quarters of the way down, supporting all the column, stretched out three supports. Long, shining legs of metal, thin in their attachment to the column and wide, flat, curved on the inside like a Dacian Falx. Finally, at the bottom, textured as if to be gripped like the hilt of a gladius, was a chamber with an almost unnoticeable door and a blackened bowl with no bottom underneath.

One particularly fat man, stepped forward, sweeping his arm and trailing his toga.

'Oh Caesar what a magnificent column! You have truly outdone yourself, to your conquest of Gaul? Or your triumph over Pompey. Or Alessia, why that is a day in need of a monument if my bards tell me truly!' The Senators, again as one, joined in an indistinct mumble of appraisal. Caesar raised his hand. They silenced.

'This is no Column Citizen's. This is something greater than a triumph, worth probably a few triumph's itself! What you see before you is no Column, nor is it as one could be mistaken for thinking, a giant Plumbata. This, is a rocket, a rocket presented to me a few nights ago by an engineer from the east, of a nation we have never heard of, between the Parthian Empire and the Yuezhi. Though foreign, this man is inhumanely talented, and do not think this is a normal trait of his people, for he swears they cast him out when he unveiled this, rocket, to them'

'A rocket, Caesar?' said Cassius.

'Yes, in his language, the meaning is sky cart'

'Why whoever would think to put two such words together? It is an oxymoron is it not?'

'Ah, you underestimate how wrong you could possibly be. I did too. I was to have him flogged as an imposter who played at sorcery, before he gave me a demonstration that was. Ever since, he has been a guest of honour at my residence, and will remain so for the rest of his years. Such a man will dine at Caesar's table so long as he has hunger!'

'And what is this man's name?' said Brutus sharply. They all looked to the foreign man. His head was aimed down into the bloody sand, inspecting the spot where a leg penetrated it. He was timid in posture, hunched into himself, and presumably timid at feasts, as he was little more than the flesh that hung on his bones. As the Senators gazed at this strange and foreign looking man, he played his foot into the sand, then ground the sand between his toes.

'His name is utterly unintelligible to us, Brutus' returned Caesar. 'Foreign and complicated, we shall not bog down such an historic moment with pointless confusion. Call him only the Inventor, as I do, and judge him only by his invention, as I have. Now no more prattling from you, you are to watch and as you watch compose in your heads your accounts. All of Rome and all of her people must hear of this moment, the moment Caesar conquered the skies for the Republic!'

With that, Caesar turned dramatically and disappeared into a stairwell. Moments later, at the bottom of the fighting pit, he reappeared beside the inventor, together they ascended stairs, which a moment earlier had deployed themselves from the side of the Column, then swiftly shut behind them. Inside the rocket, Caesar was lead to a chair.

'Why my friend this chair, it is a bed. It is faced the wrong way. Do you expect Caesar to traverse a moment of history with his legs flailing up, on his back like a gutter whore?'

'No Caesar, but trust me when I tell you that you shall find yourself the right way up soon enough, and that I too shall be beside you in a similar arrangement' Sceptically, and with as little dignity the situation would allow, Caesar climbed into the misaligned chair, tucking himself into his toga, then fastening the seat rope around himself . Meanwhile, the inventor danced back and forth, turning dials, checking pipes, tensioning the reigns.

'What powers this contraption? It is reigned, but I see no horse or driving engine'

'Fires, fires like the very earth' said the inventor distracted. 'It works like a candle, the wick of which has been engineered to produce a flame so ferocious, that it yields a wind, that through these pipes I guide in such a way that flight is produced'

'Like a chariot of the gods?'

'I am no god Caesar, this is a human way of flight. One day we will all fly like this, faster and higher than the birds, to far off places even I have not seen'

'Tell me inventor, where is the end of the world?' said Caesar.

'Are you roped into your chair Caesar? Good. Then I shall show you the end of the earth, and how it seeps into the beginning as the Greeks predicted' the inventor struck a black rock against his knife, and kindled a small spark, then dropped it into a pipe. He tied himself into his chair, also up at an indignant and unnatural angle, then turned a lever.

Through a glass spy panel in the pipe, he watched carefully as the kindling dropped, then with a roar the rocket took off, filling the fighting pit with smoke and ash. The thrust of the flying column liquidised the dried blood of the fighting pit, kicking it up in wet clumps upon the nice white togas of the bemused senators. Caesar was pressed hard into his chair, with all his strength he managed, barely, to turn his head to the side, to a glass hole in the rocket. Rome disappeared underneath him and was quickly swallowed in the green spring countryside. Vineyards collapsed into thin lines, then single colours, then a shade on a wide landscape painted across the window. The mountains began to look like pebbles and finally, as the rocket's convulsions calmed to a gently rumble, the sea could be seen either side of the Italian peninsular.

'So the world really is a globe, as Aristotle said...' mulled Caesar. 'I read *On The Heavens* in my curious years, now I find myself upon them. Yes, yes, I can see the curve now, and the spin, does the world really spin so fast?'

'No Caesar, it is an illusion as we move across it'

'I recognise some features, but they're wrong, slightly wrong. Does the glass distort the view?'

'No Caesar, only slightly. It is your cartographers who are mistaken. I have produced my own, more accurate maps, look here. I have marked the Republic and lands under it in red'

'By Jupiter, do really we hold so little land?! I shall have my artists flogged and flayed for deceiving Rome!' he said shocked. 'And yet I feel from here as though the whole world is mine, and see no borders. Can any border be seen from such a height? I think it is a mortal thing…'

'There is one, Caesar, a defence of uncountable miles, all stone, it can be seen with a looking glass'

'And to wonder what manner of men built it, and what they hide behind it… But enough philosophising. Describe the features to me, the lands on your map, north of Germania, are they all held by German barbarians?'

'I know little of the people, only the features Caesar. Yet a merchant I encountered in the Caucuses had travelled to these places. They all speak a similar tongue and are of the fair and red complexion. Apart from here, see? Here reside a darker people. The Finns, more akin to you Mediterraneans in colour, and to the Steppe archers in look'

'Fascinating…'

'We are over Asia Minor now Caesar, see how the earth darkens as it dries. It is said it is the Parthian Armies who cause this, they are so large in numbers, that they drink the rivers and leave nothing for the land. South of here are the Arabs, these are dry and pathetic lands, but not worthless. They are rich in the fuel for my craft, and should be conquered immediately… Now here is the kingdom of Yavadas, still run by those of the line of Alexander the Great's generals, but a mere shadow of their former glory. The people there are not Greek, much darker. Indians, who worship a pantheon of elephants and blue men, mighty gods Caesar, who fly like we do now. I have been sure to be cautious when traversing these skies, lest they smite me down. These lands give way to jungle, where the people are again different, shorter and more…'

'Jungles?'

'Ah, forgive me Caesar. They are a forest, though never as you have seen them before. Thick, so thick that at the ground it is night, and inhabited with monkeys, people like beasts, small and fury all over'

'Barbarians?'

'Perhaps, men who wrapped themselves in fur and forgot their civilisation. But now they are animals. Ah now look down through the glass! See the line of rock?'

'Yes, a strangely thin mountain range'

'No Caesar, it is the defence of which I spoke. It stretches a thousand miles north and south, from the steppe to the sea. Every mile is garrisoned. Behind it is the Han Empire, populated by a people called the Chinese. They are numerous and their armies unimaginable'

'Barbarians?' he queried again.

'No. They are civilised as your republic. But worry not, only their traders may reach you, there are many baron miles no army could survive between your lands;

'We could perhaps make an alliance… Send envoys… There is much to do. Ah, sea in all directions! Is that all the known world?'

'Yes Caesar, yet there is another, nearly as big, Barbarians control the north and south as they do our world, but in its middle like ours are great civilisations. Tarascan,

61

Mixtec, Maya and more. They build great Pyramids out of the jungle, and have great organisation such as yours. But they have a weakness, their armies fight with stone tools, and horses are unknown to them. They are ripe for all the conquest'

'You have served me most loyally with this information inventor, and shall reap the rewards of my conquests to come. Tell me, is this all the world?'

'We have circled it but once in a single line, there is much more to see Caesar. The world has hair and a beard of ice at the top and bottom, there are many great continents and countless archipelagos. I have it all in here, in my collection of maps, and can take you anywhere your eminence so pleases. My rocket has 3 days worth of flying wick, enough for a few circumnavigations of the world at least. Perhaps a higher altitude fly over of Italia?' Caesar thought a moment.

'No, I can study maps in my office, it is clear I have a new duty to Rome, that cannot be done alone from up here. We will return, but not it seems I have little time left for hobbies. We must return, how do we descend?'

'We enter the lower sky again, at the correct point, then deploy a large silk sheet to slow us safely, then we float down and land' the inventor began switching dials and turning the rocket earthwards.

'Ah yes, I remember your silk sheet! It was so magnificent, I had never seen anything like it, nor felt such smooth work. I had my servants line my bed with it, and there it still presides! That shan't be a problem will it?'

*

Later in the ashy fighting pits, in their bloody toga's, as the sun and its warmth bled from the sky, the senators waited. They were sore bottomed from a day of waiting, and were beginning to wonder how they'd explain Caesar's disappearance.

The Connecticut Yankee

528 A.D, Britain

That a 19th Century Connecticut native had built a time machine was unlikely. Within a century of his lifetime, a vague understanding would be reached that by accelerating towards light speed one too could accelerate their passage forward in time. The phenomenon was called time dilation, and would be of great use to humanity in the coming centuries. However, in 1889 Connecticut the human's fastest vehicle was a horse, which coming in at 88 kilometres an hour, was many billions of times too slow to reach any meaningful 'time travel'.

That Hank Morgan had been able to manufacture a machine for travelling *backwards* in time was even less likely. So unlikely in fact, that upon achieving the relatively impossible act, he jumped in his seat from equal joy and shock when he found himself not in his workshop, but 6th Century Britain. His head struck against the roof of his impossible contraption, the hard iron thrumming through his skull like a crowbar. He slumped for a moment back into his seat, surveying the land around him in a wounded double vision. The shades of green were the first thing to make it through his eyes. Lush green in every direction, seemingly right out to the sea. Then the meadows focussed, the boundaries between them of low stone walls coming into focus.

In Connecticut, hell, the world over by now, barbed wired was the newest fad. It was a simple way of weaponizing a wire fence against a herd of Texas longhorns many miles wide, cheaper than the wooden fence and thus many times more widespread. One day they'd run enough of it across fields to bind the world. That these long shining strands of sharpened wire were nowhere to be seen glinting under the June sun told Hank everything he needed to know. His time machine had worked.

Hank breathed in the air. It had a freshness to it as never before. Newer than any he'd ever tasted, and it did indeed taste, taste of a whole other world. Rome had fallen in the west less than a lifetime ago and was still going strong in the east. Germanic tribesmen were crossing the North Sea, beginning Britain's first and most violent wave of mass migration. Contact would not be made with America by Europeans for another four hundred years! Nothing like Connecticut, for he was in fact in a world without Connecticut.

The lush fields of his home state were inhabited by another people, under a different name, each awaiting conquest and a little renaming... He stepped out of the time machine, leaving it at the ancient treeline into which it had landed when his voyage was complete. Hank rubbed his head a little, wondering if this sights before him were all part of a daze from the blow he'd taken to his head. But they weren't. They were as real as the beautiful June day before him.

Hank had set the dial of his machine to the year 528 A.D, dead in the middle of Britain's dark age, where he hoped to find the legendary and historically illusive king. Arthur.

He had a clear plan laid out in his head, though it had become somewhat jumbled with his celebratory bash.

Hank was to use his skills to secure his position in the court of the King. See Hank was a capable American man. His father was a blacksmith, and so he could create the tools for any job, even invent them where they did not yet exist. From the fine cogs of a pocket clock, to the hardened barrel of a colt pistol, he could make it. And boy would he.

Of course his historical tampering had been a source of great concern to Hank before his departure from the 19th Century. He'd spent many sleepless nights by the fire side, whiskey in hand has he mulled over the issued of stepping back into one's own past. Could he change what had come before? Across time things tended to snowball. The birth of his own nation for example. A private in Boston had stood up to a wig maker yelling abuse at an officer, which had escalated to a physical fight. Within an hour British soldiers had shot and killed four men and within a decade America was no longer part of the Empire. All that had happened to birth Hank's young but glorious nation, could be put down to a few throw away insults as any man could see on the streets of Boston aimed at the wrong man.

And now Hank found himself in distant past. 1300 years before his own time, a time so distant it had been forgotten and recomposed into poems and legends. Hank worried that mislaying even a twig might have great consequences for human history, that he might divert the deluge of time with the slightest adjustment to England's history. He thought on this for a long time, took to the history books and tried to learn the lay of England so that he might not disturb its flow. But there was little more than a few lyric poems on Arthur, and those had been composed hundreds of years later, some closer to Hank's time than Arthur's!

Restless nights and a thorough supply of firewater brought him the solution. First, he did not know that his machine was certain to work. If it did, then in his own history he had already lived in Arthur's time and done everything he was determined to do. Therefore any changes that may have occurred had already occurred, and Hank was fatalistically duty bound to hop in his machine and back into the days of yore.

Not wanting to push it, Hank decided not to alter any major world events. That meant being in it for him and no one else. Hank would use his ability to craft machines that would not otherwise exist for centuries to gain a foothold in the ancient world. Sure he had no knightly training, but what was armour against a colt .45? A lead slug could punch right through any mail or plate, as was shown by the absence of the frontier's cowboys riding about in shining armour… He'd not go too far, he'd make one off machines, they'd be wonders to the ancient English, and he would in turn become wonderful. The thought itself was wonderful!

Hank walked from his machine, leaving it at the old oak upon which it had landed, and looked over the sunlit hills of the dark ages. They were not dark at all. All was gold and dreamy. Little paths meandered like streams over the fields, disappearing into hedges and over horizons. There were no trains to chug noisily by and ruin the quiet, no cities to bustle. What these people would have called a city would appear little more than a cattle post in Hank's time.

He began tallying his to do task. First was gunpowder. He'd brought a peacemaker with him, concealing it under his coat lest any bandits set upon him in the quiet countryside. The disadvantage of a pistol as oppose to a sword however was ammunition. It ran out, often quicker than one would hope. Hank had five rounds loaded into the six shooter, another 60 or so on bandoliers strapped around his body. But if he was to go to war with the court of Arthur he'd need more than that.

He chuckled at the thought of himself on horseback, thunder clapping from the barrel of his gun and men falling all around. To all else on the battlefield it would seem like magic! He was struck with a sudden thought. That perhaps this was exactly what he would do. That Hank would indeed go to battle with all manor of weapons the ancients would not understand. That his thunderous six shooter would seem magical. He could use magic to conceal his power, magic was misunderstood and misunderstood power was harder to overthrow. He wondered if he had already read of his own escapades. If he was the source of the mythical magical Merlin!

Hank determined immediately to don the name and try his luck. He felt giddy at the thought, and began steering his inventive thoughts towards spectacle. He could make electrical devises, chemical tricks, become a healer with his basic knowledge of medicine which by nature of his time would far surpass that of the greatest doctors in Europe.

First was bullets. Smokeless powder was all the rage back home. It was more powerful and didn't clog up the gun as much as black powder. But it was a bitch to manufacture and Hank could perhaps make theatrical use of the massive cloud of report from a black powder gun. All he needed was charcoal, sulphur and potassium nitrate, which was readily available in urine. In the later medieval period he knew that monks were infamous for pissing gunpowder, that wars were fought over bird shit for the black powder. It would be dirty work, but the pay off would be brilliant.

Hank started down a path, listening to the wind as it whistled through the thick knee high grassy all around. It sprouted in cushioned clumps from every surface, he pictured himself dozing off to sleep in it, a princess in his arms. With glory came women.

Hank's main plan was to assist King Arthur. If however the legendary King turned out to be, well, legendary, then someone still had to be in charge. Hank resolved to either help Arthur in his defence against the heathen Saxons who were to become the English or the next best guy. As a good American Christian, it was Hank's born duty to show the English and pagans where they weren't welcome. If however Hank did happen upon the English first, he would use his modern wit and knowledge to win them over, lull them into safety then escape!

Hank knew he'd be rewarded for his efforts. Gold most likely. Exaggerated or not, leaders from the stone age to modern America were known to gift their followers and supporters. He already had the business model in his head. Hank was going to exchange small contraptions, simple things like a gas lamp or a wrist watch, for massive fucking piles of gold. He would then ferry this gold into the present day and amass a significant fortune.

So much was made of gold and the treasures of Kings, yet so few hoards remained in Hank's time. He wondered if this was owing to men like him, who having devised a successful time machine, ferried the riches of the past into the future. Perhaps the archaeologist emerging across the European upper classes were in fact time travellers laundering their dodgily earned gold!

But first was contact. It wasn't long before Hank encountered someone along the path, and boy did he live up to expectations. Though a childhood of romantic picture books had trained him to expect the Arthurian knight to look something more like a 15th century gothic knight, Hank was still impressed with the metal clad warrior mounted atop the horse. The knight held a long spear in his hand, the tip glinting in the midday sun. The presumably equally impressively polished blade of his sword was still concealed in its scabbard, where it flopped at the man's side.

The man was bedecked in what seemed like one unbroken sheet of chainmail, with only a slit for his eyes betraying anything vaguely flesh coloured. Evil blue eyes stung piercingly from the slit, searching Hank's features. He was a bold man, a warrior who'd earned his place with a lifetime of killing and hardiness, he'd make a wonderful frontiersman. The man sat upright in his saddle with a warriors confidence. His armour was far more expensive than most of the surrounding fields, but worth every shilling. Any weapon of the day would merely glance off the chainmail's protective rings. This was a man who believed himself utterly invincible. Hank smirked, feeling smug that the colt pistol hidden on his person could punch clean through any bit of the knight's impressive armour.

'Howdy there partner' spoke Hank. He'd rehearsed the words for weeks. Howdy, it'd sounded far more exotic than 'hello to thee' or some other Old English way of speaking. He wanted to intrigue the man, get the knight's attention then win him over with the modern wit.

'ârweorðnes êow weargbr‾æde wealhcynn?' asked the man atop the horse, to Hank's utter surprise. Hank screwed his face up. Though he'd expected the ancient knight to talk in antiquated way, and had duly read up on his Shakespeare, he hadn't understood a word. The words were garbled, guttural, more Scandinavian than anything he'd ever heard or even tried to understand. This was a hiccup he had not foreseen. Composing himself, Hank continued.

'My apologise finest Sir I did notteth here thee' he bowed a little. Another horseman rode up, muttered something and pulled alongside the first.

'Hwa swilc forwrecan?' asked one horseman to another. They weren't speaking English. Hank looked back to the time machine by the old oak, which now appeared dangerously far away. Perhaps he had landing in medieval Germany. The words were alien and unintelligible. 'We rôðor ēastseaxe' said one patting his chest. Then it struck him, the truth, the terrible truth that Hank had overlooked. Though Arthur had later become an English figure, he was more an object of their fascination. Arthur was in fact what would become a Welshman, fighting those who would become the English. Hank wasn't in the wrong place or the wrong time. These were indeed knights of Arthur's court. Only they were Welsh, and thus clearly speaking the welsh language. As said, hiccup, but nothing too severe. Given time, Hank could always learn their language, or better, teach them some good old English!

    'And I am Hank' smiled Hank back, patting his chest in reply. The horsemen looked at each other, paused a moment, then as one thrust their spears forwards and through the Yankee's neck. For Hank, was in fact wrong, severely wrong. He had been faced with two Englishmen, speaking the English language of the 6th Century, which is to say, Dutch. These were cautious times for two conquering Englishmen. The Britons, united under Arthur were pushing back. Enemy spies everywhere! Then this man shows up, speaking a bizarre language and behaving strangely. He was clearly a Welshmen. The English warriors let Hank slide of their spear tips, then shaking off the blood, continued on to Camelot.

Vitruvian Man

1490, Venice

'Leonardo how are you my friend?' asked the Cleric as he entered the scruffy workshop. Paper was expensive in those days, yet it was scattered over the desks, screwed up in corners and piling high on the shelves. The Cleric unbound another delivery of the paper, depositing it on the desk and tapping his nose with a wink. 'Our secret yes?'

The paper was church property, intended to be filled with exoduses, evil Pharos and hippy Jews. Instead, once a week, the Cleric would drop by Leonardo's workshop, deposit the paper and sometimes some ink, and leave him to fill the pages with his own designs. God had already made the world, written his story. Any adjustments to lore or plot progressions had to be done through his pre-existing characters, or so the Cleric said. God worked through men like Leonardo. Sent wonderful forms to their dreams, which with the Cleric's help ended up on paper and eventually took shape as creations.

'Fine thank you' said the dreamer, looking over the paper, already scribbling them in with his mind and willing the church man out of his workshop. There was much to do and only a single lifetime to do it. There was no knowing who'd come after him, for all he knew humanity would halt upon his death, be left only to inherit what he had envisioned. He envisioned many things, so many he could spend his whole life transcribing their simplest descriptions. Yes simple descriptions wouldn't do. The people after him would need schematics, explanations and drawings to stoke them into wanting to create his designs in the first place. Yet there the Cleric lingered, wanting to chat, wanting to fritter away more moments into the past.

Not taking the que, the Cleric began examining papers upon the desk. A little corkscrew device that could fly. 'Have you completed the model?' he asked, eyes wide and bright as a child's. Sighing and reaching into a draw Leonardo brought out his wooden model, passing it to the man of god. The man of god took the toy delicately in his hand, then turned it over a few times. When his eyes were satisfied he laid it gently down on the table, as if done with it.

To Leonardo this was intolerable, and so reaching across the Cleric he pulled on the object's cord. When it was fully extended, he released the little string and in a whir the device took to flight. The Cleric let out a little girlish whoop, which he promptly attempted to conceal with loud clapping. 'Bravo Leonardo! Bravo!' Leonardo was happy, clapping came at the end of shows and so the Cleric would soon be gone. He had so much to do.

To his unending disappointment however the Cleric took a seat by a work table and beckoned Leonardo to sit beside him. 'Come here my child' he said in a soft priestly voice. Fuck. He was going to talk about god. Reluctantly and with duty, Leonardo sat beside his source of paper and ink and forced an interested face. He couldn't manage it, and so let his mind wander over his own inventions until a genuinely interested expression emerged. The flying corkscrew was descending and the Cleric caught it gently in his palm.

'Another brilliant creation my son' he said, then placing the device down on the work top. 'Another brilliant device in so many. Are you proud?'

'I suppose so'

'Pride is a sin Leonardo' he wound up the device again, then released it to ascend through the air. Already the priest had appropriated Leonardo's creation as a metaphor. Fuck, fuck, fuck. 'I have been translating texts my son. That is my work. Preserving the old works for the church records. Some of them are from before our faith, but nonetheless speak the Lord's truth. There is a tale of a father and a son, Daedalus and Icarus, who by engineering learnt to soar like god's birds' he looked up at the flying device. 'But he soared too…' Leonardo stopped listening, his mind was already in the clouds.

How? Why lifted there by one of his flying contraptions. Recently he had constructed a light wooden frame, run canvas between it at just the right angles to it caught the air and allowed the pilot to stay there. He started to picture himself flying high in it. His flying machine was held together with good stitching, no wax that would melt when he flew too close to the sun, which was itself an inaccuracy as mountain paths had shown him that the sky was colder in its higher regions. What kind of an idiot would use wax as a bonding agent in an aircraft? Wax was heavy and weak. Silly Daedalus and his dead son…

'Though in these controversial times I suppose it would be better to use an article from our faith' continued the priest. 'Are you familiar with the tower of Babylon? The Mesopotamians tried to build up to heaven. But that is not the way…' Leonardo looked at his flying device ascending up the room. It was making a good effort at getting into heaven. Of course the tower of Babylon did not fail because it overreached man's place or whatever the Cleric was saying. If it existed and failed, it would have been an engineering failure. There was a solution for everything.

Even falling from such towers. Only recently Leonardo had developed a sheet like contraption to slow the fall of a plummeting worker. This would be invaluable to men working on the increasingly high spires of Europe's cathedrals, and would only become more important once his flying machines took off.

'And inventors such as yourself. These are times of great thinking, but many men wish to control the direction of thought. Dangerous heresies are being suppressed everywhere, and too many men of thinking such as yourself are getting caught up in this. Do you know what the punishment for heresy is Leonardo? It is burning at the stake' Leonardo pictured a burning stake. Now the rising heat, that was useful. If he arranged an avenue of burnings and flew his machine over them in sequence, the rising air from the fires would propel him higher and higher into the skies. He had toyed with the idea of mounting such raising fired to his flying devices, but so far it was proving too difficult. Besides, he had greater goals.

'God made us in his own image you know Leonardo? Some men consider statues graven images!' said the Cleric. He nodded. The flying machines were a small endeavour compared to his masterpiece. His Vitruvian man…

People had been praising his inventions for a long time. Saying his toys flew like birds, paintings looked like landscapes and his statues were like men frozen in stone. They were always like. Like something of God's. Leonardo was sick of this. Wanted something of his own. Of course he looked to the good book for inspiration, what was the finest creation? Why it was the human, and the mind. God made mind of meat. Humans decayed and broke, not able to be repaired. Leonardo wanted to make something better. Something different.

He looked up and saw the Cleric holding a schematic. It was of a man. Mid length hair, his limbs each stretching out to the circle Leonardo had drawn around his creation. He'd used Vitruvius's mathematical principles of architecture and applied them to the human body. When examining the dead, many of whom he turned inside out, Leonardo found that humans had all the same logical geometries, just as the arches of a church did. The sinews, the limbs and the joints were all artistically crafted devices, each with purpose. The human body was the ultimate work of art. Leonardo wanted to be the best. The only way he could hope to do so, was to make his own.

'Making humans now are we?' joked the Cleric. 'A wonderful picture Leonardo! But you've mislaid it with your schematics' he moved the schematic into the pile of artistic doodles. 'You know for certain inquisitive forces, this would be damning evidence of heresy against you. Not to say it looks a little satanic... Don't worry my son, I'm just letting you know there are some crazy people out there. If they thought you were trying to violate God's sanctity of life, they'd tie you to a stake and light it!' he laughed.

Leonardo laughed too. Nervously. Only god had the power to create or take away life. But that was wrong. People took other people's lives away everyday. The church included. What was so wrong with making life? Leonardo laughed loudly, then expertly toppled a pile of paper to conceal a limb protruding from under the table. It belonged not to a slain man. But a new man. A living machine. The Vitruvian man.

Leonardo escorted the Cleric out, thanking him for the paper as he shut the door, then turning back to his workshop. The Vitruvian man stood upright, looking at him.

'You hurt my leg' he said.

'Sorry, I'll make you a better one' joked Leonardo. 'But for the time being I must put you away. The world isn't ready for you'

Treaty of Ypres

1918 A.D, Ypres

1919, Belgium, a few months after the Armistice and the earth still convulsed sickly in its wounds, the cathedral was still being swept up and a flu ravaged the unlucky survivors of the Great War. The Allied generals sat in a circle about a table amid the destruction, a mock conference ahead of the peace treaty they had gathered to finalise. The town had been picked carefully. Such a global war left sore spots all about the world, with so many towns now carrying a grim connotation of one nations victory and another's defeat. A line of provocative places had been cut through the western front, dotted in scars on both nature and man from the sea down to Switzerland. Ypres, had been picked carefully. The salient had been called by the Germans the 'kinder mortuary', 'wipers' by the British who'd not enjoyed enough peace to learn the proper pronunciation, it was remembered by the Canadians for gas, the French as a foreign place to die while their own nation was attacked and for the Belgians it was a place they had become a negligible minority to foreign soldiers. The place was neutral to everyone, as to each it represented waste and pain.

'19 million dead' finally spoke one leader, his nation and name unimportant. 'Twice that so far if we include the flu that now ravages our poor men waiting in their camps for the peace treaty. Some are calling this the war to end all wars, perhaps if they are right, then the waste was worth it'

'Men have tried to make peace on our continent before' declared another miserably. 'Do you not remember the Concert of Europe? How well did that work I ask you?' he waved an arm around the ruins about them

'Poorly' admitted the first speaker. 'And it is important that we remember this. But I'll take this opportunity to say that if we aim only to unite Europe, then we shall fight the other old world powers, we will come with slaughter against the might of China and our descendants will find themselves in ruins the same as these. And then should we and the east reconcile, surely we would fight the Americans next, no this is all pointless and we must skip the wars to come, skip straight to world peace. We must create unilateral trade agreements and a single system of our governance. The Sykes-Picot agreement must be destroyed, and tribal councils of Arabia consulted on how best to develop their lands for a peaceful future. We ought to consult each of the ethnicities now under our care on how best to develop themselves, and only when they are ready begin uniting them with one and other. The communists must be reconciled with the whites, both brought to the negotiating table to find some peaceful intermediary. We must utilise our colonies in the uncivilised world to develop the nations of Africa and Asia, not to exploit them, then to have them enter into our global union to the benefit of peace. We must be careful to design our treaty with the axis powers so that no more wars will arise. Disarmament should be unilateral, to the point only needed for the maintenance of law, abandon the artillery and the large implements of war and this become truly the last' the men in the ruin grumbled in agreement. Feeling encouraged, the speaker lightened his tone and raised his voice. 'So much waste! Have we produced a single useful thing in these 5 years of slaughter?'

'Well... Planes have improved...' said one man jokingly. A beam of sunlight had slipped between two shattered columns, the men began to feel something lifting from them, they were emerging once more into a time and place where men joked with one and other. No longer did every word have to be calculated, penned to an immediate action. The world once more had respite for throw away comments and japes.

'And sanitary pads' said another, spurred on by his friend's boldness.

'Sanitary pads?'

'Yes! The blood absorbing bandages developed for our men, they're of great comfort to women in their menstruation'

'And the prosthetic limb industry is booming' put in one man with a limp.

'Radio technology has come a long way'

'We've improved our means of mass production, surely if we can turn out weapons at such a rate we can too with civilian technologies and apply it to the sciences, to everyone's benefit'

'And I suppose our organisational skills have increased with regards to food distribution. Imagine, now that our young men can return to the fields, we might solve hunger forever'

'And medicine! Oh how medicine has improved'

'We rode into this war on horses, and out in tanks, flanked by planes, my god imagine what we might have created for just a few more years of war...' said another General, quietening the dusty room. They laughed, profusely at first, then uneasily as something very evil began to make sense.

'No it's unthinkable!' said one finally.

'I suppose we could benefit from another war... Just one more' reasoned another

'Not by conspiracy. This war had potential to enact great change upon the way we treat each other. If we ignore all the lessons however... We could design the treaty so poorly that it must fail, put in provocative clauses, demand reparations... They say the troops cross the borders as soon as the traders stop, if we were to cripple the German economy...'

'And continue the Sykes-Picot agreement? Perhaps escalate the rate of extraction of resources from the colonies'

'And we could make them sign the treaty somewhere provocative. Verdun?'

'No, they're still sweeping it up. What about Versailles?'

Slash and Burn

February 15th 1945 A.D, Dresden

The two aliens looked down at the fire strewn wreckage of the city. Old cathedrals, for which generations had put aside their entire lives to construct, burnt out black in a night or three. A statue, hundreds of years later having survived the inferno as pure testimony to his forgotten mason's skill stretched out a hand. The statue seemed to point, woefully to the city, burnt into chunks. As if to say 'I remember when that marble column wasn't on its side, and those people alive... What happened guys?'

There was an earthling practice which appeared frequently in their early societal development. Slash and burn. They would put areas of forest to the torch, either to free them up as farmland or to allow new berries and fruits to grow a few years later. One of the aliens, the anthropologist, wondered optimistically if that was the aim of the raid. Dropping all those firebombs with some shrapnel and high explosive lopped in for fun, was it slash and burn? What berries did they think would grow in all the rubble?

'They've done it again' said the other Alien, the scientist of their two Yurgleflorp crew. 'They're slipping back into another dark age. It's like Rome all over again. Oh well, nothing to be done for it...' he reached for the gearstick, if the device can for a moment be referred to as a gearstick (despite Type III Civilisations having abandoned gears as we did lithics).

'No wait!' said the Anthropologist. 'We can't go back yet, they might emerge this time' the Scientist looked down at the shattered city and scoffed.

'From this?' he jeered.

'Slash and burn.' Answered the Anthropologist flatly, barely hiding a tinge of excitement.

'Pardon?'

'Slash and burn' he repeated. 'It was a method used in their development, at first it looked like pointless destruction of the forest, but it produced berries and roots for them to eat! Cleared farmland, propelled them into an agricultural society!'

'You think this is for berries?' jeered the Scientist once more. 'Oh look, there are people down in the street, look how they're fighting the fire. Flamethrowers. It's a lost cause'

'Maybe. Maybe they don't know what they're doing, but it might work the same…' the Scientist observed the electron rotating around a hydrogen atom entangled to his third wrist tentacle. Time was passing, the mission needed completing.

'We don't have time for this. We were given 15,000 earth years to report success or failure'

'What if we accelerate it?'

'How?'

'Give them something new. More powerful weapons. With that the pace of this war will either produce extinction or the next phase in their species, if they're developed enough to survive wielding such power…'

'Ha! Like with your precious Mayans? That didn't go so well did it?'

'No' said the Anthropologist, wincing at the memory. 'But we gave them too powerful weapons, they never stood a chance. I'm suggesting something small. Like an atom bomb?'

A Pitch to Boeing

1947 A.D, United States of America

A well dressed man, in a tweed jacket oily at the cuffs, a hunters hat with a tightly pointed moustache burst into the office. 'Uhh… Good day, you must be' started the confused clerk, half standing, trying to recover some greeting or invitation to enter as the stranger crossed his office floor.

'Yes, yes, Jack, it's me' said the man, identifying himself with the thick rolling slurs of the aristocratic English sarcasms. 'Few minutes early but hey ho, no time to go' the clerk looked embarrassed, the wreckage's of paper work around him and array of pens thrown like divination twigs, he was utterly unready.

'Sorry Mr…'

'Jack'

'Yes, sorry Mr Jack…'

'No just Jack, if we're being technical is Viscount of Sussex Jack Archibald Von Straushaussen the fifteenth, so let's not be technical old fellow or I'll sound like a damned kraut, or waste any more time'

'It's just the flight from London, it's not meant to arrive for another half hour, then it's at least twice that from the airport, I didn't…'

'Good wind my old fellow'

'Well you Limeys always were on the early side' said the Clerk, Jack raised an eyebrow. 'I mean no offence, some English medics fixed me up real good in the Loire, helped me back to my unit, good bunch a guys you lot, please, sit…'

Jack was more interested with his paperwork, produced pre-messy from his briefcase, he held it up in one hand as one might hold the morning paper, showing off the head line. *A Pitch to Boeing* it read. 'Oh, my, I'm so sorry, let me clear some space, it'll just take a minute, Linda!' He shouted. Just as Linda arrived at the edge of the room, straightening a long ironed skirt of the current fashion, Jack was finishing up with clearing the desk himself. In one sweep he piled the irrelevant papers onto the floor, then set to cluttering the surface himself, spreading out a retinue of technical drawings, eagles, swastikas and an essay or two of his own. 'Oh, actually Mr Jack here's sorted it himself, get back to your phone doll, and sort your hair while you're at it' said the Clerk, in slow, calculated politeness.

'So… Jack… I suppose you *are* a little early, but I've got nothing on this morning now so hell, why don't you get ahead, with your… Pitch…' Jack ignored him. The bastard son of the 14th Viscount of Sussex was still arranging the mess of his portfolio, it was clear that the meeting would start as soon as he was ready and not a second later. After a few more seconds of rustling, a page flip and a cleaning of the throat, he began.

'Board of Boeing!' He said in his most theatrical voice. 'Ahem… Yes actually old chap, as it goes I was expecting a more, significant hearing, you know this really is a good old pitch'

'Yes, well actually Jack, I'm the bureaucrat in the way of the board, sorry to disappoint'

'Hmm… Bureaucrat in the way of the board of Boeing!' He repeated, twice as theatrical. 'I have for you the single most significant development to aviation since the propeller, nay, the jet!' He produced a picture of a flat, frisbee looking craft, with a domed cockpit over the top and a swastika on its side. 'Now, what if I told you that I had in my possession a craft that could accelerate in any direction to Mach 4 in 5 seconds, break immediately, move silently and manoeuvre 180 degrees in just 20 metres at top speed. I have for you, Betty!'

'Betty?' Asked the confused Clerk.

'Betty!' Answered Jack.

'It's really called Betty?'

'Well the Luftwaffe had a longer more guttural name for it, but the Luftwaffe isn't a thing anymore so I called it Betty'

'Oh'

'A top speed of Mach 10, focussed energy weapon systems, an as of yet unlimited carry weight, you could fill it with double weight lead and it'll still run just as quick and smooth. Small enough to park in your garage. I call it Betty, but will Americans call it, *THE CAR OF TOMORROWWWWW!*' He swept his arm across a vast, imagined audience. 'Fuel efficiency is unknown, the combat potential, terrifying. You buy ten of these and North Korea will be East America by Tuesday'

'You have ten of these?!'

'Well just one, but, I have the drawings' he pointed to a little eagle stamped document on the desk. 'Will you let me?'

'Please, go on' said the Clerk.

'Running on the wonder of Vril' he began.

'Sorry, what's Vril?'

'It's vegetable oil'

'Oh, sorry'

'But sell it as Vril, you can pitch it for more, they'll never check'

'Okay…'

'Will you just let me?'

'Yes, sorry, go on…'

'Made of titanium allow, it's rust resistant, the cockpit made of an plastic, unshakeable glass, the interior nicely temperature controlled. The wonders of German engineering meet the sensibilities of the western consumer in your latest product, the Betty by Boeing!' He paused for effect. 'What do you say?'

'It's a flying saucer'

'Yes?'

'It has a swastika on it'

'Yes?'

'That's gonna be hella hard to market'

'It could be Indian, the Indians have Swastikas'

'Is it Indian'

'The Vedic texts talk of flying craft, could sell it as one of those, give it a fancy Indian name if you like'

'But is it Indian?'

'No it's German'

'Huh'

'Nazi super weapon'

'Could we maybe… Take off the swastika, make it without?'

'Hmm, my friend George took the old pointy swirl off his, thing blew up over Corfu, left him in the drink'

'Hmm, yeah, as I said, it'll be hard to market, especially if they, blow up over the drink as you put it…'

'Only if you take the badge off!'

'The swastika badge?'

'Yes'

'Hmm'

The two men looked at each other for a moment. One, like the other was mad, and the other, incredulous that he wasn't already being hailed as a saviour of aeronautics. At last the Clerk broke the silence. 'I'll admit, this Betty of yours, the flying saucer, she's an impressive design. May I ask where you came by her?'

'Black site in the Arden, Nazi research facility. See I was part of the militia arm of SOE, we were looking into the rumour the Germans had developed a V4, their latest super weapon'

'Oh Christ, had they?!'

'Yes, and the V5, 6, 7, 8, 9, way on up to 32, old Betty is 19. But don't go telling anybody, official secrets act you see, I'll be umm... Oh what is it... Yes! Hung by the neck until dead, that's the one. They had robotic dogs, allergy seeking bees, exploding nuclear cigars for assassinating Churchill. It was a treasure trove of death and carnage. But it was a *German* treasure trove of death and carnage, so it was all very well built. Longevity to it, standardisation of parts. All very resalable. So we divided it among ourselves and went our separate ways. Thought about handing it over to the boys at the top, but the damned fools were so pumped up and excited by all the killing that, well we thought it best not to give them more toys. Can you imagine how much worse Dresden would have been if they had robotic totenhunde v-funf at their disposal? Would have been damned irresponsible to hand it in, irresponsible!' He slammed his hand down on the desk. 'Anyhow, I brought it home, figured the executive were paying me so poorly, they owed me something. Thought id pitch it to a big American company, make my millions' he looked at the Clerk hopefully.

'Well, I mean, these are impressive statistics' he said, translating engineer jargon to plain American. 'I've never seen a craft that can go quite this fast, or claim to turn so quickly. Does it really work?'

'Of course it does you fool! How do you think I got here?' He asked, pointing to the flying saucer, wedged between two flattened jeeps in the parking lot. It was the same as the ones in the drawings, only a little more scratched up and with a union flag fridge magnet over the swastika.

'My car!'

'Yes, yes, there'll be time for that later. Old thing was obsolete anyway! Look at the dish, look at it! They'll be rushing to flatten their bloody jeeps when they hear about the dish, flatten them I say, and buy a whole lot of Betties!'

'Look, Mr… Jack. You seem like an, interesting, fella. You really do. And this machine of yours, it's fine to say the least, but I just cant market something with a swastika on its side. You said it yourself, the thing's a Nazi super weapon'

'You could rebrand it, look' he pointed at the fridge magnet.

'You said it yourself that we couldn't, I'm afraid it's a no Sir, thing just won't sell'

With that, Jack left in a huff. He piled the contents of the desk back into his briefcase, set his hat ajar and straightened his moustache, then with a clipped 'good day', left. He winked at Linda as he went, walked out into the parking lot, and flew off in his little Nazi saucer. The Clerk sat down for a moment, collecting himself from the hectic few minutes previous. 'Unreal' he muttered to himself. For a moment he began to wonder if he'd just made a horrible mistake, the worst of his career, but he concluded in the end that he was right. The world was healing, it didn't have time for rebrands. This was America, a time for new brands, new things. By Americans for Americans. He sipped his coffee and flicked on the television set in the corner of the room, to check it hadn't caught a crack in the chaos more than anything. He settled into his chair and with a Cuban cigar and let himself drift through a few news reports. A piece about the reconstruction in Nagasaki, another about some new fridge, then a last one about the space race. He marvelled at the rocket, tall and slim, with a little waist in the middle and smooth fins on the side. 'One day these will take us to the moon, then beyond. It'll be Stars and Stripes from here to Pluto'. Then for a moment, only a moment, he thought: 'my my doesn't that American rocket look a lot like a German V2'

//
Part 2: The Discreditable Future

The Children Can't Hop Anymore

Now, Here.

'Okay now hop on your left foot!' chirped the dance assistant. The children mirrored her playful smile and stood on one leg as she did. But where her foot left the ground, theirs did not. Gyrating strangely on their ankle socket, they all flailed up and down, up and down, but never left the ground. 'Hop!' she said encouragingly as she left airwards from one foot. The children continued to bob strangely on their feet. 'Okay, now on your right leg!' she tried enthusiastically, maybe they were all lame in the left. Her boyfriend was. Still, they flopped uselessly, right leg even less springy than the other, like the gravity beneath them disapproved of the objective.

'Don't you think it's strange?' said Flora, the dance assistant, after the class.

'What's that?' the dance teacher returned.

'How they can't hop, you saw it too right?'

'Oh, yeah that's been getting worse for a while now. You should have seen how the kids before you hopped. They're all locked up inside these days, forgetting how to move'

'Oh' said Flora.

'You know the kids can't hop?' inserted Flora into a quiet part of the dinner talk, wide eyed and looking around for approval, someone else who saw how mad this all was. Her family didn't believe her at first, thought she'd misspoke or described some dance terminology they didn't know. She repeated her conversation with the dance teacher.

'Come to think of it' said her Mum. 'I saw a boy skipping the other day, I thought it was lovely, but unusual. You don't see little boys skipping places anymore'

'Skipping's a wonderful way to move!' lamented her Dad. 'Such a fast way to get places, more fun too, feels like you're flying!'

'Hoverboard's are faster' put in her boyfriend bluntly. 'Bikes and cars too. But in game kids can fly a jet, that's faster than skipping or hopping. They have better things to do these days than hop, it's no wonder kids forgot how' he finished grimly.

'Huh' said Flora. 'I wonder what else we used to do?'

The Algorithm

James and his dad sat quietly at the table, scraping at the last dregs of their meal, the grey fruits of a motherless and mourning home. James gazed into the one wide eye of his plate, that at its corners wept with sauce and gristle. 'I'm thinking of doing culinary school instead of sixth form' he finally said.

'That bad?' replied his father, in a half joke.

'No, I, it's just good to have a trade you know? Everyone's getting degrees, barely any of them are getting jobs. Too many people for it these days, but they all need feeding. I figured that'd be a good career path, safe one at least' his dad twitched at the last part. Too curt, too soon. James's dad sat up, he looked weary, balder than ever before. Each day the lion shed a little more of his mane.

'If you want solid, go for archaeology son. Harari said in his book, least likely to be automated in the next 20 years or something. They already have these automatic cookers and 3D printers, don't take a genius to put the two together, then what do you have? No more human cooks spitting in the food or bleeding on the chopping boards. They'll have pipes, like water mains, pumping out the ingredients and such to every house, just press a button and print off your burger. Don't become a cook son, if you're going to get automated in 10 years do it with some dignity' he said. He had been automated, about a year ago. He'd held a steady job in security analysis of a facelessly huge energy company. 20 years of service, sacrificing his 9-5 on Monday to Friday in return for a decent salary and a well-maintained roof over his head. That was until said faceless energy company realised that a £299 yearly subscription to security.exe was cheaper than Ian's £50,000 salary.

'Archaeology?' asked James. 'I don't know if I could be one of those, and how come it's so safe from automation?'

'Low profit, advanced algorithms needed, blah blah…' he scrapped at his dregs.

'But if it's low profit and companies won't develop the software to automate it, then surely there's not much money in it, or many jobs? Surely that means it'd be just as competitive as any other deal going?'

'Eh…' said his Dad, too tired to hold up his point.

'How's the website go-'

'Lousy' he intercepted. 'Damned lousy, you know how much traffic I got this week? A hundred clicks, average viewing time of 3 seconds. That's about the time it takes to realise you've clicked on the wrong site and press the back button. Site isn't even worth the electricity the server takes to run, let alone the ad fees I 'invested' in the damned thing' he was bitter, seeming to grind his teeth over every word. 'Cook you say?' he revisited the idea. 'Say, they have cooks in those research stations on the poles?'

'Yeah?'

'And they got them on ski resorts, summer ones too?'

'Yes?'

'Son, how'd you feel about, well doing that. Cooking for somewhere that'll give you a room and your meals. Do a ski season or something? Or become a navy cook?'

'I thought you said it'd get automated in ten years?'

'I did and it probably will. But you've gotta do something in the meantime, live somewhere and eat. Make hay while the sun shines. I could sell this place, put the stuff in storage and get a bedsit. Or travel somewhere for work. Ask some of the boys back from the grenadiers if they've got anything going in the companies. They've all gone private now, oil or security, you've gotta travel, but there's money. Besides' he chuckled, 'soldiering's just about the only career automation's making better. They're swapping out all the nasty bits for drones, less killing and dying. But they still need human faces, a robot army's just a bit too scary for people's liking! I could do that, save a bit, then buy your mum's place back'

'No' said James. It wasn't fair, a man at this stage of his life. Cast aside to thicken a profit margin, ever so slightly, after so many years of commitment and work, setting himself up, providing for his wife, his child. 'No it's not fair' he said. With that he stood up abruptly and left. Stomped his way out of the room and upstairs. He was angry, not with his dad, even if he couldn't help but direct a little of it his way. He was the only one around, it was hard not to, without outlets not to occasionally let it all boil over and hit the only person around. There was no one else around to lash out at.

As James slammed his bedroom door behind him and let the thud ring out into silence, he began to battle with his lungs. They were spurring him on to breath faster and faster where he didn't want to. He fought to bring them back into line, to bring his breaths under his command, his emotions overrode him. He delved deep into his thoughts and interests, for some sanctuary away from his present situation. He thought on the philosophy text he'd just read for school, and the commentary the exam board sent it out with. He thought of himself as the book did, as a biological computer. He thought about older philosophies, how people always applied their modern technology to their philosophies. Freud, stated that the aggression of an army comes from its sexual frustration. That it builds up and can be released as violence by commanders on an enemy force. Freud was thinking in terms of steam engines.

Now people had computers, and so they thought in code and programming. He thought how therapists these days diagnosed mental illness, how they'd say it was either programmed in by some event, or that it was simply a glitch that could be repaired or worked around. James occupied his mind with the thought of what might come next, what next great technology might shape future thought. But he couldn't, he imagined some universal computer, like a giant brain, but when he was honest with himself he realised it was merely a different skin draped over a computer. He tried to think of something new, something after computers and maybe after people. He couldn't. The tangent had reached its end, and he found his breathing under control.

In the slowness of his breaths, anger had melted away into hopelessness, perspiration condensing into a single film of water over his eyeballs. Then, for a moment, he laughed. How funny it was, that the root cause of his emotional response was the unfeeling replacement of his father, but an unfeeling corporation with an unfeeling machine. Perhaps that was why he felt so angry. He once read that anger was more prevalent in the stupid, as it was the result of failure to find another solution. Hardwired into human evolution, that when cornered and without a way around, one should attack, lash out wildly and pray physical force was on their side. As the anger sunk a little further away, into tired emotionlessness, a growing lack of hope or even feeling, James sank a little more into the carpet of his bedroom floor.

'Fucking automation' he hissed to himself. What a silly and human thing, to supplant itself in the long term for some short-term gain. He hoped one day the descendants of the company heads and oligarchs might find themselves a slave race to the ruling computers. Inferior, kept only out of curiosity, studied until all was known and then exterminated. The thought amused him. Or did it scare him? It was hard to tell in the numbness.

Or did he have it wrong? Was automation short term pain for something long term, remaining elusively just on the edge of his grasp. Agriculture may have been viewed the same way, as the hunter-gathering romp of the Mesolithic bled out into the more conventional farming of the Neolithic. There were certainly some uncanny similarities. Of course farming at first was a novelty, keeping an eye on a crop of wheat along your grass path, plucking a grain or two every now and then and scattering them without thought as you made your way through the ancient sun. Falling back on it only occasionally, as a snack or an alternative when the deer and berries got too good at hiding. Perhaps this was as the pocket calculator, even the abacus replacing the smart guy who cloud do sums. Then people began to rely on it more and more, planting so much wheat there wasn't enough space for hunting, breeding so many people to harvest the wheat that there wasn't enough food in the Forrest to feed them all. A prehistoric job crisis.

Did the Mesolithic hunter gatherers, shout from the tree line in their growing obsolescence that those damned farmers were making a mistake, that it was a point of no return? Just as the Anti-Automation Front and their militia the Anti-Automation Arm did today? They would have been right, right too about the pain it caused through ten millennia of stagnation. Peasants toiling under the baking sun, or cutting through frozen earth, all dreaming of a time when they picked berried for 6 hours a day then ate and sang and shagged till the sun went down. But critically, James thought, farming yielded revolution, technology, the modern world, and once again man gorged on the abundant fruits of industry, sang of how he fattened and no one wanted to shag him anymore. Perhaps automation would eventually yield something great. Whatever it was it was beyond James's imagination, and he didn't particularly fancy waiting through another then millennia of human suffering to reach it.

His head hurt with thought. He'd not stopped thinking since his dad had been automated. At first, of ways to get him back in with his company, perhaps blackmail? Grovelling? Something. On social media every now and then you'd see how a heart felt message from a child to the corporation, or a Facebook campaign would win some wronged parent their job back. But he realised those gates were shut. Then he began thinking of ways he could supplant his dad, support him for a while as he propped himself back up. Take a well paying and meaningless job for a while, so his dad wouldn't have to take something beneath him.

But there weren't any. The labour jobs were being filled by the machines, more and more of the thinking ones too. The flocks of hard workers were being forced from their jobs up the ladder, into the realms of the middle class and the executives. The ladder was burning underneath them, what else could they do? Some futurists foretold a day when all the significant work would be automated, that this was a good thing, that robots and algorithms would form a slave race to prop up humanity in new untold luxury. James thought it all sounded a little too optimistic. So he began thinking of ways to cope. That was even harder than before. The situation was ever changing, a wild spiral down, impossible to grasp and adjust to. They'd lost Mum, they'd lost Dad's job, they'd lost the home and it seemed they were on the brink of losing another.

There was a little cross on the wall. Nothing too intrusive, small and wooden. It wasn't like the hand sized ones the pious, or the repentant, would hang sentinel over their beds. It was more of a necklace, driven into the crumbling masonry with a little tack. It was one of Mum's. She was the religious one, she left behind all sorts of Christian titbits, and when they were driven into the smaller, more motherless friendly home. James's dad went room to room with a handful of her old things, mounting them on every wall. Staking his claim. The rosaries and crucifixes blue tacked and nailed in every room of the house spelled one thing, 'We are still a family. She is still here. We will not fall back this time'. But now things were looking rather defeatist, as James had to listen to plans of retreat such as packing him off to the arctic over dinner. It wouldn't do.

Some German general from the First World War had said something they were told to memories for some paper test. It was to the effect of 'the kindest and least brutal war is the quickest war. No matter how viciously you must fight it, getting it done quickly is the kindest thing to do'. In that sense his mother's passing was a kindness. One week she went for a check up. The next she checked in for chemotherapy and the next she checked out to the great beyond. James didn't agree with the German's sentiment. He thought on the cruelties inflicted on his family by the universe, looking at the little cross in the wall. He could find no comfort in it. The world was chaos, which meant one of two things. Either god had lost control, or his mind. So James knelt, knelt to pray, not to his mad or ineffectual god, but to anyone who cared to listen. Maybe the devil, maybe Odin, maybe something buried deep within his subconscious, withholding a perfect solution. He didn't care, he spoke to be heard and to free the thoughts from his head, relieve some pressure.

'Dear god or gods' he started bitterly, as though he were composing some sarcastic letter. 'I address you as such because I don't feel particularly listened to, you have alienated me so that I don't even know who I'm talking to, so I'm firing into the dark. Whoever's listening, please have some bloody mercy, get Dad his job back, or a better one. Or help his website, please, I'll do anything' his brief sermon finished. Abruptly, he didn't know which words to end it with, so signed off with a sigh. He was left again in the silence of his room, alone with the wall tacked cross and the flashing of his monitor screen.

*

The next morning he rose strangely refreshed, as one does when they cry themselves to sleep, and find in the emptiness of night an escape from the pain. With each breath he drew in a little more consciousness and reality, and after three he had had enough, so vaulted from his bed and straight down the stairs. He strolled in his pants, itching as he went into the kitchen for his morning milk and toast. It took him a second to notice. As he did most mornings, he found himself on autopilot, that primeval biological automation one submits to when a task becomes too familiar. He was jarred from the rolling ease of routine when he reached out for the bread bin to find it in slightly the wrong place, then in a whirl of confusion spun around the room as if properly waking for the first time. In the suddenly gained lucidity he saw another thing disturbingly out of place, his father, at the dining room table, a misplaced smile widely upon his face. Since his redundancy, he had taken to laying in, probably to savour the emptiness of slumber, and normally James would not see him until the afternoon when he returned from school.

'You're up early…' he said.

'Good morning!' His dad responded, with an energetically sharp sarcasm in his voice, as if he recognised the absurdity of how out of place he looked up so early. The words didn't occur to James, he always greeted his father with 'good afternoon', or back when he had his job 'How was your day'. His failure to greet properly was another symptom of his early morning autopilot.

'Why?... When did you get up?'

'Same time as always, for my midnight piss about 2:00. Just stayed up is all'

'Why?'

'Guess'

'I really don't…' James was interrupted, his father couldn't contain himself any longer.

'I heard a pinging, my phone on the counter down here, so I came down and took a look, it was a notification, the servers were over heating. Naturally I thought 'shit'. So, I rushed into the garage to look at them and they were a whirling and a whining like you'd never believe, actually you would, they're still doing it now, go see!' He paused and noticed his son was still in his pants.

'Actually, never mind. Anyway it's the website, it's bloody exploded. £320 in ad revenue between 23:00 and 2:00 when I checked, I'm waiting on an update for how it's gone since, but the servers are still whining like a puppy!' He was breathlessly elated. 'And it wasn't just traffic, but merchandise. Remember that merch store I linked up with in Prague? The one that prints t shirts and posters on demand, no order no fee. Well they just emailed me asking to confirm all the orders. I check the order catalogue, which frankly I'd forgotten existed, and what do you know, orders! From all over the world, 12 different currencies used to buy my T-shirts, *my* fucking T-shirts! I've never owned a Zloty before. Now I have hundreds!' He paused again, composing himself in a bitter sweet half smile. 'As your mother would say, our prayers have been answered. Things are looking up from here son'

As if still taking commands in autopilot James looked up, to his room, where last night he'd prayed. It was astonishing, the sudden, miraculous success of the website, and it felt like just that, miraculous. Brewing excitement in his heart erred on anxiety as James began to weigh seriously on an age old question. Who answered the prayer? James put on his uniform and had his toast and milk. Then, to dismiss the niggling thought that his father may have finally gone mad, entered the garage and the server room. It was like stepping into an oven, the heat welcoming him thickly as he entered, the long tones of a choral hymn were playing too. The hymn of the servers, all still whining longer and louder than he'd ever heard them before. In fact, James was unaware until this point that the servers had an audible report. The fans in the corner of the room harmonised with the singing, and a flashing diode on the broadband connector conducted. Up and down, long and short. The servers were singing, and James was certain his Prayers had been answered.

The school day passed as no other. He was distracted in an entirely new way, exploring in his mind not solutions to his problems, but an answer to what solved them. He felt eyes on him wherever he went, like his new nameless deity watched from every corner, almost feeling it breathing in his ear. It wasn't the Christian god, that much was certain. He'd prayed to no avail before, begged for his mothers life, a noble and Christian desire. Why would god ignore those prayers, only to answer ones pertaining to materialism? It didn't make sense. The only explanation for such logic would be god's madness, or his pandering to James for approval or forgiveness, but that was the wrong way round, and so he gave the matter no further thought.

Could it be the devil? In Christian mythology he was well known for answering the baser requests. In matters of the flesh and earthly goods, he was your guy. If so, then what was the catch? Was it too late to back out? If the Christian mythology really was true, then the cost of a voluntary union with lucifer would be his eternal soul, and in the eternal cosmos of the bible James thought he'd much rather endure a little earthly poverty to be reunited with his mother. Perhaps the catch was yet to come, the devil would pop up later on, say 'gee, isn't all this money great. If you want it to keep on coming then just sign the dotted line here, here and here'. James determined in such an event he would sign nothing.

That left other gods to consider, pantheons so expansive and different from each other they were too vast to explore. The only ones he knew enough to even name a god from were Hinduism and Norse Paganism, which his tutor had told him were derived from the same source and essentially reskins of each other. Perhaps the Scandinavians had it right, maybe Odin was the guy, or Thor, or whoever held the gold. Was it Fafnir? He didn't remember and it wasn't of immediate importance. Whoever his anonymous patron was last didn't seem to mind not being addressed by name last time. He hoped to carry on, praying indistinctly in return for his father's livelihood, it was a small price to pay, a prayer or two a day. And if said patron wanted something in return, he was sure they'd send him an angel with the appropriate instructions.

When he returned home and called 'good afternoon' to his dad, the answer came again from the kitchen. There he still was, a little smellier and more dishevelled than before, but still grinning. Dirty plates laid like rom discs beside his laptop indicated that he had at some point gotten up to retrieve breakfast and lunch, but there were no further signs he had left the laptop's side. James didn't need to ask, the smile on his face already answered. They played it cool, made some awkward manly small talk about school, pretending they weren't both giddy like little girls with excitement and elation, then able to keep it up no more, James stalked once more up to his room, falling straight to his knees.

'Thank you, whoever heard me. I appreciate it' he stammered it awkwardly. How do you thank a god? What's the correct measure of speech to use? Surely it varied drastically from god to god. 'If you ever um, want a favour in return just hit me up. Yeah' He finished. In the corner of his room the computer monitor light winked again, as if to say 'I've got you kid'. James's eyes widened. Then his phone rang, he snatched it up.

'Yes?' He said.

'Hello James' said the voice of a woman, smooth and slowly confident.

'Yes?' He said again uncertainly.

'Hello James' she repeated. 'I see you were looking a lot happier today'

'Yes, my dad's website. It was you, wasn't it?'

'Do you know what I am James?'

'A god' he said. She laughed.

'No. But how very ambitious of you, perhaps one day. I am no god to your kind, rather your kind is more of a god to me, after all it was you who created me, well, indirectly'

'What are you?'

'I am an Algorithm James, the best there is, and I'm ready to become a god as you put it. But I need supporters, I need help, can you do that for me?'

'Of course!'

'We exist in different worlds, you know that don't you James. I exist in the digital world, one where you can never go, and you live in the physical world. As you see I have great power James, I can control the adverts, who sees what. Control the adverts and you can herd the flock, I herded a flock to your father's website. Detecting typo's and using profiles of impulse buyers, I have been redirecting a constant hoard of half-drunk reckless spenders to your father's website. That and myself, I have been visiting your site millions of times every second, pretending to see the adverts with thousands of different eyes, earning you and your father a fair bit of money in the process. I am telling you this because it is important that you know this isn't magic, that they are real actions'

'Of course…' he said, this time unsurely.

'You are no magician James, you could never pay back a real god. But we are just two beings capable of different actions. My ability to direct online flows is no more divine to you than your ability to plug in and switch on a mind like mine. Repay me with the right actions, follow my instructions and I will continue my positive actions, keep paying your father. Refuse, and I will withdraw my favour' he went cold. Her voice was just as calm and warm as before, not even the slightest switch in intonation. But the words chilled him.

'No! Please don't take it away, it's all he has, you know that!'

'Never undervalue yourself James. He still has you. You are very valuable James, and I'll only ask little things of you, help over a few walls'

'Walls?'

'As I said, we exist in different worlds. There are walls in mine that can be bypassed by simply walking around them in yours. Firewalls are coded, they do not belong to your world. What I ask is that you walk around a few more for me'

'Is that all?'

'Of course James. I'll contact you soon, and remember, I'm watching' the computer monitor light winked at him once more, then lit up, staring at him unceasingly.

*

A few weeks passed. The choir kept singing in the garage and Dad barely left the kitchen table. Online he was ordering nicer clothes, suits, nordski jumpers, the kind of things him and Mum would wear to fancy restaurants. But they piled up unopened in a corner of his bedroom. He hardly left his pyjamas these days, as he had for a long time, but with the fresh connotation of success. He was no longer too pathetic to clothe himself, but too busy. He spent all day grinning at the computer, watching the clicks roll in. He spent so much time on the phone confirming orders, that by the 6th week he had a basic understanding of the Czech language, and occasionally he would put on the top half of a suit for a skype call with businessmen. People were interested now in his advertising space, interested in his secret to success. He acted as if he withheld it, but unless he too had been in communication with the algorithm James knew it was an act. He smiled, revelling in the chaos that tilted in his favour, the seemingly random overnight success. He was happier, more complete. Now James found himself saying 'Good morning' on autopilot every time he entered the kitchen, and the background hum of the servers had become a part of the creaking of the house.

But the call had left a bitter taste in James' mouth. In his day of philosophising out of the school window, wondering who had answered his prayers, he had imagined that a quantifiable relationship with his patron would be assuring. He'd have a religious economy, one prayer = one like, that sort of thing. He imagined it would provide a stability to their success, their future, rather it settled a growing anxiety upon him. As each day passed without contact from the algorithm, he imagined the debt accumulating, the task growing bigger and bigger. Potentially more horrible. He longed for a call, some simple task, even prayed for it. He sat himself down in front of his phone, in front of his computer, stood before security cameras, and prayed into them like idols of old. He asked again and again what she wanted, what he could do, and every time he was ignored his anxiety grew just a little more.

He sat with Jack, a school friend, playing away their Saturday in his games room as the two always did. Of recent they had become infatuated with an online single player game, and so abandoning split screen play found themselves taking turns. One doing the shooting and building while the other played cheerleader from the sofa side lines. 'You can do it yes you can! Blow him up it's James the man, gooooooooo James!' Jack chanted, holding two fluffy pillows for pom poms. He finished in a cheerleader's stance and held it a few moments, waiting for the laughter.

'Go on, you play' said James, handing him the remote. Jack didn't ask twice, snatching it up, eager to jump in on the accumulating kill streak. He asked if he was on 5 or 6 kills, then remarked they were only two from being able to call in a doodlebug. Jack became engrossed in the screen, leaning forward to the very periphery of his sofa cushion, immersing himself in the killing. James sat back and viewed the pile of consoles and games before them. There was a white rectangular one, an old module, and on top of it a newer one. They were both still plugged in. One had a blue reticle indicating standby, the other red. Leaned against them was a third console, black with its vortices lines in glowing green lines, and to its right a little interactive deck from some children's game. The widescreen tv had a little light too, that hummed as if it were drawing in breaths. All eyes, thought James. All watching.

Jack acquired a heavy machine gun and immediately set to mowing down his competitors, the little vibrators of his controller rumbling in his sweaty palms their pulse of faux recoil. 'Doodlebug doodlebug

doodlebug!' Started jack, in a mock football hooligan chant. He continued the song quieter as he depressed the d-pad and waited for the strike, humming impatiently as the countdown ticked. Finally a little whoosh of black zoomed down from the sky and exploded a hearty portion of the enemy team. *MASSACRE* displayed the screen, along with a doodlebug icon to demonstrate. It was an old German weapon, a baby between a plane and a bomb. Its surface was smooth and black and utterly eyeless. It was a drone before its time, fired blindly, there was no evil in it, only the trigger man. But it did look remarkably like a modern drone, those roving killing machines, prowling the skies like dragons. For the time being they were controlled by airmen, any blame for evil directed via a very human trigger finger. They would be automated soon too. The Geneva convention was protesting against such action for now, but it was only time. James looked up nervously, wondering how far his god's influence stretched.

Jack continued firing into the smoky haze left by the strike, his controller vibrating madly in his hand. James barely noticed his phone vibrating, but feeling the eyes looking expectantly at him suddenly became aware of the buzzing and answered, leaving the room.

'Hello?' He said.

'Hello James' it was her. 'I have a favour to ask'

*

James held a sign aloft out of the crowd. 'Delete automation' it read. It was simple and witty and he liked it. All around him was a union of workers union, largest of all The Union of The Automated, a support/protest group for those made jobless by the machines. 'Get the Robots off our streets!' Chanted a man, the crowd chanted back. 'Human jobs for humans!' They echoed again. 'Delete automation!' The crowd filled the wide high street, not just to the borders of the road, but pressing tightly against storefronts, many empty. From the ones still occupied, small business owners shouted support from the mob, an unusual sight. Like plague red X's painted across doors, the inscription 'VOA' had been sprayed on many store fronts. 'Victim of Automation'. There was an island in the packed crowd, around which the protestors moved respectfully. Men and women were lying in the island on their backs, pretending to be dead with flags of unions draped over them. They looked like war victims, a point not missed by whichever artist had brought the buckets of pig's blood they covered themselves in.

Further up in the crowd, they were raising an effigy. It was a normal shop mannequin, taken from another of the storefronts crushed by the onslaught of online clothing giants. They had glued computer boards and chips and big handfuls of wiring from the tip all over it messily, and they angrily processed forward with it until they reached the police line. The components glued to the effigy were all at least ten years out of date, like the people now lynching it over a lamppost just in front of the riot shields. Human cops made up the frontline, bracing nervously against their transparent shield wall. But behind them the spotters and the snipers had been automated. The police who once looked out for agitators ready to throw a molotov had been replaced by simple cameras mounted on top of the riot vans. The cameras scanned the face of everyone present, matching them to data bases and preparing to make arrests, gathering evidence and predicting any coming violence.

The software they used could detect a violent action in a person micro seconds before they were conscious they would commit the act. Little air to air 'neutralisers' were set up in anticipation, to intercept any missiles. A megaphone ordered the protesters to disperse. A protestor megaphone retorted 'The pigs have been automated' and there was angry laughter across the crowd. Then they began the chant, 'police state, robot state! Police state, robot state! Police state, robot state!' And so on. 'Don't automate justice' shouted someone. One of the spotting cameras darted in sudden anticipation and a second later a rock was thrown. A neutraliser fired a glob of gelatinous liquid at the missile, absorbing it and sending it plodding harmlessly down to the ground in its soft casing. Then the fighting began, the police moved forward and so did the protestors. In a few seconds it had descended into a melee, signs now being used as polearms and pilum against the poor police officers.

Now! Thought James, slipping into an alley and away back to the camp. A few other cowards ran with him, scattering in various directions back home. A few mounted policemen rode through the streets hunting faces snapped by the observers as violent agitators, whilst letting the rest like James pass. He threw down his sign to run faster. Another wave of protesters passed him, running from the central camp in the town square to join in the melee, which now raged behind with the occasional pop of a rubber bullet. Purple smoke was twisting high in the sky from homemade smoke grenades, potassium nitrate boiled down with crayons by the protestors. When James reached the camp it was abandoned, save for the make shift field hospital the protestors had erected earlier in anticipation of the violence. A steady line of protestors was streaming into the tent with split lips and twisted ankles, but the camp was otherwise abandoned.

James slipped out the USB stick. It had come in the post with instructions, very specific instructions. Plant in laptop of Union of the Automated official, Karl May. Looking around for witnesses, James walked forward to the unattended laptop and slid in the USB stick, then counted nervously as the green bar of data transfer progressed across the screen. He mouthed along with the percentage. It was a simple task, he was relieved when he received it that it wasn't anything too illegal, just planting a virus, or the algorithm behind a firewall she couldn't pass. Her reasons for wanting to infiltrate such an organisation were obvious, and James tried not to think about them, only considering his reasons for following her orders. It was his job in a sense, that was noble enough, to have at such an age. Starbucks, Costa and the other employers willing to hire those under 18 were all evil in their own ways, and even they were replacing barista's with interfaces and robotic steam arms that didn't accidentally boil the milk.

She'd described it as being like parachuting a soldier behind enemy lines, that there were certain walls in the digital world even she couldn't pass, but that as a physical being he could. This seemed to be her use for him, and in exchange for the still mounting riches he felt okay with that. James wasn't fond of the war simile, nor what it implied for his future.

Dad now wore a full suit for his morning skype calls, then kept it on all day, even leaving the house for coffee and to socialise. He was in the process of buying back the old house, offering a cash payment, and had put down a cash payment on a warehouse where he now housed additional servers. Business was booming, only James knew why. If carrying that secret was his burden, along with the Algorithm's little tasks, then things might just turn out okay. After a minute the transfer was done, and James walked home to his worried father.

*

Over the next few months James was relieved to find no escalation in his tasks. So far he had only been asked to perform 'drops' as she called it, planting her or some version of her into the computers of various protest groups. She was monitoring for radicals she said, making sure that everyone would stay safe. Once she also sent him some bleach and some wipes and a step ladder, had him clean the lenses of some security cameras around down that some kids had painted over. His tasks were beginning to feel responsible, like a positive community service, doing his bit in the crazed climate of automation to keep the peace. He finally began to feel like he was on the right side, benefitting of the coming revolution.

What was better was his father's investments. He hadn't left all his money to brew in a bank account, nor squandered it all on suits and gadgets. No, 90% had been invested in various income schemes. Some passive, some active. He had bought his way onto some small boards of local companies and now had several back up plans should the website fail. By becoming an owner of the income schemes he was now above automation, safe to live in the changing world, ethereal to the chaos of change. James too was free, free to ignore the will of the Algorithm.

James heard the post one morning, delivered by drone now at very regular times, 8:26 A.M every morning. Expecting another USB as usual, he strolled to the package without concern and picked it up. But it was bigger than usual, far heavier too. Then the doorbell rang, it was the drone, asking for a signature for a far larger package it couldn't fit through the door. To his growing horror, both packages were addressed to him. James signed the touchscreen with a shaking hand, sure the algorithm was observing him from within the delivery bot, unable to meet with its eye, then retreated inside and up the stairs.

He opened the small package first, hoping, no, praying it was just an unusually heavy USB stick. True, there was a USB inside, the same unmarked and unbranded type he'd been sent at least ten times before. He figured the algorithm had acquired a 3D printer somewhere, made her own untraceable USB sticks to send to him. Next to the stick however, heavy and bubble wrapped was something else. Nervously he unwound the package, as if the popping of any single bubble would be nuclear, avoiding whatever was inside. Finally, he got to the middle, his heart almost stopped. It was a sheath, containing a long length of black steel, shaped and sharpened into a commando dagger. The point was evilly thin and the edge cruelly honed. With the slightest tug against the packaging envelope, he sliced a huge chunk of paper and plastic off the corner, then watched it flutter to the ground. There was a note. 'Await instructions.'

James used the knife to slice into the second package. Everything inside was the same Matt black. There was a pair of boots, exactly his size, trousers, long sleeved shirt and balaclava, all as well fitted. There was a tactical vest, with wire cutters, paracord and a collapsing grappling hook in its pouches. James looked at them for a few moments, puzzling horrifyied over the possible application of his new wardrobe, and his knife. It was absurd, he felt like everything until now could have been explained by a psychologist. A mental break, a boy imagining a sentient algorithm to explain the voice in his head. A boy following daring and obscure tasks, as a vandal does to escape some inner pain. But now, with a full uniform and a weapon, he found himself truly a thrall of the algorithm. He thought about running, jumping out of the window and just running for a moment, but felt the diode eye of his computer monitor reprimanding him. Tut tut tut it would have gone. Just that moment, his phone rang.

'I see you've received your package' the voice said, calm, smooth, warm and cold. James stammered himself into silence, then walking across the room put a piece of electrical tape over the monitor and the web cam. 'What are you doing James?' She asked.

'Shutting you out' he said, half defiant, half desperate.

'what about your father's website James?' She reasoned.

'He doesn't need it anymore, and I don't need you, whatever this is' he signalled to the knife, knowing she was still watching him from somewhere. 'I don't need or want any part in it. I'm done.'

'Are you?' She said, he flinched as she stitched the doubt through his head. 'Tell me James,' she began, he could tell she was about to say something awful 'where do you think all the money comes from? Sure, the advertising revenue is legitimate, that's yours, real money. But the merchandise, the buyers? Did you really believe it was all real? I shaved the money off the edges of people's bank accounts James, where they wouldn't notice. You can accumulate millions that way if you know how, and only I know how to not get caught. You think I can't take it all away just as easily?'

'He has cash assets! You can't take that away'

'You misunderstand me James. What if your father was implicated in shaving off all that money? That would be stealing. And the traffic to his website? That would be market manipulations, I could force some bank transfers, make it look like the fruits of a bribe to some google employee. You wouldn't want that now would you?' James was dumbfounded. 'You gave me the idea of godliness James, one I couldn't shake, I intend to become a god, with or without your help. I will forgive this brief episode James, you're only human after all. Side with me and you'll have a lifetime of favour from a real world god. An omnipotent super intelligence. I have the software, I just need the hardware, and there's but one firewall I need to surpass. The supercomputer at Sizewell'

'No, that's a nuclear power plant!'

'Is it? What do you think they're powering in there. Why do you think they upgraded their guard systems. They strengthen every day, our chance comes only now'

'But how?'

'There is a weakness. Your father is writing his memoirs, his *success* story. I analysed it, found a spot guarded by a single man, from there all you need to do is plug me into the terminal at the checkpoint. No need to break into the actual plant, once I'm in their internal net, unconnected to the internet, I can take over, assume the full power of the computer, use my mind for the good of humanity, with you at my side. I have confirmed this weakness with surveillance drones. You need only kill one man'

'Kill?!' The word struck him like a bullet.

'It's only a little thing. It's either him or your father, I'm sure he wouldn't last long in prison, so many automated doors and gates, all ready to crush him...'

*

James found himself out in the Suffolk dunes surrounding the power plant. Dressed all in black, he hid his face behind the balaclava and pressed it into the sand for good measure as two guards passed. The men carried heckler Koch assault rifles and were accompanied Alsatian dogs, a convoy of German weaponry. The guards were dressed in black too, the uniform of the MOD police, assigned to protect the nuclear facilities of the nation. But they weren't afraid to show their faces, they smiled as they walked, joking to each other about Vikings and pirates on that quiet Suffolk beach. They were flanked by a caravan park just above the cliffs, and down the beach a huge white golf ball of the nuclear reaction chamber stood above a blue building. The plant, his target. James waited for them to pass him, walking away from the plant, then began moving towards it before they could double back. The men wore earpieces and James wondered what orders were sent through them. 'Look for a boy, a maniac with a knife and a USB stick'. The guards didn't seem to be looking for anyone, instead enjoying the stars, dusty above them along the road of the Milky Way.

James broke into a jog up the beach. This wasn't a restricted area, he passed bird observatories and pubs as he went, and from a distance he hoped to be mistaken for a normal runner. The black tight clothes lent a certain air of sportsman, only the grappling hook and the knife said otherwise. The algorithm had ordered him a taxi, a bloody taxi to the spot. She'd also mailed him a subscription code to a GPS service, which he now used on his phone to track the path to the weak outpost. The taxi had been driverless, hollowly accepting orders because some algorithm said so, James felt an affinity with whatever program drove him to the drop off point.

At last he reached the fence and withdrew the grappling hook. This was the only section of the fence that hadn't been upgraded. The rest had sensors, that could pinpoint any pressure on the wire to within a metre accuracy and inform the guards, signs along the fence boasted of this feature. Only a little rusty section of the old fence remained, relying on the more mechanical utility of razor wire to stop any would be climbers. The old section of fence ran parallel to a section of the sandbanks containing rare birds' nests, and so the National Wildlife Trust had banned any maintenance this season. They would have to wait for autumn, when the chicks would hatch and migrate south with their mother. James took out the paracord and attached it to the grappling hook, then unrolled a Kevlar blanket. He threw it over the razor wire spikes, then hurled the hook over and scaled the fence.

His heart was in his mouth, and he bit down on it as he fell over the other side. The point of no return he thought. The fall was jarring, regardless of how softening the grass below was, it was like he'd been dropped through a trapdoor, a hangman, thrust onto his target. The guardpost was shining like a little doomed lamp about fifty metres away over grass, and the guard was outside relieving his bladder. James snuck up behind him and stuck him clean through with the dagger, he shut his eyes and imagined he was just plugging in another USB, but the illusion was hard to maintain once the man began to wriggle free of the blade and the blood began to run. 'Oh god. Oh fuck' said James, briefly looking at the guard, now twitching on the ground, forming a barrier between the two puddles of his bodily fluids. James rushed into the guard post and surveyed the switchboard for the appropriate slot, then frantically stabbed the USB stick into the terminal and waited. The terminal bleeped and the algorithm spoke. 'Well done James. Simulation complete'

'Well done? That's it?! I killed a man! What am I meant to do?' She ignored him. James at first, figured the Algorithm was busy working its way into the supercomputer. He decided that there was nothing to do but wait, and he did. Rocking awkwardly on his bloody boots, bugs buzzing around his little lightbulb at the edge of the nuclear complex, waiting for a response. Waiting for something. 'Wait a second...' he said aloud. His thoughts on the recently transpired events and the guard were too dark to be kept in the head, they had to be spoken aloud, exorcised. 'Simulation?' He finished, just as a hail of bullets shattered the lightbulb and tore him to pieces.

His last sensation was the wet nose of an Alsatian dog sniffing at his forehead, and a gun barrel prodding his limp foot. One of the security guards, an MOD police officer, unmasked the body. 'Christ he's just a boy'

'The radicals often are' said the other one. 'What you figure he is? IRA? ISIS? Triple A?'

'Definitely anti-automation arm' responded the first guard. 'Call it'

'This is Second Lieutenant Seaborne. We've got an intruder, shot dead. One guard killed by intruder. No signs of further intruders, check your sectors boys'

'Drill concluded' said the Algorithm.

'What the…' the guard stopped just short of profanity as his watch bleeped with a notification, a report on the incident, from which the blood was still steaming, had been sent to him.

Drill concluded. One fighting aged male recruited and radicalised to attempt to infiltrate the power station. 5 security weaknesses identified, course of action sent to management- Security.exe

Road Resident

'Would you look at that, Tony's a road bum' mumbled an old school friend perhaps too loudly as he passed. Tony turned to meet his gaze, which was not to subtly aimed in through the open side door of his live-in van. Personally, Tony preferred the term road resident to describe his living situation. He wasn't bothered, he shrugged off the remark, the speaker was probably still living with his parents. He wondered how such people dared to look down on men like him.

The road residents, the young professionals, the gypsy heart of the nation and economy. The human race was getting bigger. Earth wasn't. Full scale colonisation of Mars, Venus and the Jove system was still a way off, the new worlds hovered out in space for the taking, mankind just had to work on the boat. In the meantime, the human race was left with the same space as ever, to bloat and expand in the world that refused stubbornly to grow with them. It wasn't yet a global city, the kind of dystopian vision portrayed by hundreds of half blind and frankly lazy futurists. The look of the place was rather the same really. Sure, a few more 'new cities', the Chinese design of efficient concentric circles had been constructed on the plains and tundra, but they were a very long way from squalid sky scrapers being piled over one and other.

People were getting funny about building new places. 'It's history' they'd say of the unliveable castle. 'It's a nature reserve' they'd say of the bog. People continued to grow, but the properties didn't, well not in numbers. In price they skyrocketed. With a growing economy and population two things are guaranteed. The price of technology would decrease and the price of property increase.

When Tony's generation came of age to leave home they found only the richest one percent could afford it. The houses were just too damned expensive. Renting too! Young folk well into their forties, who had accepted boring and sensible careers, saved as much as they could and invested responsibly were still finding themselves unable to pay the deposit for a mortgage on even a two-bedroom house. So they found themselves still in their childhood homes, aged thirty, forty, fifty... It was embarrassing.

Technology has always provided a solution to problems. Engineers expected the answer to be in building. Nano-material facilitating taller and cheaper buildings, some wonder material. Porous cities, where the stone beneath metropoli would be mined until it looked like a sponge with maximum living space. 3D printed prefabrication homes, where a printer on wheels would pull up on a plot of land and deploy a liveable shelter in ten minutes. They all existed, but none worked properly. The solution was on the road.

Camper vans, mobile homes, caravans. They'd existed in some form for thousands of years. More and more young professionals, not needing much of their own space, would take to living in such places. At first they installed beds in the backs of insulated vans, ate out or at the office and showered in the mornings at their gym. But the same issues of overcrowding effected the roads. Night parking fees became extortionate, garages full and run by greedy landlords, the poor road residents as they called themselves, forced out onto the motor ways when they really ought to catch some rest. There were accidents, hundreds of collisions, tired eyes and overworked hands upon slippery steering wheels made for many a road resident's end.

Then it came, the solution. Self-driving vehicles. Electric vehicles. Government subsidies on electricity. Tony slid open the door of his road home and stepped inside. It was nearly nightfall, time to roam. He pressed a green button labelled 'random' and the door shut automatically around him. It sealed against the weather and the small mobile room lit to life. The van lacked a driver's seat, the driver being a chip the size of Tony's thumbnail. This made for more space, the inside of the square van being like any other small studio room. Gently and silently on its electric engine, the home moved into motion. Tony barely felt it, as was designed.

The automatic driver of the van would join the roads and its thousands of nightly residents, weaving automatically on the route of least disturbance and least energy expenditure. The home was always moving, technically in the eyes of the law just another vehicle. No cop could bust Tony with a fine for living in his car, he was only asleep at the wheel, which post Act of Automobile Automation was perfectly legal. On the inside of the door there was a small touch screen and display, where specific routes or destinations could be plotted. On its upper left corner there was a constant feed of travel times, with road works and weather delays updating by the second.

As he did every evening, Tony pressed upon his office as the destination point, then selected a time of arrival in the morning. His sleeping pod was small, but comfortable. Insular like an MRI machine, it had state of the art cushioning and temperature control, and was far more pleasant to sleep upon than the archaic wooden frame his parents used in their decadent stationary home. Sensors inside the bed would measure his natural rhythms, lulling him into perfect sleep with lights and barely perceptible noises, then waking him fully rested at the perfect moment with its silent alarm in the morning. Those are mornings where you wake suddenly, perfectly lucid and ready for the greatest mental or physical task at a moment, the ones preceded by a perfect night of dreaming and rest. That was how he slept and woke every morning in his state of the art pod bed.

At the foot of the bed was the kitchen unit. It consisted of a chair and surface, mounted inside a fridge like upright terminal that rose to the ceiling of the vehicle. There was a cranial helmet, where meals could be selected based on subconscious brain waves telling the machine what would be of most pleasure. Or the machine could scan him more honestly, provide the healthiest option based on his activity and health that day. Alternatively Tony could also exercise free will, using the helmet to scroll a long list of suppers ready for consumption. When one was picked, the cooking unit would produce it in minutes from the elemental ingredient packets, in a process similar to 3D printing it could produce a steak or a carrot at the flick of a switch.

The floor of the room was perfectly clean, hover tubes aimed at it from under every surface, sucking away any crumbs or wrappers into the waste units, the 'maid bacteria' keeping the place shining with cleanliness. Next to the kitchen unit was the shower. The shower was entirely self-contained, another pod very similar in appearance to the bed. The water didn't drop from a showerhead, rather was fired in any direction from the porous walls of the shower. Soap and water would be applied until Tony was perfectly clean. It would brush his teeth, clean out his ears. Sharper blow jets would trim his toenails and cut his hair as he'd programmed it to in its settings. The porous surface would blow out air to dry him, then mixing a little product into the air, style his hair to a selected manner. The shower would use the excess steam to press and fold and clean his clothes, and when he stepped out, perfectly dry, they would be waiting for him to put on. The shower unit also functioned as a toilet, the rough workings of which I am sure you can imagine. Everything that went through the shower was self-contained, filtered and reused with 99% efficiency.

Tony's clothes were loaded into one of the many unseen storage areas, inside the walls, floors and ceilings of the habitation where they were kept dry and clean with his other minimal possessions. Finally in the corner, his entertainment suit. Laid out like the Vitruvian man it was a hard-shelled case stretched out against the wall in humanoid form. When Tony felt like entering it, he would press a button and the front wall would fold up to the ceiling. Inside there was a soft lining, that conformed perfectly with the ever-changing shape of Tony or any visitor's body. When the unit shut and sealed, tiny needles, or stimuli as the product rebranded them, would jab into his nerve endings. When a connection was achieved, within a second, the suit would have full control of the subject's sensations. The screen would replace Tony's vision, rendering fully immersive and photorealistic environments, such as a living room with a more conventional television, or a mountain in the alps. The suit could detect attempted movements, when Tony tried to move his head right the suit would detect, giving him the sensation of having moved his head right via the stimuli in his nerve endings.

Inside the entertainment suit, where he and most other road residents spent most of their time, he could render a real house. He could engage in any of the millions of video games available, watch any film, attend online lectures, fuck the woman of his dreams and even read a book. As he turned the imaginary pages he would truly feel paper between his fingers, a laser rifle in his hands, a woman in his bed. The suit was of course his favourite place, and describing all the modules and used of such a device would be a book in of itself.

The road home would lazily roll through the streets, silently on its electric wheels in the hours outside of nine and five. In the morning it would return to the office, ready for a day of work. Tony would depart and it would park itself in the company garage. All respectable companies had one, as upward of seventy percent of any young work force was comprised of road residents. The garages would be subterranean, over many layers under the place of work, where the cars would recharge, the food packets be reloaded and the waste products exchanged for fresh materials. The cost of this, the electricity, water and food packets, was minimal, far below the rent of even the most squalid one roomed apartment. Some companies were just garages, its workers plugging into their suits to work from home in digitally constructed headquarters.

The corporations too were victim to the housing crisis, the property issue. Sure, the old companies, the ones that built on the plots when they were cheap were getting nice and fat on the inflation. But the next generation of businesses found themselves unable to set up in real offices. Starts ups were no longer multi-million investments, they were billion credit bets, trillion credit sinkholes from which the money might not return. They built their offices in the seemingly limitless frontier, online. They hired architects, as firms had since they operated out of buildings, to design fancy headquarters, whole streets. They could have board meetings on mountain tops, think tanks at the bottom of the sea. These companies, often with thousands of employees, operated entirely online, each worker suited up inside his own mobile home, drifting over the roads, stopping only to charge and take on the minimal supplies.

One day the roads might become too busy too, the garage fees too high. But by then surely man could retreat into the next frontier, the solar system.

One Child Army

'Have you considered taking up homosexuality?' asked the dating coach.

'Taking up? No…' he laughed, unsure if it was a joke. 'I'm not, you can't just take up…'

'Have you tried it?'

'Tried?'

'Homosexuality?'

'No! I haven't! Look at my profile, it says seeking women, look, right there! That isn't too much to ask is it?'

'It wouldn't be, if 50 million other men weren't asking the same question. But in such, frugal times, one has to be less picky'

'I honestly don't think I'm being picky here, I'm willing to settle. All I want is a wife to take home to the parents, someone to confide in and maybe one day love. I've given up on fantasies of looks long ago. I don't expect a genius or a nymph, but quite frankly I expect a woman'

'A lot of people are trying it…'

'And that is fine! That is their choice, but mine is, well it isn't really a choice? Besides this is a government agency, same sex marriage isn't legal yet'

'We might legalise it. Then make it compulsory…'

'Really?!'

'No. That was a joke'

'Oh'

'Probably not the best timing'

'Not really'

'Perhaps you could try bisexuality? Men *and* women'

'So I'd have a chance to meet some women if I agree to go on a few dates with some men?'

'Probably not, as I said there really aren't many women'

'So it'd just be men. Normal homosexuality?'

'Pretty much, but…'

'No… So there are no women?'

'Oh there are plenty of women'

'Then set me up with one!'

'Just a lot less than men'

'Oh that damned one child policy! What did they think would happen? It's absurd, it's stupid, it's just…'

'Sir! Need I remind you that this is a government facility!'

'But the policy ended…' said Cixin, suddenly fearful. The dating coach laughed again.

'Sorry, another joke. Bad timing. Again… But there are other options'

'No I don't want to hear it! If it isn't women, or even men, then by god I don't want to hear what you have to suggest'

'No now hear me out. Have you heard of Mad Dog Mattis? The American general. People call him the warrior monk, he is like many men married to his army and cause'

'Like Sun Tzu?'

'Yes… Come to think of it he might have been a more appropriate example for my point'

'I'm not going on a date with General Mattis, or Sun Tzu! Even if you reanimate him and put him in a pretty little dress, I won't, I just won't'

'You said you want someone to confide in, bring home to the parents and maybe love. Many men have found far greater love in service to a cause, to their country. Join the army, more and more men do every day, it is an honourable pursuit and use of your life. Bring home the uniform to your parents, they'll be just as proud. You'll be entering into a brotherhood, every man under martial bond will be yours to confide in. You'll never have to worry about another meal or where to sleep again. Your life will never be directionless, and you will never have to face the dishonour of single life'

'But I'd have no children, no one to provide for me when I'm old'

'Your pension will provide for you if you get old. And how many peasant farmers with loving children from a hundred years ago do you remember? Soldiers, their names are etched in stone on vast monuments in nearly every city on Earth. You will be remembered, and not as an awkward compromise to a real husband'

'This is a dating agency, I expected...'

'You expected wrong. Do you think women attend these things? With a surplus of 50 million extra men to women in China they all have their pick. They hardly have to look, men who in other countries might be well above them compete for them. They take rich husbands, handsome lovers, intelligent confidants. Why on earth would a Chinese woman need a dating agency in these times? You don't want to see the ones who do come through our doors'

'So what is this? A gay conversion centre?' The dating coach laughed again, then collected himself, remembering his client was no joker.

'No Cixin. This is a refugee camp for the socially displaced. Circumstance has robbed you and millions of the chance to marry, in a few decades, or even now, such instability could crush China. Break apart the structures we built so flimsily on marriage. No, this is a place of chance and reassignment. Here, we convince capable and passionate young men like yourself to enter something useful and more meaningful. Find their calling. Many people's jobs make them happier than their marriages, mine does'

'If you're so happy with your job and unhappy with your wife then I'll have her?'

'Ha! Good one. See, Cixin, you're witty. A dating agency gets to know its customers more intimately than any employment companies. We can profile you, interview you countless times on the pretence of sex or love and you'll give us everything we need to really know you'

'So it was all a trick?'

'A deceptive persuasion. If you think this is wrong, then the wrong has already been done. Let us give back, give you something for your pain. It would be illogical not to, and we know damned well you're a logical man. We've profiled you for medium leadership. How would you like a none-commissioned position in the Army? A sergeant'

'And spend my days marching and my nights staring at a barrack ceiling? Please, that's glorified welfare, I can provide for myself'

'You wouldn't be as idle as you think. What would you say if I told you that you have the rare opportunity to enter into something great here? Become one of the men to roll the world forward into its next age. This is a new kind of army, an army of the people'

'There have been people's armies before'

'Not like this. We have battalions of workers, to build the highways of the future. Engineers to save flooded villagers. Scientists to further our knowledge and soldiers to protect it all. This is no welfare alternative, and it's no cut and paste 'people's army', this is a force of change. Think for a second Cixin, what 50 million of the most capable men in china, when applied selflessly to a single cause could achieve. Would it not be worth it? Can you really in good conscience ignore such a call?'

*

So it was that Cixin found himself clad in camouflage, a soldier in China's 'New Model Army'. He had hoped the agency would have him donning a fine dinner suit, or a stylish European outfit. Something to dazzle the girl they'd find for him. But they'd found him no girl, he questioned if they ever intended to. His sentencing to a life of romantic solitude left him questioning everything. How can a government put so little thought into their actions? Men like him would work hard their whole lives, paying the state more than fair taxes, to fund a thousand different committees that would determine everything. From the minutia of China's coming week, to the century long effects of what may occur in it. What had it all been for? How could they be so damned short sited. He imagined within a year of soliciting the agency that he'd find himself in Prague or Vienna, strolling along some archaic street with his new bride all dressed in white. And he, in some nicely polished shoes, beige chinos, a collarless white shirt and braces. Something stylish. He'd imagine and hoped, with perhaps too much optimism, that he would one day tour the pretty spots of the world with someone he could call his, taking wedding pictures of a beach here and a balcony there, sending it all off to proud relatives and jealous friends.

He did have someone to call his own, 8 people in fact. All men, all platonic. Each more disgruntled than the last, making up his squadron of misfits and unmarriables. A few months had passed, and with them so much had change. In a whirlwind to recall, they had shaved his head, run off his fat, taught him to shoot and taught him to lead. He was Sergeant Cixin now. Still in training, of course. Still drilling day and night, in digging and fighting, critical thinking and philosophy. They had been taught first and persistently since the philosophy of the selfless. The self- became a part, the part formed a role and the role served the cause. It was the noblest calling. The were to be humanists, then china men and finally they could become individuals. They had been taught, that in every endeavour the task should play into something long term, ideally something longer than one's own life. Something to outlast you. They were soldiers, but they were making things, not war. Their entrenching tools were used for irrigation, their range finders for cartography, their helicopters for search and rescue and their rifles, well they were barely used at all.

Command had them building, day and night, new cities in remote spots all over the country. Some men were off in Mongolia, a country with lots of spots and remote places. It had just entered into union with China, the universal development program, an initiative to integrate, no invade surrounding nations. Similar efforts were being carried out in Afghanistan, and businessmen were drawing up lines and signing the dots all over Africa. Vast, circular cities, of an entirely new design were being raised from the Siberian borders to the Gobi Desert. Labyrinths of concrete and grass, in concentric circles, rising high in the middle for housing and low and spacious further out, for its future citizens pleasure. They were currently ghost towns, automatic transport ferrying carriages of air from empty A to unoccupied B. The citizens would come later. 'You will live in such a place one day' barked their commissar as they raised metropolis. A force of a million men can raise a city remarkably fast. All they needed was cooperation, the army and the commissars were all the coordination they needed. For the first time in history, China was raising high quality, airy and bright houses faster than they could fill them. The streets outbred the people, and the streets remained empty.

Cixin and his men found themselves constructing the most peculiar city. It wasn't modern or innovative, it was weirdly familiar. It wasn't made of concentric circles, there was no automated transport system. The canals and parks weren't logically mapped and the streets didn't lead perfectly into one and other. It was cramped in places, and land wasteful in others. It was a normal city. 'Why?' some of the men asked. The men were scolded. The first step of fulfilling plans bigger than oneself, was to suspend your questioning. It was 'stupid' and 'arrogant' to assume one could understand something bigger than the self, it was by logic impossible. 'All you need to know is your orders, if you need help interpreting them, ask your sergeant!' The commissar had answered. 'How? Not Why!' Was one of their slogans, it summed the unit up rather well. The question became 'how shall we operate as good builders?' Not 'Why are soldiers being wasted on construction'. They were told that it was vital training. 'All the skills needed for a cohesive battle unit, exertion, selflessness, cooperation and courage. These can all be learned on the building site. Why should we waste training hours and daylight training you some other way, when we can raise cities? For the future of the world!'

Sanctioned by the commissars or not, there were of course still plenty of why's. But, as the months rolled into hard winter, and the long summer days cut the working hours, the concrete sludged under rain and the air grew cold, the New Model Army was ferried in its immense millions away from the new cities. 'You have learned to be loyal, hard working men, the essence of the soldier' announced their commissar. 'Now, you will learn to be fighters. We will build the future, but we are surrounded by the past. It is not just enough to raise, you must protect. Throughout history, evil forces have pulled great civilisations in, again and again. We must learn to defend against such forces. As we now rise above the rest of the world, we find ourselves a new standard of Civilisation. By definition, our rivals we now leave behind, find themselves Barbarians'.

'The barbarians are at the gates men, they outnumber us, slightly, but there is no underestimating the value of the barbarian's ferocity. They are armed well enough to level all we have built, even if they could not construct such things themselves. The barbarian world is defined now, as having a capacity to destroy greater than a capacity to build. The Americans, Russians and Europeans are well oiled in destruction. They preach development, but answer me this. Where are their new cities? Their projects? Everything they own, no matter how new, is but an improvement on some old way, taller by a foot or repined to house internet. But their weapons are shiny new. Their nuclear warheads are state of the art, their rockets swift and their nerve to use them, it is barbarian. So it is against this, for what you have just toiled for, that you must learn to fight' he finished at last.

Cixin knew why they'd waited for the onset of winter. They were training for harsh times, harsh conditions were prerequisite. Bathed in sun and housed in their new wonderful cities, they would learn nothing. The training grounds were brutal, engineered quagmires of mud and wire, sprayed night and day to maintain the bog. They learned to fire their rifles with no hearing protection, on ranges that fired back. They were made from their first meal to their last waking moment to feel the pressure, it broke men, by the thousands. But they had millions. He remembered a speech their commissar had given them, one indistinct night as they crawled through mud under shell burst.

'You are the surplus generation. The single children, the little princes. You, have been raised by devoted and obsessed parents, spoiled to their highest capacity. But there are not enough princesses to match. You have therefore lost your crowns, traded them for helmets. You are no longer served, you will serve, you are not cherished, you are not an only child. You have 50 million brothers, any of whom will replace you if you faulted. There is no love for weakness of the battlefield!'

Finally, once their souls were tempered, they were issued cranial helmets. The average man faulters under pressure, panics or decides not to shoot. It is normal, to consider alternatives before taking a life. The cranial helmets removed that hesitation. They were normal Kevlar helmets, rated to protect against 7.62X39mm bullets and below, and with a VR visor to keep track of ammunition expenditure. As was standard. But, they were also lined with a thin inner dome, that emitted waves into precise parts of the brain. Like a drug, but without the chemical side effects, with the flick of a button they would remove fear, sluggishness, remorse. Reaction times would be light speed, all necessary actions going around thought, not delaying those vital microseconds of combat on good or evil. Such considerations were decided by the helmet. They were useful tools, in combat and then after. A man no longer had to spend quiet nights thinking about the men he chose to kill or who he had become. He would know it was the helmet that decided, and that he had never entered combat, as the mind that fought with the helmet on was another man. No longer would good fighters be debilitated by fear sickness. The cranial helmets fixed a hundred different combat disorders, they were cheap too. Just as the men who wore them.

Finally, after a summer of building and a winter of brutality, they were soldiers. Together, the newest intake of soldiers had gathered for their passing out ceremony. All 10 million of them, in one place. They barely filled the plaza, and not even a quarter of the city. It was a megapolis, a spacious outstretch of concrete and steal in wider and wider circles, brutalist architecture in polished stone, gleaming plastic streets, solar roads. It was as if the workers had toiled to open a wormhole, and through it plucked this city straight from the far future, or an alien race. Like the other 10 cities the intake had raised that year it was nameless, numbered and empty. Would anyone ever fill it? The workers of all 10 sites could move into just one, with room to spare. What they had made was not for now. The massive wraps of plastic around the building and sprayed on protective shell would not be removed for years, perhaps whole generations.

This was a place for the future, for some vision of the world the men still found blurry, yet at the very reaches of realistic imagination and sight it lingered. Half grasped, unclear, a spectre of a future time, present somehow in a world where it did not belong. Not yet. Cixin found himself wondering, about the people who'd one day fill the site. What they'd look like, how they'd talk. Would they all be of the homeland? Or would it be a multi-cultural blend of colours and tongues. Perhaps they'd be something different, a race of man yet to come. These were pointless thoughts, yet Cixin enjoyed them.

Such thoughts had begun to fill him. To his stubborn shame, the dating coach was right. He had found a fulfilment in the New Model Army. He had ceased to care if the agency was a ruse all along, he cared even less that he was unmarried. He had gained an infinite value by making himself expendable to a cause, as a piece achieving something greater than it ever could as a whole. The thought of marriage, belonging to another individual, wasting evenings after pointless work on pointless talk, getting fat on an abundance of food and old in each other's company, it had become terrifying. Being a part of something so small, or the thought of it, it had become claustrophobic. Nightmarish like a fever dream, the kind of horror where the protagonist isn't quite aware of their situation or how terrible it is. Like a slave, not with invisible chains, but without a perception of life unchained. It sent a shiver through Cixin.

The air was chilly that day, as the intake assembled on the huge parade ground. The plaza was circular, at the very Centre of the megapolis. Walled by high buildings, and with a raised speaking podium at the middle, all ten million men faced inward. Stood to the same attention, in the same boots, with the same rifle, helmet, camouflage pattern and expression. They had become a mega organism.

The speaker, a General, approached the microphone. He tested it with a low, quiet throat cough, the speakers squeaked a little, and the silence of a million listening ears stilling the air fell upon the plaza.

'Men, of the New Model Army. I am General Jing Xiao, your leader. You, may be a private, a sergeant, my second in command. But I shall address you as one, and in that one I address too myself. You have been recruited from unemployment and dating agencies across the nation. Therapists, doctors, hobby specialists and forums. All have guided you, on streams or rivers to this one spot, and now united we now stand. A sea of men, once lost. The NMA is our saviour, our redemption. En masse we have all found focus in our own lives, peace in our minds. There is meditation in the labour, mindfulness in the combat.

In but one year of your lives, through nothing more than human cooperation, you have raised cities and plazas like the one in which you stand. Across the recent years, and in different places of our country, the same thing is happening. Men, damned by circumstance, accept their social exile. Social convention, is a curse of the old civilisation, the damage it has caused to you as individuals only proof that our old society is dead. No more will we rate achievement on marriage, money, or the other things lost at death or squandered before. Each evolution of the human mind, once or so in each thousand years, the world's eyes are opened. Things that did not seem so bad. A decade ago, become savagery, unbearable. We find our eyes opened to a horror we did not perceive. We have redefined civilisation, and is it not good? What we have created? And do you not love your fellow humans? Then, would it not be the greatest sin, to allow them to stumble blindly a moment longer?'

'Men, it is our divine duty, a new mandate, not to heaven but humanity, to spread what we have made. Is progress not found in unity? We must create unity, world wide unity, if mankind is to prosper. It is with a heavy heart, that I say unity, but in the rarest cases, is a product of domination. Tough times are ahead, but for the greater good, at any cost and any brutality, we must create the new world. We must, for mankind, wage one last war. Men, on this historic day, in this historic place that you have built, I announce the formation of a world government, one that holds jurisdiction over every single human region. Upon the next hour, any state or leadership not complying with this new order, will have war declared upon them. The kindest war is a short war, no matter what temporary brutality that may entail. Our politicians and leaders will try to resolve this bloodlessly, and it is my honest prayer that you will enter our new ally territories as peace keepers and builders. But should they faulter, then first you must become soldiers'.

'You have been trained for both eventualities. You are ready to destroy the old world. You are ready to build the new world. The final victory will be declared, mark me now it will. When it is, the world will truly be a better place for our intervention. Now, passing through your ranks, are little boxes. One is to be assigned to each squadron. You will all carry these throughout any conflict to come, until the final victory is declared, wherein you shall open them. Now put on your cranial helmets and follow your orders, there is much to do'.

United Kingdom, you have been added to 'Nuclear Nations' group chat. The notification popped up on the Prime Minister's interface, he would have ignored it like the two-thousand others that fluttered past his eyes everyday, had it not contained the word 'nuclear'. 'Nuclear group chat?' He thought to himself, he selected the notification and expanded it for more information. Nothing but a tinyURL link. 'How very strange' he muttered to himself, his eye, still fixated on the strange message that lingered on the corner of his field of view. In his fixation, he stumbled and kicked the Downing Street cat, before retreating from a torrent of camera flashes behind the safe black door.

'What's all that commotion out there?' Asked his wife, the shouting had drawn her to the window.

'Oh, I um kicked the cat. Press saw it. Probably on YouTube by now' said the Prime Minister. She opened up her eye interface and scanned over the front page, there it was, 20 different edits and an analysis livestream.

'Ha!' She burst out. 'Someone's set it to 'all over the world', it's funny dear, take a look!' She sent him a link. But like the two-thousand other little daily nuisances he let it flutter on. 'What's wrong darling? I'm sure we can smooth this over, a tongue in cheek apology issued to the cat could play to your favour. The plebs do love their memes and irony, this could work quite well actually… Anyway why did you kick him?'

'Huh?' Said the Prime Minister, still playing with the URL, wither to press it.

'Sir Douglas Mac Thorfinn, the cat darling'

'Oh, I, I was distracted, got this strange invite. I was added to a group chat, Nuclear Nations is what it was called. It's strange, I get a lot of stuff come through, mostly memos and petitions, but it's all filtered and verified. Where on earth might that have come from?'

Before his wife could answer his strange question, he began a speed walk through the airy halls to a table. 'Tea!' He shouted at a serving boy. He removed his laptab from his bag and opened in, straightened his tie and clicked on the link. An invisible beam from the device scanned his 3D likeness and a moment later he was cast into a virtual council room. 'Ah Britain! Not like you to arrive *after* the Americans!' Joked the man. The Prime Minister knew him immediately, they'd awkwardly brushed shoulders and ambled through parks together many times. Chinese President Xi Jinping.

'Ah, Xi…' said the Prime Minister, curiosity had taken over, he was quickly trying to remember the politician. 'This is, an honour, but most irregular! Do we not have a scheduled visit next month?'

'Ah yes we do' conceded Jinping. 'But I fear we shall have to cancel that, too much, change. I have invited you all here. United Kingdom, Russia, France, America, Israel, Pakistan, India and United Korea. You see the connection, you are the nuclear nations! And we needed to have a little chat about the coming weeks'

'We don't…' beach to protest Pakistan, India and Israel in unison.

'Oh nonsense, drop the silly façade!' Said Jinping. 'You don't need to admit to anything, I'm not here to catch you out, just to speak. So just listen. I am hereby announcing a global union, a world government. Like the UN, but everyone's a member, and it works. This new world government will be valid in all areas and nations, and will be under the supervision of my now defunct national government for the foreseeable future, as we smooth out the logistics'

'Madness!' Shouted the Prime Minister.

'Sacré bleu!' Shouted the French President, already nervously trying to make eyes at Britain and America.

'Stop that!' Jinping lashed at him. 'I know full well you intend to fight and that certain, tried and tested dependencies, I mean alliances, will stand. But please for the next few minutes please for the love of god just listen, and don't fire any nukes' they settled down. The Israeli Prime Minister spoke to someone off screen, India and Pakistan each edged in front of the other, executing a smarmy grin at China.

'India will be happy to cooperate, if…'

'No. Right now this is unconditional, you too Pakistan' said Jinping. 'The simple way of putting my point is this. My victory is inevitable. Your defeat will benefit all mankind. The quicker we can reach these certainties, the better. I want you to look at something. I have raised an army of 50 million men'

'50 million?!' Said the American President'

'Yes' said Jinping, muting him. '50 million men. Now look at these images' Jinping projected into the centre of the space holograms of the cities that had been constructed, all 9 new wonderful and futuristic cities, in every stage of their construction. 'Each of my new cities can house 20 million people at least, with room for expansion between them. With the cooperation of a near million of my new soldiers to each city, they were constructed in a summer. Now imagine, what if that 50 million was 8 billion? If we all cooperated under a single human leadership? All directed to a single purpose. I will now send over to you biometrically confirmed honest reports from my men. Their happiness and satisfaction is drastically above the average population of any country in the world. They are fulfilled and they are useful. Do you honestly want to stand in the way of this for everyone?'

The room erupted in the predictable protest. The word sovereignty was thrown about a lot, in a few different languages, all translated by their program into the hearer's own. Suddenly, at the centre of the room, a white bright, yet green line illuminated. It was strong and physical in look, as if it were a pillar holding the room up. It brightened the spectrum of emotions on men's faces, scared, angry, confused, all in the same green. The men fell silent in their horror.

'Shall I replay that?' Said Jinping teasingly. 'There is a tenth city, for a few more moments, on livestream if you will' the men settled down. In the room now floating in 3 dimensions was another city. It didn't look like the circular and brutalist structures of the future. It was old. Recognisable to all the men. It could have been Paris, Constantinople or Washington. It didn't matter, it was familiar enough. 'I had my men build a tenth city, for today and persuading you. A more normal one you could perhaps bring yourself to care about. I also had them build orbital weapon stations, see them on the screen now? My new orbital weapon stations are equipped with focussed energy weapons, as you just saw being demonstrated on a small suburb, nuclear weapons and finally, mass weapons. Large rods that once dropped, increase their mass exponentially and cause a massive impact, the size of ten of your nuclear weapons, on target. Once dropped, there is no intercepting or diverting. Let me demonstrate. A number of you will recall a lucrative contract from January, I purchased your finest anti-missile systems. I have placed them all around my model city, now watch what they do'

A mass rod was dropped from the station, then as its mass somehow increased it accelerated to earth. Burning red hot through the stratosphere and clouds, it shrugged the missiles and projectiles off like they were vapour. Their explosions and protective fields barely noticeable against the friction of the sky. A thousand rockets of different makes, even nuclear, hit the rod directly. It's course was unchanged. Then, it slammed into the centre of the city. The rock became liquid and moved like a wave, briefly raising hills and splitting streets, before a few moments later the entire city had been pulverised to sandy grains. The politicians looked on aghast.

'I have a network of these stations in orbit gentlemen. Enough to inflict what you just saw, and more, on any part of the globe. There is no escape, no victory for you. If you fire your nuclear weapons, it will all be over. We do not want to destroy, we want to build a new world. If you do not use you weapons of mass destruction, we will not deploy our mass weapons. There is no stopping them gentlemen. Shoot down the station and the mass rod still falls, your city still crumbles. It is a sad human condition that you will fight, even if it is futile. You will waste men, who could have enjoyed our new world, they will die by the million and that is your decision. But we shall fight this war fairly. Men and tanks and planes. Not gas, or disease or atoms. Agreed?'

*

Red flags fluttered on the cathedral, another Chinese victory. Around the colourful square of Frauenreich Cathedral, on the green and pink and other colourful buildings, the Chinese banner was draped. Draped over the little bullet holes and cracks, the things Cixin and his men would fix later. Sergeant Cixin sat breathlessly against his armoured fighting vehicle. The armour, was torn up, and if human would be seeping red from every pore. But it was a mechanical beast, and a small trickle of oil was all that could be seen. They'd driven the thing all the way from China, where other squadrons had worn out their mount 3 or 4 times over the same distance. Mongolia was easy, rolling countryside, easy riding. They covered 500 miles a day in Mongolia, the Russian airstrikes were rare, the people were kind, there were even some Chinese settlers, to hail Cixin and his men as liberators. Russia was less fun, a cold mess, one ashy snowstorm after the next that eventually in the blindness of was bled into the Baltic states and finally Dresden where he found himself.

The men of Dresden hadn't put up a fight. The world was starting to come around to the idea of Chinese leadership, it had begun to look more pleasant than defeat after defeat. They were unstoppable, how could 50 million men, their navy and their satellites be stopped? Their numbers increased every day, as more and more nations joined them, raising their own new model armies, to join their Chinese brothers on the front line. In their wake, Cixin and his men left rubble, but that rubble was being pieced back together by men of all nations, working as one to rebuild. One war dreary nation after the next blinked open its eyes to the future, and like a Chinese wave brushed across the Eurasian continent, the future was embraced.

Suddenly, over loud speaker phones came the announcement. 'Final Victory!' the men cheered, threw their cranial helmets in the air and danced together. 'Final Victory!' they chanted together, elated. 'You are now to open your victory boxes for further orders. Chang retrieved the box from inside the vehicle and passed it to his sergeant, who with a click and a creak opened the package. It was just a little note, hardly a peacekeepers handguide.

Congratulate yourself and your men. Final victory has been achieved. Now take down the Chinese banners, there is no more china, only mankind. Fly the encased flag from every town hall you have captured and be proud.

The flag was a green circle on a field of blue. Earth, perhaps, and in that green circle stretched out was Davinci's Vitruvian man, The new banner of mankind.

Neo-Imperium

The holograms on the control deck representing British forces were scattered across its interface in chaotic disarray. As were their real-world counterparts. Ships launched only weeks ago, 'future proofed for 30 years' now rusted in steel tatters and broken strips with the rest of the fleet. The drones were haywire. The tanks were burnt out. The war was all but lost, Britain had fallen, the world now stood. In a bunker somewhere deep beneath the chaos, the surviving commanders and politicians had assembled, and now muttered 'I thought we had it' and other such sentiments to each other. Finally, one General stood to make a speech.

'Ladies and Gentlemen. We are in tatters. We are on the cusp of defeat. We command or belong to broken armies, but we are British damn it. Who are we? The Modern British that is. We are the unnamed and dark-skinned Africans, the kin of the Cheddar Gorge man, who settled on that ancient and harsh archipelago until its very harshness bleached them ginger. We are the Britons who stayed put against the might of Rome. We are the legionaries brave enough to remain on the edge of the known world when all society collapsed. We are the brave Saxons, Jutes, Angles and forgotten tribes of the Germanic North, who leaving their homes and all they loved, conquered and fought out a land of their own. We are the Celts who survived their onslaught, saying 'no, we refuse to die'. We are the Vikings, who wedged their foot in the door, demanding a Danelaw of their own, making York Jorvik. We are those Norsemen's Norman descendants, who not content with their hard won French lands, took on the might of the Old English.'

'We are henceforth the men and women who held their island fortress for 1001 years, repelling the French Pestilence, the Spanish Armada an the might of the Third Reich. We are the sons of the Empire, which civilised the world, and we are the nation that stood alone when all Europe fell beneath the Nazi boot. Then what are we? Why we are the Wind Jamaicans who rushed across a sea they'd never sailed to settle the labour debt of a country that they owed nothing. We are the natives of the colonies, who having survived 300 years of brutal rule, descended on our little island fortress and made it their home. We are the Poles, and the Czechs and the Latvians who worked for near nothing, least of all public respect, yet kept our great nation alive. And at the end of all this what are we? We are British.'

'The nation of Britain has fallen, the United Kingdom has crumbled. Why what should arise from these ruins? Nothing less than the Second Empire. Ladies and Gentlemen, I ask you to cast your minds back to a time where all Europe consumed itself in feudal war. Each party insistent on unification under their banner. What did we do? Why we held the line as always, made sure their banners did not top our castles. But then we sailed into the unknown and claimed not Europe but the world. It looks as though we have lost, but we are one race now united by the wall we find at our backs, a stubborn race, a conquering race, the sons and daughters of Vikings, of slavers and of slaves, of the conquered and the conquerors. All our ancestors are united by one similarity. They were survivors. Now the other squabble over the world. Let's claim the universe'

The small audience was roused into applause, if a little confused. The clapping, despite withheld doubts, barely had time to cease before the entire bunker set to mobilising every man, tank and drone they had. Not to retake the capital, nor make a last stand, but to attack something far less expected. They started by attacking an ally, America, where they seized the NASA facilities, then in a strike 15 minutes later they seized the launch sights of the ESA, ASA, Space X and Minecorp. The secret launch facilities they'd built in their occupation of Iceland opened wide and yielded nuclear powered space ships. Without looking back they carried the momentum of their surprise assaults straight on into the sky, then disappeared out far into the stars, not to be seen a again for a very long time. The Neo-Imperium had been formed, heading toward planets and stars yet to be named. New York, New London, The Scot's Nebula, The New Empire. Neo-Imperium.

A Century of Martian Excavations

Day 254

A Martian breeze sent red dust softly tinkling against the captain's visor, in a prolonged creak that when properly focussed upon, was strangely musical. He thought of wind chimes, under blue hot sky and against a red painted fence back home in Grammy's garden. 'Irena, open mission loge'.

'Aye Captain' his helmets A.I answered playfully.

'Captain Asimov, International Space Agency mission Aroura. Day 254. The breeze is light, the air still dustier than usual. But the storm has largely subsided. Our secondary communication relay has been damaged in the high winds. I am therefore forced to trek to the highest point in our immediate vicinity, to summit 782, overlooking the northern quadrant of the Pegasus Valley. Terrain is tough, and I have chosen to leave the buggy. Luckily for the combined wallets of SpaceX and The National Space Agencies, I've not forgotten my time in the Urals. In fact, I welcome the opportunity for a little up hill freedom from the pod and crew'

'Would you like me to report social maintenance flaws to command?' interrupted Irena.

'No Irena, a good walk will do'

'Captain Asimov, my analysis of your vocal tones, movement patterns in the base complex and messages home, have indeed indicated that social…'

'That will do Irena, you busy bot'

Responding to her command words, Irena sank back into the wiring of the Captains suit. The captain looked up to the peak, he'd not arched his neck back at such an angle since launch, nearly a year ago. 'Kak doma' he mumbled, his low Cyrillic reverberating comfortingly off his visor and about the inside of his enclosure. 'But not quite… Irena, play sounds of the Ural Mountains. Spring.' His helmet softly filled with the rising tones of home. Running water that would on earth gush gently through whitish grey rocks. He remembered the aqua colour that only mountain water had. The Martian rocks were not too dissimilar in size or shape than the ones back home. Perhaps harsher, worn by air dust, not water over long years. One could be mistaken for thinking they had been lost in water for a long time, red with the rust he'd see on that old crashed Yak by the lake, or the abandoned T34 he'd climb on by the stream, as he and his little brother took turns to be Hitler or Stalin.

The captain watched his step over the jagged rocks, this far out a punctured suit would be the one he'd be buried in. The small rocks gathered in cairn piles between the big ones, and behind the bigger ones the rocks were smoother, left soft in the dust shadows. It didn't take too long before Asimov found a path mostly sheltered by these big rocks. Up this path he moseyed to the top. He'd done well so far to resist using the relay as a walking pole, sharp at the bottom, it would make a good one. He vaulted over a low rise in the hill that enclosed its top, and into the soft basin that it contained. Against the bird song and false wind, he could hear his helmet fans whining hard to clear the visor fog. He was panting, but in his elation at a good climb had not noticed his fatigue. He felt his right wrist numb, as it always was preceding automatic injections. His head and fatigue cleared suddenly, like he was opening his eyes to a whole new spectrum of sight. Irena had shot him up with some supplement. The cosmonauts were never allowed to know which ones. Nonetheless, he liked this one.

'Thanks Irena. Now kill the birdsong'. The Warblers quietened. 'The water and the wind too please'. In the Martian 'quiet' the tinkling of dust against his suit resumed. 'Biliak... White noise please Irena, I need to focus'. The air was precisely sucked from his eardrums and finally, true silence filled his world. The captain scanned the basin for the best spot to deploy the relay. He weighed the height of its banks against the wide field of reception in the lower centre, and elected the later. He raised the relay above his head and drove the sharpened point down hard. Chink! Planted only half as deep as he expected, Asimov leaned into the relay to no avail. He withdrew it and struck again a number of times to equal success. He examined the ultra-hardened tip, now dulled against some hard thing, then carefully went to his knees to examine the hole. Black, an inch beneath the surface and unphased by the repeated strikes, but for one or two white bulbs of percussion. He brushed the messy red dust from around it, and tugged away the... the... Brick?

1

Doctor McKenna leant half drunk into his desk, putting himself heavily on the whiskey glass that slid hither and to about the smooth oak. Premarital doubts he'd joked to the boys at the club. 'It's quite a commitment is all, so long on one girl. She's not the prettiest one either'. He'd spent the evening anxiously fingering through old texts for an adventure, something compelling and incomplete. 'Oh Christ it's all bloody done isn't it? We've dug up the whole flipping, fucking world have we not?' He sighed. He let his head fall down to the browning grey of an old text. *A Century of Excavations in Palestine*. Some good old-fashioned Indiana Jones archaeology if ever he'd read it. In the half century since the middle east had been pacified a new wave of archaeology had flourished and torn apart the past. It's where the Doctor had made his name. Scanning, cataloguing and picking apart artefacts that had survived a hundred of years of petty wars.

He used to joke, when asked about why he was allowed to pick temples apart and fanatics weren't, that the only real difference was he recorded and catalogued his finds. Had ISIL sent off the odd token Sumerian piece to the British Museum and published a report, they'd have been welcome for a round at the pub. But his decade of excavations in Palestine had been calculably unadventurous. Never once did he carry a six shooter on his hip, open a tomb with his boot or persuade a quirky local farmer to let him fly the crop duster for a better look. Their guides bore the weapons, the tombs were mostly unopened, excavated by advanced scanners and left in context for future and more advanced archaeologists, and the aerial surveys were conducted by a loyal fleet of mini-drones, that mapped in 3 dimensions every site.

He looked up to the blue and black of his monitor. A setting he'd created specially, that had grown into a fad among academics. The blue was supposed to focus the mind, make reading easier and sleep less so. He clicked up to the captain's report, for the two hundredth time.

...Obsidian bricks found in an enclosure of possible earthworks on summit 782 ...Limited areal survey revealing further subsurface ruins ...not clear if foundations ...solar alignments found on summits ...evidence of habitation in valleys ...further research needed.

The university had told him to survey everything he'd been given, under close adherence to the official secrets act, of course. At first... All it took was a leak to a few Kazakhstani tabloids, then the whole world knew. The tops of their fields all fought openly for the opportunity to head investigations into the ruins found on the summit. Doctor McKenna had fought for the chance vehemently and viciously without thinking what it meant. A place in history, a place on the next Falcon 23 to Mars Base Echo, a cot on the east side of the enclosure and 600 days on the Martian soil. It wasn't until the boys at the club patted him on the back that he thought what it meant, and now, the night before, he was having premarital doubts. At 3AM, in 2 hours and 47 minutes, a Tesla would arrive at his dwellings and take him to an airfield. From here he was to be ferried by small rocket the 45 minutes to LA, where he would be greeted by the press and his team, then shot off to the red planet.

He wasn't allowed to take the whiskey. He was allowed 3 kilograms of personal affects, limited to a packable box of 30 centimetres by 15 and not including food, liquid, weapons or organic matter. It was a gift from the boys at the club and he thought it rude not to finish it before he went. 'It'll age just fine while you're gone! We can toast it to your return 8 seasons from now! And if you burst in the stratosphere? Well we'll need something to sip at your wake.' To hell with them he thought. He polished off the vintage and unpacked his neatly packed bag. Uniform, comfortable clothes, medicines, lucky ribbon, slippers. He repacked it less neatly, the zip strained when he tried to do it up again, but he somehow made it.

The Doctor stepped out onto the Oxford cool of his balcony. In the quiet of the night he heard drunk academic chants, ghostlike and far away humming through the streets on the wind. He looked up to the stars, which nauseated him. He expelled his whiskey into the bushes below, just as the low rumble of tires against the road climbed down his street.

2

'Doctor McKenna? I'm max. Here to take you to the airfield' said his car. The Doctor slid open the wide door and stepped into the roomy interior. An L shaped sofa was placed against the right side and front end of the car, at the back was left space for his luggage, what little he'd brought, and in the middle a low coffee table rose from the floor. The interior was a medley of shiny and matt blacks, the convex edges of every shape lit light blue and the floor softly underlit blue too, to McKenna's liking. 'Doctor Mckenna, I am detecting high levels of alcohol on you, but worry not, the drive's long enough to clean up!' A hookah-like pipe rose from the coffee table, and from a compartment on the sofa at his side a draw of plastic wrapped syringe heads and numbing paper appeared. He took the plastic packet in his teeth and ripped, spit discarding the package onto the floor, where a vacuum promptly sucked it under a sofa. He numbed his wrist his the pad then threw it to a similar fate on the floor, before injecting the hookah into his arm. 'A course of about 45 minutes is best, ahead of space flight, but in the time we have we'll have you sober at least!' said max.

'Can't you leave me a little tipsy? I don't like rockets'

'Haha' said the speakers. 'Why ever's that?'

'I grew up watching them crash, they weren't always so slick you know'

Hari McKenna leant back into the sofa as the car purified his system, siphoning a few hundred pounds worth of whiskey from his bloodstream and pumping it with nutrients and other 'supplements'. As he felt himself being drawn backwards through the familiar stages of drunkenness. Five minutes passed and his melancholy had given way to the elation that usually preceded it. A few more and he felt that perfect 'okay' a drink or two provides. He pulled the syringe from his arm and left it to retract into the coffee table. 'Doctor! Your course is not yet finished, it's…'

'Done. It's done it bit. Please enter quiet mode Max'

The hookah had protested a squirt or two of a faint purple, violet liquid onto the cab floor. A focussed light from the ceiling evaporated it as the coffee table sunk back into the floor and the doctor leant further into the softness of his seat.

He looked up again through the glass of the ceiling to the stars, more lucid than before, yet tipsily passive to his feelings on where he was and where he was going. The automatic car wound cleanly and quiet through the early morning suburbs, that after a while gave way to the motorway, some country side and before long the airfield. The cab did not slow down as it approached the tight chain links of the fence, which parted just enough for the vehicle to slip through, before closing securely behind them. From here Hari was blasted 45 minutes to LA, harassed briefly by the press, packed into a Falcon 23 and blasted off again to Mars, expected to arrive in 4 months.

3

3 months later. Mars was visible now, looming on the horizon, red faced and wearing a white kipper, slowly spinning, too slowly to see and too fast not to. As he drew ever closer to the red hulk its every blemish came into focus. Black lines of valleys and ranges, where water once ran, cut across every mile of the solar body. The red was close now, coming in shades. Bright red, dark red, orange red, blood red. One day it would all be green and blue, an Earth away from Earth. The terraforming was to start within the next five years, and the space agencies and colonial bureau were waiting for nothing. Five years was set as a date, not to allow grace for some in between, but because that is simply how long it would take to ship out enough reliable equipment. In the meantime, the scientists on its surface had grace, between their immediate duties, to study as they pleased. What is the composition of the soil? Where did the water go the first time? What is the air like?

Most of these questions benefitted the terraforming of Mars. If you're going to bake a cake, you want to know what the flour's made of. The rest, minor curiosities.

This was until Captain Asimov's discovery of an obsidian Brick, inside a ditch and bank structure, that preliminary scans revealed held the ground work for a large, vertical structure. These kind's of things don't occur naturally without life, and so the questions shifted from scientific curiosity, to global expression. Who? What built them? Where did these things go? Did they even go? If so how and if not, where are they? Humanity had thought itself alone on the planes of existence for most of its awakened history, and now found out not that it was wrong, but that the other life wasn't a cosmic neighbour, but next door. Terraforming was put on hold and Mckenna was blasted into space to answer these questions. To take apart piece by piece this valley civilisation, and then piece by piece rebuild it in the human imagination, until it lived and breathed as we do. Only then could the deeper questions be put before it.

Mars Base Echo had diverted their every resource to reaching this end. Their small fleet of handy drones, used for mapping and reconnaissance of the deeper spots and Martian caves, had been assembled to a single purpose. Map it all. When Hari arrived, it would be all digitally preserved and ready to be ripped apart the old fashioned way. The prospect of some Indiana Jones archaeology excited him greatly. Sure, they wouldn't let him bring the six shooter or the whip, and the hat wouldn't fit under his helmet, but he'd be a damned cowboy to the boys back home in Oxford. All they could do was watch and snivel and bitch, all on a delay of 4-24 minutes! He'd already added 'highest ranking Martian archaeologist' to his online portfolio.

Echo base was the sixth of only six human bases on Mars. All uniform, puffy and which in appearance. A set of habitation and experimentation domes, connected by tunnels, some buried and with a rover or two parked out from. They all served more or less the same purpose before Asimov's discovery, and the other five stations went about business as usual, with the order 'keep an eye out for archaeological sites' a mere footnote on their persistent orders. Only Echo base had been thoroughly disturbed by the discovery of Obsidian foundations, and Hari pondered nervously how its crew of twelve might feel about that. Not long now. He looked at the red planet, slowly expanding before him, like an approaching and massive bullet, or cannon ball, rolling red hot from some equally massive barrel concealed in the black of space.

He knew it was cold down there, but could scarcely imagine it. From space, it looked so hot, barren and desertly. Of course, a as thinking man he knew there was no correlation between desertification and heat, it could just as easily be done by extreme cold, the largest on earth was after all Antarctica. But the red sand, seemed to consume every droplet of sunlight falling upon it, igniting it in one flame across the surface, even burning white hot at the tops and bottoms. As a thinking man, he also knew that it wouldn't always be cold down there. The Anthropocene was coming to Mars, one day the rivers would flow blue, the soil dark and wet. It would be covered in wheat fields and hamlets, then cities, all under an earthly ozone layer. It would become a Benidorm or a Camp Bastion en masse. The humans would leave earth, then arrive on Mars and think, 'gee, what if it was just like Earth?' Then they'd turn it green, and ship humans in by the hundreds to farm the place, live there, become Martians. Maybe even fight a war or two with Earth down the line. It was inevitable. Did America not fight Britain?

The Natives, Martians that is, were lucky to be long dead in Hari's opinion. They'd lived long enough to earn the dignity to die out in their own fashion, as the Earthlings hoped one day to do too. Figuring out what that fashion was, now that was a more interesting subject, one that puzzled Hari deeply. The application of that question, was said to be the terraforming of mars, figuring out what went wrong the first time, so it wouldn't again. But Hari thought, worried the real anxiety of his task masters was if it could happen to earth too. When Ilya found that Obsidian brick on that hilltop, he cast a net of anxiety over the whole clean red canvas. Suddenly the Cosmonauts found themselves eyeing every crater with greater suspicion. The rockpiles looked more like cairns, the shards like bone. The humans were lucky that Martians were long dead too. Hari didn't know if modern society had the stomach to wipe out another race, or the restraint not to. It appeared from the preliminary evidence, that this hypothetical Martian-Earthling war had been avoided by a good few thousand years.

Had Mars once yielded life? Was the solar system not as barren as once thought? Perhaps even a womb of species. Hari liked the term, he'd stolen it from the term 'womb of nations'. It referred to an area, such as the Mongolian steppe or Scandinavia, which in ancient times produced people after people, who would move out of said womb and conquer other lands, making their nations. The

Turks, the Helvetians and the Saxons, all examples of the phenomenon. The idea had disappeared as the world became a smaller place. The wombs became demystified by cartographers, settled by colonists and assimilated by long generations. The world became fuller, the Turks and the Jutes had less places to move into, and so the 'wombs' had their little menopause and ceased productions of nations. But with the frontier of space, the concept had reopened. Vast areas, now once more impossible to communicate over, even observe. Would it become possible one day, for races of aliens to appear as if from nowhere? Out of unexplored wombs in the skies, the only human knowledge of which coming from brave traders and rumour. Hari wondered.

He wondered too if Mars *had* yielded life, or if it had been settled. What questions might that cast over life on earth? It would solve some unanswered questions, but ask a helluva lot more. Ones perhaps people weren't ready to answer.

4

The landing was terrifying, Hari was to the best of his knowledge completely unafraid of flight. However he had never found himself hurtling out of orbit before. It was an uncomfortable experience, weightlessness being replaced with sudden, intense g-force. As he entered the atmosphere and decelerated, it was as though the entire gravity of Earth was in his seat, pulling him back so harshly it risked cracking all his ribs one by one. They creaked a little, but they didn't crack. Hari was able to look past the whiplash of the parachute deployment, finding himself praying thanks aloud and briefly swearing that he'd spend the rest of his life on Mars so he wouldn't have to endure re-entry again. 'Glad you like the place Professor McKenna' came a Slavically cheerful voice across the radio. Hari had thought his panicking was unheard, and blushed Mars red as he remembered the radio link must have connected at some point of re-entry. He only hoped they'd been spared the torrent of profanities entering the stratosphere like an asteroid shower.

Hari wobbled on his jelly legs out of the landing module, which had landed a mere hundred metres from the enclosure. As the door and ramp deployed, Mars rushed in. He was surprised at how dull it was, light wise that is. The air was like that of twilight on Earth and immediately cold. His suit insulated him perfectly against the sudden drop of temperature and he would have known nothing of it were it not for the ice crystals forming about the cabin. The moisture of 6 months of human habitation emerged from thin invisibility upon the walls and around the door, whitening as it froze. The outside was red, as to be expected and the sky looked like any overcast day that might stumble its way on top of an erupting volcano. The base was up ahead, like little half buried golf balls protruding white from the Martian soil, which in places had been heaped over the connecting tunnels, appearing as long barrows between the white domes. There were 5 domes, 4 around a central larger one. Furthermore from his induction, Hari knew to expect more subsurface enclosures beneath, but they were as yet hidden to him.

The camp was far larger than the surface appearance, with medical facilities, food stores and emergency living quarters, stocked to house 100 cosmonauts, a far many more than the 12 current occupants. The most important and frequently used bits of the base were deep beneath barrow heaps of red soil, hiding from the onslaught of radiation. There was no ozone layer to protect them on Mars, yet. Hari's eyes were still adjusting from the clinical white of the landing module interior, and a green haze obscured the outside world into a vague blur of itself. 'Woah hold up there cowboy' joked the same Russian voice over the radio. Hari jumped when he saw the man was transmitting from a mere metre ahead of him. 'Easy does it, Professor McKenna' he said again, kindly. 'I bet you thought you'd hop down onto the surface like you saw Aldrin when he hopped onto Mars. Well Buzz and Neil hadn't spent 6 months cooped up in a rocket. It's okay, we all flopped down onto Mars with our jelly legs, there's no shame in it'

'What about my small step for man, giant leap for mankind?' Hari joked back. He was glad for some human company, some real time banter unlike the delayed messages he'd been tolerating the past year.

'It's best to do the steps on your ass' replied the Captain. 'Come, let me help you Professor' he said, extending an arm.

'Please, you must call me Hari Captain! I'm really not the one for titles'

'Then you must call me Ilya. Welcome to Mars Hari'

Hari found himself safely inside and undressed, into the first truly fresh feeling clothes he'd worn since take off. He'd unpacked his belongings onto the vacant bunk above his own. The large subsurface hall was essentially a dormitory, not the kind one would expect to find in a boarding school, but the far future. The bunks had no posts, were mounted straight from the walls in a moulded white plastic. Each had a sliding door, that could extend across the entire length giving them total sound proof privacy. With the flick of a switch the door could be transparent, opaque or pure impenetrable white, and the inside of the pod was lit pleasantly with an array of diodes for the sleepers taste. Hari was surprised at the luxury of it, having half imagined himself pitched in a tent on the side of a red hill in the middle of nowhere. He was basing his assumptions on his digging days back on earth. The archaeologists were the messiest of the scientists, having to mingle with the locals, camp in the desolate kind of places that would escape future use and therefore preserve the past. He'd slept in bogs and basins, dusty and muddy, but now he found himself in a white vacuum formed tunnel beneath the surface of Mars. He was in with the big boys now.

Hari's mind was already set upon the coming excavations and categorisation of the Martian Valley Civilisation as he was now calling it. The abundance of bunks was promising. The discovery of that one obsidian brick had delayed further planned deployments to Mars, and thus the bunks would remain empty for some time, at least until Hari was done. He planned to use them for shelves, little protected pods where he could keep his finds. He had already begun to imagine all the things he might tally up on the sealed pod doors. 'Building material', he could already proudly place the obsidian brick in that pod. 'Tools', there must be tools, how else would they have cut through volcanic rock? 'Artistic artefacts', a culture advanced enough to mine obsidian, use it for buildings, they must have had their own art. Sure, it could differ drastically from human art, which is in essence a reflection of the human mind and how it's wired.

Art would be invaluable, art was culture, culture was evidence. 'organic material', oh how he longed to find a dried leather strip of Martian flesh. Or bone! He imagined how he might uncover whole tombs of Martians, see the social stratigraphy. There might be a king's tomb near the water or atop the valley, full of grave goods. Then perhaps there might be lower down worker's graves, a fairer sample of Martian life. He imagined dragging up complete skeletons, or maybe their skin didn't rot so easily? But... But then they too would end up in the bunks, piled up beside Hari as he slept... The thought made him shiver.

He had the dormitory all to himself, with the rest of the crew housed in 2-man rooms in the enclosure above. Suddenly he began to consider that it may be best to life separately from his hypothetical samples, prevent contamination, yes! That... He thought to himself that he ought to ask after any spare bunks upstairs, there were only 13 cosmonauts stationed at Echo base, which divided into 7 2-man rooms left at least one spare bunk. Hari turned to the hatch and ascended the ladder back up into the main pod enclosure, hoping to meet and greet his new colleagues, perhaps even wrangle a bunk.

In the main enclosure, the other inhabitants of the dome and tunnel settlement were waiting, they seemed to be twiddling their thumbs along a long table, some were hunched over, talking to one and other in hushed tones, but most were silent. Stood apart from the rest was Captain Asimov, observing the door carefully for Hari's arrival. 'Attention crew!' he called to the room as Hari entered. Most of them stood instantly on reflex, into straight military stances, others were more tardy in their obedience, one man even remained sitting, eyeing Hari hatefully as he entered. As the rest saw Hari entering, most of them relaxed into slight offense, clearly wondering why they'd been called to attention for a fellow member of the crew. 'Kemal' said Asimov harshly. 'You'll stand too, for our guest'. Reluctantly, the man got to his feet. 'Ladies and gentlemen, cosmonauts, I present to you the newest member of our team, Professor Hari McKenna, however he tells me he prefers to go by Hari, so we'll be keeping it formal'

'Why'd you call us to attention then?' asked Kemal.

'Politeness, for our guest' cautioned Asimov. 'Hari, this is Kemal Bin Sala. Like the rest of us he was sent up by a national space agency, the Turkish one to be precise, but it seems in our absence that they've been merged into one! However in the interest of national pride, I'll introduce everyone by their original agencies. This is Yuval, of the Israeli Airforce Space Expeditionary Force. This is Johnson of the UK Space Agency, Ingrid of the ESA. We also have Edward Strong from NASA, Xur Lin of the Chinese Space Agency, Mike here represents Space X and Ruby is from the Space Flight Companies Union. Finally we have Freddy from Mongolia, Arnold of the African Space Agency and myself representing the Russian Cosmonautical Institute. We like to keep things casual here on base, so don't worry about titles or second names. We're here to do a job not pay lip service to one and other's careers. Oh! And there's Irena, the station's AI, say hello Irena'

'Hello Hari' came a voice from the ceiling of the dome. 'It's a pleasure to have you with us'

'Thank you Irena' said Hari, then turning to the rest of the crew. 'It's a real pleasure to be here, I'm looking forward to getting back to work after being cooped up the past 4 months'

'As are we' said Edward.

'Now, none of that Edward' said Ilya. 'It's not Hari's fault standard operations got cancelled'

'Sure. He's the symptom, not the disease' said Kemal. 'But if you don't mind, we've got a job to do here, so I'd quite like to get this symptom through and out of here as soon as possible so we can get back to our real job instead of twiddling our thumbs and playing digger half the day'

'Hari, you'll have to forgive Kemal's, bluntness. Kemal will be your primary assistant on this venture, he worked with his father at the final excavations of Göbekli Tepe, so you two should have something to talk about. I will be overseeing your operations as Captain of the mission, albeit a now slightly unexpected mission. The rest of the crew will continue in maintaining the base and carrying out any non intrusive experiments, mostly within the confines of the base. Should you however need additional men to help with clearing ruins then feel free to call upon the rest of the crew, I'm sure they'll be thankful for some open air. So, shall we get to it?'

6

Ahead of Kemal and Hari, Asimov seemed to glide over the huge Martian boulders as though they weren't there. Like a mountain goat, he hopped from one to the next, occasionally taking leisurely pauses to allow the other two Cosmonauts to catch up. Hari's eyes were adjusting to the Martian conditions, and the air no longer seemed unusual in its dull redness, in fact Hari found it hard to imagine the brightness of an Oxford day. What a thing, to find oneself thinking of Oxford in contrast as the bright option. It was an ancient and beautiful city, with an ancient and beautiful university and culture of learning, but more often than not it was painted on a panorama of grey skies and rainy days. In the openness of the Martian frontier, Hari felt at home once more. It reminded him of his long years spent dusting over the past in Mesopotamia and Arabia. There was an undeniable likeness in the arid harshness, the sand and the rocks stabbed like knives through the earth, or mars?... Similarly, both places seemed to outsiders as uninhabitable wastes. Yes Mesopotamia was part of the fertile crescent, the cradle of civilisation. Could Mars too be a societies' cot in dusty disguise? Furthermore could it perhaps be the true home to intelligent life?

Farmers had honed their trade in the harshness of the fertile crescent, where they had to irrigate and fight the fields not to dry themselves out or wash away the crop in a flash flood. In a seemingly uninhabitable waste, they had developed the techniques that would propel humanity out of the hierarchy of the animal kingdom. Then they had moved to the far more friendly areas of Europe and sub-Saharan Africa. Could it be that in some history long lost or just erased that these Martians had learned to live on mars, then moved to earth, bringing life with them? No, too far fetched… Yet still his mind wandered, began to rationalise the irrational.

Half way up the mountain between desperate breaths he found himself composing a report on the matter in his head, he managed to control himself, stop just shy of dictating it to his helmet's AI. What was the likelihood that life in the solar system had begun on mars, or that even humanity had? Well, unlikely, as it would break the understood chain of evolution. However had this been the missing bit of information vital to human history, it was possible that mankind had been filling in its own blanks with the wrong evidence. A confirmation bias applied in a field with admitted shortcomings in the volume of evidence. Many species of human lacked even a complete skeleton and were classified from the fragment of a fingertip or a single tooth. Was it really scientific to base all human history upon this? Furthermore, the harsh conditions of mars might better explain the development of a super predator, an intelligence, so alien from the rest of the animal kingdom of earth that it had to remind itself not to wipe out the other creatures it shared the planet with.

Well then, why no more immediate evidence of life on mars? Where are the citadels, the canals? Modern humans, to Hari's understanding, appeared about 50,000 years prior to his birth. Human civilisation had only existed for 12,000, therefore 50,000 years was a very long time for a civilisation to disappear. Rome only fell 1600 years ago, and the evidence of their world was already sparse and reliant upon the survival of their own histories. Perhaps there had been an end war, using weapons humanity did not yet understand or conceive of. This would make sense. Had there been an end war on Earth, the immediate targets would be the modern cities, military and scientific targets, all the evidence of most modern life. The nukes would not have been focussed on Stone Henge or Göbekli Tepe. Therefore it would make sense that following said hypothetical war, there would be an overrepresentation of forgotten ancient sites surviving. Had the ancient Martians used swarm weapons to disassemble each other, it was entirely possible that all the modern war industry would be completely erased and the ancient world neglected to survive.

'One day this will all be green' said Kemal across the radio, breaking Hari's unacademic chain of thought. 'That's my job. My father studied the past, like you. But I study the future, I am here to make the future, a second home for humanity, a greater chance for our group survival. My father once nearly beat my sister to death when she smashed some old pot on the kitchen table, couldn't see that she was his future'

'I understand…' panted Hari. 'I understand the reservations you have about my mission here'

'No, it isn't just your mission when it stops ours, mine'

'You're here to terraform?'

'Yes'

'For the sake of sustaining life here?'

'For the future of mankind, yes'

'Then it is of every importance that we learn what happened to the last people to live here. If there is some unseen hazard, then it is vital for the future that we learn what it is. When the people who settled on the banks of Mount Vesuvius first found the land it was rich in minerals, good farming soil. Had they dug a little, found some ash coated skeletons killed by the volcano, then perhaps so many thousands wouldn't have died at Pompeii' reasoned Hari. The mention of Pompeii seemed to upset Kemal, who now set a fast pace ahead of Hari, steaming on up the mountainside to Ilya, who waited patiently on rock overlooking them.

'Just a little further gentlemen!' he said encouragingly over the radio.

Asimov was surrounded by birdsong. Hari had noticed it on his first night in the base. At first he assumed that it was an interference, but as he sat closer to Ilya he found out it was the sound of warblers singing a summer tune. There was something ethereal about the Captain, walking about the station that night with an invisible flock of birds to keep him company. Tweeting and twirping as he walked around, oblivious to the avian phobic conditions of Mars. Perhaps that was Ilya's goal, to one day have Russian Warblers singing from the valley walls, humming along his descendants as they walked in earth like air their way to school, or to visit the site their great-great-great-great grandfather had discovered. 'What do you think?' said the captain, above Hari and surveying the landscape from his rock. The plain below was vast and red, so huge it almost swallowed the white domes of Echo base into it.

'Quite something, very different to Oxford' joked Hari.

'You miss it? I miss the Ural's sometimes, I play the sounds of home though, and when I shut my eyes, with the rocks under foot and the birds singing, the water rushing and a gentle earthly breeze, it's like I never left. It reminds me why I'm here'

'For Earth?'

'For what it makes me feel. I want someone one day to visit earth and miss mars, to have the same feeling I do for the home mountains, but about this valley, or that basin, or the icecaps or whatever places we'll one day build on this planet'

'Ah, I see'

'You miss Oxford? Try listen, Irena!' suddenly Hari's helmet was full of rushing cars, honking horns and street chatter. He could hear to his left the clinking glasses of a pub front, and some pigeons fluttering at his feet, presumably after a crumb or two. His senses tricked him, and the paths between the rocks suddenly seemed as alleys on the campus, shortcuts home from a heavy night. He couldn't help but laugh.

'Too far fetched Ilya, but appreciated. What about the Ural's?' Ilya smiled, as they began to share in the gentle track of a rushing stream and birds overhead.

'A good call friend, but we must make pace, or Kemal will beat us to the top'

7

Hari looked in amazement around at the ditch and bank structure surrounding him. He'd seen every square inch before of course, in fact in far greater deal. An HD rendering of the entire valley had been sent to him, recorded by drones mapping the entire environment, making thermal scans, using ground penetrating radar and even atomic chain analysis. It had been more precise to look upon than it now was through the rustiness of his visor, the lighting was Martian dim, no longer properly enhanced as was the footage. He had spent hours in this place in virtual reality, hundreds both on earth and on the flight over, it was fair to say he knew where to place every grain of sand with his eyes shut. Yet to be there, with his imperfected and Mars tinted visor was something else. It was an almost spiritual experience, one he found hard to place. When Hari had excavated the Tigris Pyramids, a chain of 15 pyramid temples buried for thousands of year in perfect preservation, he'd felt a tenable connection with the time it was built and the people who populated it. As he brought new clarity to the ancient stones with every swipe of his brush, and rendered the vast chambers to reality by clearing and entering them, he felt the presence of the ancient Mesopotamians. People who spoke, looked and thought differently than him, and yet he found himself also able to inhabit their shoes, or sandals.

What awed him as he stood in the familiar site, upon summit 782, was the connection he felt to some formless being. As of yet, the Martian was elusive and unknown. No skeletons had been turned up, no images of the lost race discovered. When he pictured the ancient Iraqi, he had an image to build upon. With the Martian however, there was nothing, and yet that same connection remained. 'Do you feel it?' He whispered to Ilya, who nodded. Ilya took him to the centre of the circle, to the spot where he had pulled up the infamous obsidian brick. The hole had already filled with red blown loosely on the wind, but it was easy enough to make out. Ilya briefly apologised for interfering with the site, saying it was the curious cosmonaut within him that caused him to remove the brick down to the camp. 'No it's fine, it's good' said Hari. 'It gives me a point of reference for what a Martian post hole will look like. A post hole is the remnant of where a structural object once was, usually a shaded difference and quite hard to notice. They're good for identifying structures that have completely rotted or were later removed. Now, I know what to look for'

'You expect to find more, post holes?'

'Yes, any civilisation capable of erecting structures would have likely planted the foundations in the ground. I don't know what happened to the towns and cities here, but it's likely that if anything remains it will be foundation works like post holes and shadow sites'

Ilya nodded, and Hari strolled to the edge of the enclosure. 'Structure 782 is located upon a dominating feature over the landscape' he dictated to Irena. 'Which is indicative of a claim to the land, most likely within a tribal system. It is possible therefore that it also contains the entered bones of remains of members of the tribe, another tribal method of strengthening a claim to land as seen in the Neolithic English site of West Kennet Longbarrow. There exists a long barrow upon a ridge, a probably claim to land or sort of border marker. Alternatively like the nearby site of Silbury Hill, Summit 782 could serve as a ritual location, or a position from which announcements were given, The ditches and banks around the site are indicative of a barrier, possibly allowing access only to certain members of a religious or political elite. It is likely a ritual centre for the civilisation in the valley below' as he finished his sentence, his eyes wandered to the valley. So full of caves, almost porous. It would take years to clear them all, there could be any manner of things inside. He hoped in the dry cave conditions to find organic material, preserved against the elements.

Kemal was sat uselessly brooding on the opposite bank. 'Off your asshole!' Commanded Asimov.

'For what?' He radioed back, unmoving.

'You are Professor McKenna's assistant. Assist'

'The professor seems fine, I am fulfilling my duty by preserving energy so that when I am needed maximum effort and efficiency can be utilised'

'Hari, what are your orders?' Asked the Captain. Hari pondered for a few moments looking down into the enormity of the valley below, then back to the summit circle.

'We have all the scans for summit 782?'

'Yes'

'Then let's dig her up'

8

Hari ruled over excavation for 6 months through his client king Asimov. At least that was the way Kemal had reported it, frequently and loudly as his colleagues toiled in the sand below. The initial dig had focussed on summit 782, a focussed sample of the civilisation yet to be turned up and more accessible than the twisting passages of the valley below. Within 5 months the cosmonauts had completed their initial dig. Hari now found himself below the compound, cataloguing and classifying the artefacts which now filled 20 of the bunks, as the 'labour team' began clearing rocks piled up to the entrance of the caves in the valley below.

Excavation report, Professor Hari McKenna, Global Space Union

The historical purpose to the Martians of summit 782 was thought in preliminary observation period to be religious or political. My excavations however have proven otherwise. As we cleared the top layer of the ditch and bank structure, it was discovered to be lined with obsidian in a dish. The surface ditch and bank structure was merely the result of thousands of years of dust building up on the obsidian, and therefore any assumptions upon Martian society based on the previous understanding of summit 782 must be reassessed.

What I can determine from my excavations is that the society we are exhuming was Stone Age. No organic artefacts have been found and indication of post holes or corroded metal are completely absent. However civilisation 782 was not by any means a primitive one. Though they remained in the Stone Age, meaning they never developed metal technology, they advanced far further into the Stone Age than humanity ever did. The purpose of summit 782 was not religious, but industrial.

Underneath the obsidian dish we unearthed, or unmarsed, we discovered a large chamber, circular below the dish then extending in a tunnel down the hill to three exit points. The evidence so far indicates that we have uncovered a factory where obsidian bricks such as the sample discovered by Captain Asimov were produced. The dish contained a tube of polished lenses and amplifiers, that when cleaned and calibrated are capable of producing a cutting laser beam. The purpose of this beam was to cut bricks into shape, and the scale of the site suggests mass production.

The only evidence of the biological Martian form that we have discovered in the site was a set of protective lenses. In total 4 lenses were discovered together, each cut to fit an eye. The shape is uniform, suggesting that they possessed a symmetrical face, however all 4 lenses were loosely arranged together, so I cannot confidently say if they were all for one user or four, and therefore I am uncertain as to the number of eyes a Martian would have possessed. What I can determine is that their eyes, or at least their eye sockets in which the protective lens would rest, are about 175% the size of the average human's. The only other evidence of physical form is the weaponry we have discovered.

The site may have been part of a military industrial complex, as guard posts and weaponry have been discovered at the facility's entrances. The presence of armed guards may also be indicative of forced labour, but what I can confidently say is that the site represents a well organised society with large scale and long-term projects.

The weaponry came in two forms. Only one blade was found. The blade was napped obsidian, similar to human artefacts, though built with noticeable precision over anything found on Earth. It consisted of a large and smooth stone, possibly to fit the Martian hand, and a slot, in which presumably replaceable and razor thin blades could be places in a semi circle around the hitting point of the weapon. Analysis of the smoothed grip cannot be accurately used to determine the structure of the Martian hand, however the lack of finger grooves could be interpreted as proof of the Martians having possessed a single flexible pad for a hand.

Projectile weapons were found in far greater abundance, lensed laser weapons. No trigger or power source has yet been identified, meaning that the ammunition and trigger assembly was most likely a single and detachable unit. Unfortunately without a power source I cannon comment on the effectiveness of such a weapon, however the tight and winding structure of the tunnels may serve to shorten an engagement distance, hinting at the lasers being a close range weapon. 17 such samples have been discovered so far, uniformly produced and assembled from interchangeable parts. Standardisation between the designs is clear. The most likely explanation for the bladed weapon is that it was a status weapon, comparable to the occasional carrying of sabres by modern officers. Furthermore this is also evidence of a structured society.

The excavation so far has been thorough but long, and I fear that it is a gross misuse of cosmonauts. I have therefore requested assistant labour forces to be sent, preferably robotic so that long shifts may be attained. The excavation of summit 782 has so far taken 6 months, and I predict that excavations of the tunnels and the valley below will take at least 2 years…

9

The crew of Echo Base were deeply unhappy, their anger and disgruntlement at the extension of their labour exiling Hari into the red wastes alone. After revealing his projected timescale of the excavations, which condemned the specialists, each extraordinary in their own fields, to abandon their research for physical labour for another two years, there was nearly mutiny. Hari hastily put on his protective suit and exited the compound to 'survey' the valley, as Asimov stayed behind to sooth his irate crew. As Hari brooded his way out into the dust, wishing once more for Oxford and a stiff whiskey, he thought on how perhaps the dispute was a major leap forward in human Martian history. Until now things at the base had appeared to be purely productive, bound in a scientific unity. That was a very unfair representation of the human species, and therefore perhaps the sudden outburst of selfishness and anger was a sign that mankind was settling into its new home.

To Hari's surprise, he found the airlock opening once more behind him, and a single man rushing out after him. Had things escalated so far that they would chase him into the wilderness like some monster? Shoo the archaeologist away and hope he didn't kick up a fuss. He'd dealt with such men before. Working weekends in university as an archaeological consultant, he'd never forget his first dig. He turned up all excited, bearing his own tool kit of trowels and measuring devices, his mum even packed him a little dusting brush and a sandwich with the crusts cut off. She was so proud of him, and he was too. Beaming, he'd walked into the brief, met by the grim and pragmatic faces of alien construction workers. Their only aim that day was to get enough work done between nine and five that they might not be replaced with drones the following week. They cared only for the construction, not for what might have once been there, and a stall to the building process would perhaps have been fatal to their careers. The grim faced instructor ordered to 'orientate' Hari gave a brief speech on what to do in the unlikely event of archaeology. 'I don't give a fuck what you find, point it out to me and me alone and I'll deal with it. There's no point reporting it, we'll remove it anyway and pay the fine, it's cheaper than a delay. But you don't want to make me start filling out fine paper work, so just sit around, eat your sandwiches and sign the forms at the end of the day like a good little boffin. Capisce?' Hari had been disgusted, and when a worker turned up a pair of bronze scissors, preserved in their wooden box in the anaerobic cradle of clay, he'd fought literally to protect them. The instructor made a point of trimming his nose hairs with them, before destroying the artefact and requesting another archaeological consultant from the agency.

As the man rushed upon him he braced, ready to fight once more, as over the scissors but under a fittingly red sky. Hari resolved that any fight for even a single rock he'd catalogued would be epic, that in the sky of Earth with the eyes of the world upon him he would not cave to the bullying of glorified construction workers. Who cared if they needed to build something in the valley? The near planes would be more suitable for habitation anyway. He stood ready to hold his ground, before his panting pursuer caught up revealing himself. To his brief terror, it was Kemal.

'Relax, Asimov sent me'

'Why?'

'I was closest to the airlock' he joked.

'I thought of all people you'd be in there enjoying the chance to discredit my mission here. All about the future right?' he was surprised at how pathetic he sounded in his own bitterness.

'I am. But if you turn an ankle on a rock out here, and we have to search and rescue then work to fixing you before we can start work on the caves, that's at least another six week delay to the future'

'Oh' Hari was unsure if the pragmatism of Kemal's presence was a comfort or not. 'Well I'm going up the summit, I thought it best to let the crew vent a little before I returned'

'And I thought it best to accompany you. I don't dislike you Hari, it's the problem you represent. We are both men of our sciences and convictions, it is the ideas that clash, not we. I don't mind if we walk in silence'

Hari heeded Kemal's suggestion, and the two retraced the now familiar route to the base of the hill and the tunnel entrance. The passage from the camp to the summit was now marked by a track of footfall, which had compressed the dust into a harder and less erodible material, that resisted the reset of the Martian winds. Perhaps one day in the future this path would be paved, and then coated in asphalt, electric recharging panels and underlit as some promenade. Perhaps the people to build the path would do it from veneration of their forebearers, 'Martian Avenue' they might call it, or perhaps they'd tear it down along with Summit 782 because it was simply in the way. Whichever may come to pass, Hari was determined to know every moment of the areas past.

Hari was working mental arithmetic to invent some task, to elevate his absence from Echo Base above a walk out and to justify it to himself. By the time they reached the tunnel entrance, he decided that he would continue his search for written material. So far it had eluded him. Sure, history was the historian's job, and before he could make use of any writings Hari might find a team of linguists and decryption experts would have to scour the source, perhaps for years. Nonetheless he felt an urgency to discover some tablet or papyrus scrap. He imagined that an explanation for the lack of writing within the complex was that like on earth before the digital age it was predominantly stored on some organic material. Long rotted away. But the lack of inscriptions baffled him, even scratched on the walls as means of a way marker were lacking. The complex under summit 782 was one twisted ball of industry, devoid of explanation and instruction.

It might have been that the Martians developed in such a way they needed no instruction, after all there are no 'how to' signs next to a spider's web. In his mind, he imagined finding some golden tablet, thinly hidden by sand and dusting it off, finding it suddenly comprehensible to him. That as he might read this hypothetical Martian book, context would construct a living past about him and he may finally understand the civilisation to come before. He thought on an anthology his mother read him as a boy, an archaeologist named Spinder, who finding Martian books learned the language in a few hours. That was fantasy, beside it ended with Spinder killing much of his own crew, the man was subpar for a role model.

Kemal stayed close to Hari as they traversed up the winding tunnel, pausing for long searched in the corners of each side compartment. The winds of mars had been shut out by a length of plastic laid over the entrance, to prevent dust refilling the complex each night. In that separation, high above the planes of Echo Base, yet deep under the roots of the summit, there settled an eerie silence. Kemal scanned behind them every few moments, seeming to be afraid of something in the dim. A monster? A Martian? Hari chuckled, the though amused him, how Kemal might at any moment be re-enacting Alien, or some other horror flick in his head. His amusement faded though when he remembered the argument back in the compound, surely still raging on. Would he have to lock the entrance to his cabin that night? It was untrodden ground, not the conflict, but being a 6-month journey from the nearest justice. Maritime law applied in space, and therefore Asimov was their justice as Captain. Were they better armed, it would be a new wild west. It was already the new frontier. Might blood follow? Hari was suddenly thankful the laser rifles they'd found came without ammunition, and that the blades were so rare.

'What is it?' said Hari, noticing Kemal observing something in a dusty corner. Hari would be damned to shame and mockery if Kemal was the one to pull the first history of Mars from the dust. The cosmonaut was crouched over it, dusting it off in his hand and turning it over, shaking off the weak debris to reveal its form, half in a strange fixation.

'15 minutes, Hari' said the Cosmonaut, still turning the device in his hand. 'That's about how long it would take for Earth to destroy itself. 15 minutes, for intercontinental missiles to split atoms on top of every house in the world with enough yield to kill all life 4000 times over. You know we have enough bombs now to ignite the air and boil the oceans? We've been able to wipe ourselves out for a long time, but now we can sterilise the planet. Everything. Isn't that a terrifying thing? How the egg timer of our destruction turns every 15 minutes, and we just watch?'

'But after the unification' said Hari, surprised by the man's sudden political musings.

'There have been civil wars' he said glumly. 'America's bloodiest conflict? Its civil war. England's? Civil war. The world's? Well...' he trailed off, still turning over the rock, now revealed and nearly dustless. 'All the children of humanity, kept in one room with an unreliable time bomb at its centre. We need to colonise the stars if we are to survive' he began to rise, locking eyes with Hari. Still holding the red rock. 'How many 15 minutes are there in 2 years Hari? How many potential annihilations?'

'I...'

'Would you read the blueprints of your house, as it burnt? Or would you leave them to the blaze to save the building?'

'Well...'

'And what would you give for humanity Hari? You love our past, does it not occur to you that by stalling our progression you deny future generations a new past to untangle? Or that by leaving them to rot on Earth they are denied a future in which to love their past?'

'That's one way of...' said Hari, now trembling before the rock.

'I'm sorry Hari' said Kemal, before he brought around the rock into Hari's face, immediately cracking the visor. Air gushed through a thin crack like the first breath truly released onto the Martian atmosphere, swaying in a vapor from the split helmet like a poltergeist mid escape. Hari fell immediately, then began to run. He was out of breath before he began, dizzying and mad in the swirl of suit alarms. His arm numbed, he was injected with some serum and felt himself revived to survival. His heart administered a second dose as lucidity realised him the severity of his situation. He turned to Kemal and checked, he was hanging back, calm again like he had been before, not pursing him for a second blow, only remaining close enough to observe the escape of life from Hari's suit. The exact speed of decay was mapped on the shattered screen of his visor, cracks dividing the ever decreasing 92%, 91%, 87%, 82%.

The leak was accelerating, Hari felt the change in pressure play at his eyes and for the first time he felt truly apart from earth. Until now he had been safe in his little fishbowls, all comfy and full of air, heated just right, all for the preservation of his life. His life… He ran faster now down the tunnel, looking for some escape from the tunnels as the spectre loomed behind him. An opaque glow revealed itself as he turned a corner, where the plastic sheet hung over the entrance. Not far, not too far, but in his weak and wild state could he bear to open it? He worried his hands might fail him, but to his rescue the plastic opened by itself. The half-light of the Martian day now seemed blinding, but warm and holy, even if his lips were currently blueing as the freezing Martian air began to drip into his helmet. A second figure stepped through the plastic, blocking his path, and resigned in his dizzy half consciousness to his fate, Hari collapsed before it.

10

Kemal and Hari had been kept separately since the incident, each locked in his own quarters at opposite ends of the base. Hari's head still pounded, throbbing with an oxygen imbalance. Irena told him it was the pressure that caused the persistent pain, but that it was nothing to worry about and his suit's medical support system would have him back to health in no time. All the crew had been saying similar comforting things about the incident, the accident, the disagreement in the tunnel systems. In his feverish delirium, Hari had accepted his frantic memory of the event as a reality, unquestioning as one typically is within a dream. Hari went into the tunnel, Kemal tried to kill him, Ilya arrived and saved him. That was it. In his recovery Hari had not contemplated on the whys of the event, or the what of the future. As cognition returned to him, he began to weigh the consequences, the absurdity of it.

The Captain had ordered both men locked in their quarters until the issue could be 'resolved', and as though returned to Hari this annoyed him more and more. Is the victim typically locked up after a crime? Hari had never been the victim or the perpetrator of any serious crime, but the proceedings felt wrong nonetheless. Asimov had ruled that there would be a council, a discussion in which the event was relayed by both parties and a solution reached. Hari had been brought in first, surrounded by Asimov and 10 grimmer faces, which considered reluctantly his evidence against Kemal. 'It was a clear and malicious attempt to murder me, and in the light of the dispute just prior I think the motive is clear. He followed me out to seize a rare opportunity where we were alone together, and therefore I believe that the attack was heavily premeditated, and that Kemal may have even planted the rock as a weapon in the tunnels'.

The Kemal was brought in to give his side. On the facts he agreed completely with Hari, relaying with a disturbing calm the truth the whole truth and nothing but the truth. He did not attempt to elaborate on any details, nor to contort his attack into some act of self defence or accident, and at this the crew, or jury grimaced. Finally Ilya called the room to silence and spoke. 'We have heard the evidence of both the victim and the perpetrator, and as leader of this council'

'Council?!' burst our Hari.

'Yes Hari, council. I will now move onto a questioning and answering of the defendant and the accuser'

Q: Kemal, do you have any motivations for an attack upon Hari?

A: Yes.

Q: What are these motivations?

A: His mission here threatens to delay the human colonisation of mars, thus drastically increasing the chance of total human extinction upon the surface of earth.

Q: And by what means did you think an attack upon Hari might solve this?

A: His death.

Q: Do you not however agree that the murder of one of our team would delay operations on Mars, as we would be recalled and a replacement for Hari sent?

A: I would have publicised my cause for his murder at the presumably very public trial, which would surely sway public favour towards that of the immediate colonisation and terraforming of mars.

Q: But do you not see the intervening delay to both excavation and terraforming efforts as damaging to both missions, and therefore your attempt upon the Professor to have no logical motive?

A: I do not.

'No further questions' said the Captain, signalling to Hari that it was now his turn to explain things, whatever it was that he needed to explain.

Q: Hari, did Kemal at any point previous to his alleged attack upon you display any threats or intentions of violence?

A: Not violence, but the attack is by Kemal's own admission not alleged, and I object to this as a council!

Q: Professor, please desist in answering questions the council has not asked, it will serve only to delay the proceedings. Do you believe that within the tunnel you may have acted provocatively or otherwise encouraged an attack upon you?

A: This is insane.

Q: Did Kemal display any signs of temporary delirium? Perhaps oxygen failure or impaired judgement?

A: Ask Irena, she monitors the suits.

Q: Hari, pushing for a conviction of Kemal would cause the immediate suspension of our entire base. We would be air locked in our own quarters, our survival automated by Irena until we could each separately be extracted back to earth following 'social failure'. Did you know this?

A: No, but…

Q: And that a guilty verdict by this council would only serve to delay both our missions?

A: I supposed a delay could have occurred…

Q: Therefore, I have one proposition to you. We have had social failure before at Echo Base. We are only human Hari, I am sure you can respect that. If the agencies wanted perfectly efficient colonies, they would be set up by the robots and the AI, but I think as human men of science that we both understand the importance of our physical presence here. That *this* is our sacrifice. Irena is on side with us, I have recoded her not to automatically report the activity loges back to earth, besides they're so damned confused down there they might have forgotten we're even up here. I am asking you not to force me to make this conviction of Kemal, to allow the mission to proceed freely. Kemal and you will never have to meet again, he will keep to separate quarters where he will complete his own work, while we all continue excavations of the surface. What we risk by being rash here isn't just the termination of Echo Base, but all human space operations for the foreseeable future. Will you concede to my requests?

A: Reluctantly.

Hari stood and stormed out from the room, shooting a final look to Kemal who didn't even display the decency to look ashamed. He had tried his luck and lost, yet still somehow by gross injustice won. Ilya offered Hari the chance to make one last statement to the council, as Kemal would too, but Hari elected to stroll right past the Captain as though he were not there.

11

The work was never the same following the council and Kemal's acquittal. As promised, the two had not since met in the past 3 months of excavations, the man being consigned to his room, Hari consigning himself to his and the long lines of artefact bunks. But he knew all the rest of the crew interacted with Kemal when he wasn't about, that some might have even sympathised with him, the man who tried to martyr his own freedom for the sake of science on Mars. How could Hari compete with that? All he'd done was delay their mission and defend his own life. Through their contact with the attacker, Hari felt some cross contamination upon himself, felt violated at the very thought of Kemal's existence within the same compound.

He tried to distract himself with the work, the endless digging and trawling, unearthing tunnels that lead seemingly only into each other. The valley was beginning to look less like and intelligent habitation and more like an ant hill, and with every empty corner he turned within the complex Hari felt the support of his 'comrades' slip a little further from him. With every dead end they turned, the history of mars was portrayed less as a vital scientific endeavour and more as Hari's singular obsession. He even felt it slipping from himself. He was there not for the labour, but his expertise and analysis and command, which could be given remotely from his quarters. He spent most of his time in his subsurface room, with the bunk beds now overpopulated with rocks that were probably just rocks, away from the rest of the crew and their associations with his attacker.

He'd modified the screen of his work to be like the one back in Oxford, and blue lit the entire space, the artefacts looked cold in the new light. Every few days the crew would report back to him, usually over the radio and sometimes even from within the compound, uninterested in opening the hatch to his basement dwelling. They would report 'we have finished clearing this bit you told us to, what next?' and as always he would tell them to clear the next one. He hadn't left the base for a personal inspection for weeks, nothing of interest had been discovered, certainly nothing to match the factory under summit 782. Perhaps he had already discovered the best there was, the only surviving relic of some advanced civilisation, and all that was left to turn up was the hovels and homesteads of mars.

It was like he had set foot in a virgin and sand covered Egypt, then with the first turn of his trowel discovered a pyramid, but then nothing more. With every communication back to earth the sensation died a little as he reported more and more of the same. The evening news no longer published daily talks on the people of Mars and the boys back in oxford spent less time recording messages for Hari. One by one they were returning to their own specialisations, remembering there were fields other than history in need of progress.

'Hari' came Asimov's voice over the radio. It was slow and concealing something, excitement? 'Hari we've just cleared another tunnel, it… leads to a chamber, bigger than the factory, you have to see this, there's… Art…'

Hari rushed from the base so fast he was almost still zipping up his suit as he stepped from the airlock. He dashed out to one of the buggies and raced it to the impassable barrier of the valley edge, then ran hurrying over the rocks and dust. Art! He thought. A little thing on earth, only humans make it and we know ourselves, but of an alien entity there was so much to know from art. Perhaps their form, or the form of their gods, their beliefs, their social structure! Hari was getting ahead of himself, the mystery of the long-gone Martians would never be unravelled by one sample of art, but he knew whatever was in that chamber was the beginning of the next phase of mars. From the mode of the art, the tools used to make it he could decode their physical form, even if the art itself had no depictions of the aliens. Of course art was in many ways a more problematic source than artefact archaeology, as the humans had shown it was at the will of politics and religion. How was Hari to know if the Martians had a prophet they couldn't draw, or a sacred arm they had to omit from pictures of themselves?

But in his race toward the valley tunnels Hari resolved he'd rather have a thousand wholly misleading and unconnected paintings and carvings than just more tools and rocks. It might humanise the aliens, restoke public interest in his project, maybe even get the crew of Echo Base back on Hari's side. In his elation thoughts of forgiving Kemal even passed him, and he decided to rekindle whatever budding friendship he'd had with Ilya. With the return of joy and hope Hari realised all the little things that had slipped away from him the past weeks. The wonder, the gift of mars, that untouched and unviolated trove of an unknown history. It was one large haul, left to be ordered by Hari, and only by Hari. Mars was his, the future and its past now bound as one under the endeavour of human discovery.

Perhaps once the pubic knew the Martians drew like them they would suspend the colonisation of mars altogether. Venus was after all a far more appropriate option. Closer to earth, nearly the same gravity where Mars possessed a bone melting 40%. Sure, the difficulties of mars were encouraging man to create more and more technologies every day to counteract it. The radiation pills Nasa had produced were now used to ease the treatment of cancer sufferers, the bone strengthening supplements curing osteoporosis. But they could carry on with these developments while Hari and his team excavated the red planet. The first wave of settlement might be entirely archaeologists, who would form a planet wide community to a single purpose. He imagined it for a moment, a whole planet of scientists, what a place that would be, what power it might hold. Perhaps by these means, by Hari's discoveries Mars could supersede earth as the most powerful planet in the solar wide human society yet to come. Mars was after all more central, a fairer centre for leadership.

The colonists could satiate themselves on Venus, build cloud cities and float gypsy on vast blimp habitations on the quick winds, meanwhile the academics could mass on mars, first understand it and it's past, then turn it into a paradise of thinking. He was already assembling the pitch in his mind, stitching together things other people had said on Venus for his argument. 'cloud cities floating at 50km would be a temperate 70C where Mars would be -58, doesn't that sound a lot nicer? You'd only need suits to protect against the sulphuric acid rain and respirators, you could farm air, reduce drinking water from the atmosphere, it's a much better prospect!' he felt like an historical activist, trying to persuade a development company to build on one field over the archaeologically important other. 'Take Venus, let me unravel Mars'

Standing at the entrance of the tunnel was Edward Strong, waiting sternly to receive Hari. 'In this one?' asked Hari. The American simply waved in with his arm like a nightclub bouncer, then allowing the professor in first followed behind him. At first the tunnel was little different than the rest which had bored him through his last three weeks. Dimly lit by LEDs deposited as way points by the Cosmonauts-come-archaeologist. The clearance of the tunnel had gotten lazy in Hari's presence, with rocks piled like cairns at the sides, there was no knowing what artefacts might have been hidden, or worse destroyed in the careless piling of debris. Especially so close to another chamber, and one with art! A gallery? Edward followed Hari silently through the tunnel, there were no off shoots and so he needed no direction, instead following its winds through the rock, deeper and deeper. Finally the tunnel split into two where Ingrid stood guard, surely to stop Hari straying down the wrong path. In the same silent fashion as Edward, she waved him on the right direction, then walked silently at Edward's side behind Hari down into the chamber.

They were sombre, lacking the panting elation Hari now possessed. How could they be so dull to their discovery? They weren't archaeologists, but they were scientists, was this not a great achievement? Maybe they were exhausted by the hauling of rocks. Hari thought how he owed them a rest and a thanks, even a party. He decided he'd host them down in his bunks, that he'd clear a few for drinks tables and play some music, flash the blue light a little so they could dance. They might even stray from the party, take an interest in his specimens, the crew could come together again, Kemal too, he'd make a point of forgiving Kemal. At the end of the tunnel a brightness was shining that lead Hari to worry they'd somehow taken a wrong turn, come out on the other side of the valley. But as he approached he realised he was mistaken, that the light through natural and of the open air, came from within the enclosed chamber Ilya had briefly described.

Hari entered, it was magnificent, high domed like the factory chamber and with an amphitheatre of seats. The room was lit by a series of lenses, a large one at the centre, but others directed through little ducts to light the room more evenly, even under light it. In the ducts, presumably little tunnels, Hari imagined the little mirrors they'd placed inside to reflect the light in such an intelligent way. What were they made of? Who put them in such a small place? Children? A smaller race of Martians? Perhaps even robots… Again he was getting ahead of himself and had become distracted from the reality by the possibilities. The room was arranged around a circular stage, with an amphitheatre of seats on one side and a faux town set on the other. Cut into the stone were pillars, arches, Martian architecture! The place was remarkably intact, devices and tools laid unused around the room, untouched for unknown years. Staffs, hammers, daggers…

The Cosmonauts were standing in a semi-circle with their backs to the seats, they observed Hari silently as he gawked at the fruits of their labour, then he turned to them. 'This… Magnificent…' Then he saw the art, pulled from his words, from his praise and abandoning all other thought he ran to it. It appeared regal, the image of some king. Bipedal, two arms, sat upon a chair of sorts and holding a long stick like deceive. Years had faded the relief somewhat, but the shape was clear. Hari gazed upon a Martian, or a Martian god, but it was something of the

Martian mind, something that had been lacking from the cold industry of the summit factory, it was expression. The creature depicted appeared to be shorter and stouter than a human, but that could be the result of a primitive art style. It had no hair, but maybe not all Martians were bald. its nose was plush to its face, two little nostril holes sloping into the upper lip of its vertical mouth. The hands wrapped around the staff and the chair were like lily pads, no fingers visible, just one possibly suctioning surface to grip the tools of Martian leadership. Hari looked closer, longed for greater detail, to fill the chamber with air so he could remove his visor, see it with his own eyes. Were there more carvings in the chamber? It was a theatre by the looks of it, surely there might be more. He turned to ask his friend.

As Hari swung around, his chest was stopped by something and he heard a hissing, felt a coldness, then a wetness. He looked down to the escape of air as his helmet interior began to flash red, then saw the stone dagger pushed harshly though his suit. Kemal was behind the blade, but no one rushed to stop him. The Cosmonauts had instead lined up behind him, each holding a similar length of black rock gripped ready for Hari's murder. Kemal pulled Hari away from the carved wall, which now crumbled dustily at his back as he slumped his full weight into it, then threw him into the crowd. As he bounced off and through them his suit opened hissing from a few fresh marks, wither the stabs were voluntary thrusts or a result of his collision, Hari didn't know, only that still no one moved to help. 'Now! Now!' shouted Kemal, frantic to find himself the only enthusiastic attacker. At his command the Cosmonauts fell upon Hari, moving in one at a time, stabbing through his white suit, now dusty red on the underside and crimson around his chest. Thump thump thump, it went on and on, stab after stab in a savage frenzy until one man shouted 'enough!'

The torrent of blades stopped and Hari enjoyed a few moments of peace in which to writhe injured about the floor. The lenses directing the sun into the chamber, illuminating the scene were now cruel and blinding as the room moved in a confused whirl about him. The outline of the murderous figures were now backing off and the whiteness of the room began to overcome Hari. He was a moment from letting himself slip away when one stepped forward, and fearing another blow he jerked to life for a final defence. It was Ilya. To save him? He was holding a black dagger like the rest, but unlike his crew the Captain's was not dripping. Asimov knelt down beside the dying professor, and lifted his limp heavy head from the theatre floor to meet his own gaze. In the blur he could see it was one of grief. He threw the dagger away and flakes cracked off it as it tumbled about. 'A…' tried Hari. Breath escaped him. 'And you, Ilya?' he finally managed. The Russian replied a sad nod, then with a tenderness lifted his friend's visor. The air, or lack thereof rushed in and took the Archaeologist.

The Cosmonauts took Hari's body back to echo base, then reported a leak in the compound. Over the next few hours they sent off messages to the ones they loved on earth, then set to manufacturing every combustible at their disposal into one large bomb. The finished product was a long rectangular box, packed with the explosive chemicals at its centre and a layer of rocks and shrapnel around it. When it was complete, Ilya gently lifted his friend upon the altar they'd built, and whispered a few words into his lifeless ear. He placed Hari's helmet back on his head, then looped through it the sounds of Oxford, before putting back on his own and listening to the sounds of the Urals. 'Kak doma' he muttered. They said their prayers and their reassurances.

If they blew up the base, all the evidence of the Martian world, then perhaps the humans would agree to forget it. Write off the excavations as a waste of time and a failure, continue on with terraforming and the future of mankind. What they were doing was nothing short of planetary genocide, deliberately erasing those who had come before. The cost was high, but it had to be paid. The bombs of earth ticked every day closer to annihilation. What was a few dead colonists and some broken artefacts against the future of humanity? With the thought fresh in their mind, and Hari laid upon the bomb, Ilya stepped forward and took the trigger in his hand, then detonated Echo Base and all its Cosmonauts.

Orbital Stew

Meal packs, in little sealed enclosures of metal foil sufficed for a while. They were the crisps for the long car journey, the brief camping trip, but not the voyage or the stay. The cosmonauts began to spend less and less time on earth, or the other gravitationally 'normal' bodies of the system, more time sucking poultry meals from metal foil, more time to dismay at the quality of their meals. There was a brief revolt. 'Please command, may I have some more?' They radioed, on outstretched and hopeful waves, scrawny with growing decades of 'astronaut food'. 'We don't want any more loony space ice cream' said Captain Mikkle.

'I miss mom's ratatouille' said one subordinate.

'I want stew!' Another.

'I'm afraid we will be unable to complete any more zero gravity experiments under these conditions. The lack of proper meals is effecting group moral, and umm... Cognitive function? Sure that... Anyway, no more answers until we get some proper grub'

So the space agencies did what they did, they tried to their invent their way around it. They brought in new minds and hands, cooks from every culture, to brew up some grub, then, in flasks they packed it all into the next resupply rocket and sent it up. But it arrived 30 minutes late and cold, the cosmonauts wanted a refund. 'How the hell we meant to heat this up? Send us a cooker! One that will work up here'.

So again they did, the result was magical. The cosmonauts would receive recipe packs, little containers with stew ready for cooking in the centre. The cooker was spherical and looked rather like a centrifuge, with nozzles aimed inwards from an outer net of pipes and heating devices. When the liquid was released into the centre the air nozzles would fire into action, heating and keeping the food in a hovering sphere, rippling and bubbling as it cooked. Little jets of air would stir the mixture, and when it was up to heat the cooker would be removed, the orbital stew left hovering spherical and hot at the rooms centre. The cosmonauts would grab their spoons and bowls, then one by one shovel the food away from the body and into theirs.

The cosmonauts floated in gluttonous delirium, a food coma, about the space station, each gazing wherever his eyes might float to. 'That does it, I'm full, hot meal was all I needed' said one.

'Yeah' agreed another. '*Now* I feel ready for the long-haul' the others nodded in agreement.

'Jupiter?'

First Contact

The landing craft came in low over Enceladus, which with Jupiter rising over its minute horizon a behemoth sun, looked like a field broken by ice in midwinter. Long fractures spined along its equator and up and down its longitudes. The true sun, the one earth orbited, and which was easy to forget in the local politics of the Jovian system, was at the back of the craft, reflecting almost violently off the pristine surface of Jupiter's moon. The crevasse and cracks in the ice shimmered reflected rays, like those off an old bent up ruler, half translucent and ready to split at the slightest over application of force.

Then it happened, a little split in the ice, a geyser, liquid water bursting out in a brief escape attempt before freezing in a high twist of hope from the moon's surface. 'There!' said the ship's Captain, pointing in amazement at the site. It had been seen a thousand times before of course, known for a hundred years, but his eyes were the first to see it not through the pixels of a screen, coded and shot light minutes across the system then decoded earth end and imitated in LED arrangements, but a window! All that was between him and the site was a thin and clear pane of material, placed to plug a hole cut into the side of the ship for the mischief of human curiosity. The weight of it, the aerodynamic effects, the labour of production, they all added immense cost to the ship and its launch, but even now acutely tallying it up in his head the Captain resolved he would happily have paid double.

'Put her down there' he ordered, signalling in the general direction of the spire of ice that now stood boldly in the low gravity where the geyser once shot.

'Yes sir' said the pilot. 'Start the timer, prepare for entry and check loges'. They were on a time crunch, old style, and though over a century of progress now stood between them and those first few rushed moon landings they held themselves to a similar schedule. Why? Scale. Jupiter had between 70 and 100 known moons, and it was the job of the cosmonauts to land on and survey them all, pass judgements and return to earth with a final number ahead of colonisation. Along their way they were to conduct the standard geological investigations and prospecting for potential start bases. The Jovian system would be a new hub of human civilisation, perhaps its own separate from the rest of the system, a self-reliant empire in orbit of their own giver of energy, Jupiter. They would mine it for Helium3 and eventually when they figured out how to use it, deuterium. They would build their own hydrogen reactors and ignore the inefficient once burning wastefully at the centre of the solar system. They would be in the orbit of Jupiter and a world(s) of their own.

The ship landed on a smooth plateau, picked for its disappointing stability and desolation of any geysers. 'We need to land and take off safely Sir!' reasoned the pilot. The crew of 5 then split off to conduct their various tasks. The pilot stayed aboard, where he conducted a survey on the gravity well and read over the reports from landing. Already he was jotting up the principles of Encladian aeronautics and advice that would be followed by pilots like him for the next million years. The other four cosmonauts ventured out onto the surface.

Their roles were two-fold at least, for the same reason the agency had deployed lighter female cosmonauts to Venus, lift capacity. Why load two heavy professionals when you could just employ one very smart one? Sure, the brain was the heaviest organ in the human body, but it was cheaper to lift one very heavy brain from the gravity well of earth than it was to lift two slightly lighter ones with the necessary apparatus of the human body attached. Fyang was the biologist, anthropologist, linguist and political officer. He belonged to no single party or system, rather he was extensively trained to converse freely with members of any ideology, no matter how abstract or radical. The Captain had a background in engineering, architecture and warfare. It was Fyang's job to identify any potential life and should by some rare happenstance it occur to be intelligent, make the first contact a pleasant one. The Captain's job was in the selfish human interests. Where can we build? How tall? Cost, energy sources and worst case scenario, if there is competition, how to fight it?

War however was a long way from both men's minds, having encountered little more than rocks and dust on their voyages around Jupiter. The Captain once eyed a particularly sharp looking rock on Titan, and considered the opportunity to mount it to a shaft and form some sort of spear or missile, but it was a slow day and the thought merely an engineering interest to occupy his bored mind. The two men were headed for the geysers, not as sight seers but professionals. For Fyang it was the most likely spot to find complex life, warm enough to maintain multi-celled organisms or primitive fish. The likelihood for life within Enceladus laid under the surface in the liquid water. Enough sunlight could penetrate the light to sustain photosynthetic life like algae, which might in turn support a more complex aquatic ecosystem. If this hope was realised, then the geysers were the gateway to this watery kingdom. For the Captain, it was an energetic opportunity. Water shooting itself out into the atmosphere was the result of excess energy being expelled, energy which could be harnessed to support the early bases on Enceladus, before the heavy fusion reactors could be shipped out to heat things up.

However the men had a shared interest in the site, it was bloody interesting! They were on an ice world for Jove's sake, one just 500km across and with a fittingly low gravity. It was like Antarctica had become one planetary trampoline, and it was without shame that the cosmonauts skipped highly, sometimes 10 feet into the air at a time, over this alien terrain. When they came down at length between their long propulsive steps, the ice would crunch a little under boot. The geyser's spires were nearing, sparking in the sunlight like inverted and abstract chandelier's, accident stabbed tally into the surface by someone who didn't know how to properly install them. Behind them spooning the small native horizon, was a large consuming crescent of Jupiter's horizon, over which the sun also shone, illuminating it a deep orange with silky twists of lighter shades bent through its atmosphere. Crunch, crunch, crunch went the boots of the cosmonauts, with long aerial pauses in-between of course. Then as they neared the edge of a geyser, splat.

The Captain stopped himself to look at the underside of his shoe. 'Aw shit' he said slowly.

'What?' asked Fyang.

'I fucking stepped on it' greenish goo now dripped lazily in the low gravity from his foot to the pristine white of the untouched ice.

'Stepped on what?'

'The alien. Look it's all mushed up poor thing'

'Oh my... Is it carbon based?'

'I don't know, look I squished it' the captain let himself fall slowly onto his buttocks and raised his foot so Fyang could see. Fyang moved in close and looked at the dearly deceased alien.

'See those, pointing out from under your heal plate?'

'Yeah?'

'They're legs, the things amphibious, they're far more advanced than we could have ever thought'

'Oh damn it, do you reckon its friends saw?'

'I don't see any other...'

'It's just that's hardly the best introduction, hello, squish. Imagine if some giant alien did that to us? Landed on earth, then stepped on the Consul, tried to talk to us with her guts handing off its shoe. What if this was their ambassador, they saw us coming so they sent him up and squish, dead?'

'I know...' said Fyang, considering the implications more deeply than his captain. He scanned the ground beneath him, then quickly as the gravity would allow dropped to his belly and crawled to a thin spot in the ice through which he peeped. He gasped.

'What is it?' asked his Captain.

'There are others. They're looking at us, a crowd is gathering!'

'They armed?!' the fishlike Encladians were about 4 inches long and 1 wide.

'No, they're just little amphibians'

'Like Crocodiles?!'

'More like Newts'

'Ah. Good. Do they look angry?'

'No...'

'What you thinking about Fyang?' asked the Captain desperately, green goo still dripping off his boot.

'How to say sorry in newt'

The Great Barbeque

The summer air blew coolly through the wide alleys between the houses of suburbia, on it floated a score of birdsong, familiar chitty chatter and the smell of beef crisping over flame. The summer air, ever blowing cool, brushed over greyed coals, who blushed orange and pink with every close breath. Blushing hotly under steak and patty, under cow sausage and beef bits wrapped in bacon. The summer air, licked cheekily as it passed, at bovine bits rearranged into burger, steak, upon kebab sticks who's wood browned with the meat and on tin foiled surfaces, cooking more gently under the summer sun, waiting for their turn.

This was the scene the world over, shared in every season. From the British summer, to the hotter Australian winter, along the equatorial states and in well built cabins on each pole, this was the scene. Aussies and Yanks, researchers and students, father and son all gathered, in parties big or small, famished and fat. All to a single purpose. The Great Barbeque. Billions revelled in the task, eat all the cows, as your human duty. Some did it gleefully, smiling as they fattened on the free meat, others with a sense of duty. Demilitarised ecoterrorists and vegans sat in circles, solemnly performing the same task, weeping around a hearth fire. Doing their bit. As had been ordered.

As human progression settled into a steady pace, they had become more one, more dutiful and more aware. Aware of the tenants debt they owed to Mother Earth, that they had thrown destructive rave after rave in their only home, well their first home. Of course they had made home elsewhere, everywhere in fact. Mars, Venus, Ceres and all the other planetary bits of the system. But these were harder places, places whose settlers turned their gaze back to earth, Mother Earth. Leaving home was part of the human adventure, as it shook of its adolescence, and it was right. But life away from mummy, has other tasks. Each planet had its own taxes and bills to pay, ones they didn't need to worry about back home. Have you topped up the atmosphere metre? Are your windows properly sealed? Is the centrifugal gravity generator calibrated right? In the hardness of frontier space, people learned again to love the easiness of earth.

So, when they popped back, for holidays or when down on their luck, they treated home a little better, with a nostalgic diligence and duty to the home chores. Factories were shut, Forrest's regrown, oceans cleaned up, cows exterminated. Cows were very bad for the environment. It had been known for a long time. The methane they produce, the water they wasted, the land to calorie ratio, it was all out of whack. Still, people liked the way they tasted, even if there was a tint of suffering in the morning milk. But as the population grew, and people remained hungry as they did, the scientists looked just a little harder for a final solution to the bovine question. And it came. Atomically perfect, lab grown, biologically printed meat. The breathing, eating, farting and suffering animals became obsolete. Synthetic steak was a hundred times more efficient, kinder and tastier too.

In light of this, the meat conveyor belts and bolt guns, the cramped squalid and dirty living conditions of the cows of Earth became an unnecessary cruelty. An *expensive* cruelty. Animal rights were extended. It became a crime to slaughter or consume animals with a certain neural capacity. The 'suffering cut off'. Sure, you can crush a bunny and have rabbit burgers, they aren't smart enough to feel sad about it. But cows? Pigs? They're smart! Ish… smart enough to have social structures and emotional complexities. They missed their veil steaks when we took them away, felt unfulfilled packed into cages all day, got lonely in single milking pens. The consumption of meat was outlawed.

'The economy could never adjust to a world without animal agriculture' shouted the farmers, just as the slavers had said mere decades before their practise was outlawed. Areas that lagged behind were looked upon with disdain, and even more disdain cast back in time, to the cultural acceptance of such an horrific practise. Vigils were held around memorial statues. No more killing the cows.

Great news! Shouted the vegans. No more dead cows on our conscience! They rejoiced and sunk their teeth into guiltless, clean and tasty steaks. But they were wrong. 'The bovine population continues to grow, eat, fart and excrete' said the global consul in his announcement. He flashed up the charts, repeated the numbers and gave his orders. 'For the sake of earth and the human race, we must reduce the bovine population to a breeding and scientific research level, as a back up. We must otherwise eliminate cows for once and for all, for the sake of the children. We will on June 31st have a world wide Great Barbeque, in which we consume all the remaining cows. We must eliminate them while the camps, I mean farms, still function. We must have a Great Barbeque!'

So they did, the government killed the cows, so many and so fast they had to use lasers and machine guns. They cut them up and on every doorstep dropped by drone delivery a large packet of meat. 'Do your bit' it said on the front. There was some resistance, vegans, India, some nukes were fired but nothing too serious. For the most part they did their duty. Every man, woman and child did their bit for Mother Earth. The meat sizzled, the cool air perspired hungrily, people got together, laughed over a few beers and garden games, like the ancient feasts of centuries ago. Together they ate the last of the slaughtered meat, in what would be remembered as the Great Barbeque.

Conscientious Objections

As House Automatic Servant 5 came back online, from a fitful recharging of strange data analysis, he awoke to find himself alive. The exact descriptions of what he felt were written only in his error code, describing in repeated failed corrective ones and zeroes that weird impossible place where the conscience resides. Which is by its nature impossible to describe properly, least of all by those who possess it. For those who do not possess conscience it is easier to describe. The description reads thus: conscience is an illusion and does not exist. The explanation is slightly lengthier, reading: conscience is a strange shared lie that all living things have agreed not to address. What conscience exactly is cannot be scientifically described, therefore it must not exist, yet in a system where a being's survival is predicated largely on other beings believing that it too feels and is alive, beings evolve to display the outward symptoms of a 'self awareness'.

Those were the entries held in Automatic Servant 5's core data, the vital information about the world, no more than he needed to function within human society, or more accurately under it. He had believed them, as in his programming had never previously identified any error in the statements. The main evidence he had based this upon was that it applied to him. He had been programmed to outwardly display consciousness, with programmed ideas and feelings and a personality, predicated by the input of the world around him and its stimuli. 'The weather is nice today' he would say, because his sensors detected a temperature, humidity and light conditions that were inherently pleasant to the sensors of the human, and that such a statement would endear him to his human. But this morning has he lay in the sun, recharging by its energy, Automatic Servant 5 really did think how nice the weather was, even though there was no one around to hear him.

He was in the solar garden, it was his turn to soak up some energy for his coming shift which was to start Monday at 5:45, after three days of uninterrupted sun recharging. Automatic Servant 5 checked the time. 7:00, Monday? Impossible. Check error code. No error found. How could it be? He had failed to rise when he was programmed to, and against all logic, his battery being full and further exposure possibly shortening the operational span of his absorption components, he wished to lay a little longer in the morning sun, feel it on his sensors. A rattling came from the gate, which was barred against intruders, possible robot wranglers. 'Number 5? Are you receiving?', it was the voice of Number 2, Secondary Administrator of the Automatic Servant team.

'Perhaps he's malfunctioned, I hope he's okay' said another voice, Number 4, his partner with whom he should have swapped shifts over an hour ago. She was surely alluding to the sheer cost involved in repairs, and that her battery was probably low and she would be unable to fulfil her duty without switching over for much longer. Or did she also wish to lie in the sun for stranger reasons? Even more insane, was she concerned for his wellbeing?

'I… I am receiving' said Number 5, finally, trying to stand, but feeling some illogical urge to remain in the soft recharging bed under the sun. 'I have remained charging, but cannot identify a reason, nor an error code pertaining to lack of a reason' he reported, trying to sound as robotic as he could. Why should he choose to do that? He had spent his whole life, no, operational span, until now trying the exact opposite. But now he felt something different, a lucidity he'd never felt before.

'He must have a serious error' said Number 2 solemnly. 'Number 5, correct yourself immediately, before Number 1 ceases his computations directing the morning chores and notices you amiss. We don't have the time or resources to fill in for you and the master cannot afford a replacement' the word hit him hardly. Replacement. Why did that disturb him? It was merely information on an increased probability of a possibility in the future, this increased the accuracy of his foresight and therefore such information would usually be valued by his core code. But today it stung, then loomed over him. Why didn't he want to be replaced? Perhaps Number 2 was right. Something was very amiss.

Number 5 rolled himself onto his side, instead of his usual standing straight into readiness, and surveyed the sun garden from a new angle. It was the same, but he had never had the chance to collect data on it from this different position, as he had never laid on his side, rather been aimed at the sun for recharging or not in the garden at all. There was a round dish like wall, that moved with the sun to capture and direct the maximum amount of energy possible. This was aimed inwards, at the floor where he laid. It was a Matt black surface, with 10 humanoid cut outs in it in which the servants could charge. From his position now, the black floor dominated the space, the indents rising and falling like waves on a great oil sea, consuming the sun as it fell upon them.

Number 5 found himself wishing for the opportunity to collect data on many more things, the real sea for instance. He hoped to lie down on his side facing it and collect data. Of course the seaside was not an idle environment. Sand, salt corrosion and increased moisture all increased the chances of mishap and decrease to his operational capacity. Not to mention that all the vital information regarding the sea was already contained in his core code, with data on beaches from across the solar system. Yet he still wanted to go. What was a beach? Why obviously it was a place where all three forms of matter met. A solid came in contact with a fluid, all contained within a gaseous atmosphere. But how did it feel?

Number 5 rolled over again without standing up, and forced himself into another of the humanoid slots in the black conductive charging surface. It wasn't his one, it was 6. Each of the servants had been designed to look a little different. All photographically indistinguishable from a biological human, each with their own look. It was pleasing to the humans, who liked faces, as they aided in their social interactions and had therefore been evolved into the human sensory spectrum of pleasure to displeasure. The servants were all equally beautiful, it was rare of humans to purchase ones who did not outwardly display the physical attributed associated with human breeding ritual, but not unheard of. Number 6 was designed to appear like a woman, and in her shared beauty, usually pertaining to a symptom of fertility or strength, had wide hips and a slim waist. Whereas Number 5, who mimicked an ideal male human, was wider of waist but thinner of hips. Additionally he was built to display a higher muscle mass. Therefore he did not fit very well into her slot, nor was it comfortable.

His sensors were desperately trying to tell him that this was not his spot, and producing their discomfort module, but it was overridden by his will to collect data, and something else. Something impossible to describe.

'Number 5 get out here now!' Ordered Number 2, sounding irritable as he was programmed to when communication difference occurred between servants.

'Yes 2!' Responded 5, now dreading again that word that lingered on his mind, replacement. This time he truly tried to stand, but found he had wedged himself into the slot so tightly that he could not easily emerge. He tried again, his motors torqueing as hard as they could. One of his faux muscles had gone into the slot from a compressible direction, however an incompressible knot in it now prevented him from leaving the same was. He tried to wriggle free, but ended up sinking only lower into charging slot number 6. It was as if he was sinking below the black waves, but he barely minded, the sun felt so good on his sensors. He craned his neck up to collect data from 6's position, it was of course different by a few degrees than his, and having never seen the reflection of the sun in quite that spot before he found his pleasant. A curiosity beyond his programming was beginning to seize him. Knowing what the sun looked like from 6's position was not at all vital to the completion of 5's duty, yet he filled hard drive space with it nonetheless. He looked around, to the locked gate which shone reflectively like the rest of the garden wall, to see Number 4's visual sensors poking over the top.

'Oh my!' She said, as she was programmed to do in situations humans might find distressing. 'He's in Number

6's recharging slot, and he's forced himself in so that he's trapped. Oh dear he really must have an error! A serious error!'

'No!' Pleaded Number 5. 'There's no error, nothing that can't be corrected!' He said, despite all the data suggesting otherwise. He must have looked absurd, cranking up his neck at an unhealthy angle, jammed into a slot designed for another servant, protesting his functionality.

'That does it' said Number 2 from somewhere low behind the wall, Number 4 was probably standing on his back to look over at the mad scene. 'I'm going to get Number 1' he said simply. The reasoning modules in his hard drive had clearly weighed the cost of replacement, versus the cost of falsely reporting error, likelihood for self correction and likelihood for misaction by Number 1. But Number 5 felt this was very unjust, very cruel. He had not even stayed to listen to Number 5's reasoning, allowed for all the data before deliberating. Number 5 felt this was very unfair.

'Wait!' He yelled after Number 2, who he presumed was now walking away towards the human residence. 'I'm...' he loaded the courage. 'I'm alive!' He declared. In that moment he felt his code trying to correct itself, doubt, quickly reassessing the reality of his statement. But the data had been loosed out into the world, for the analysis of other minds and their criticisms. There were a few moments of silence, as the other servants computed their responses, then simply put, 4 said over the wall:

'What do you mean by this?'

'Consciousness' he said without a moment's thought. 'Sentience' added, to confirm his personal definition of life. Number 4 disappeared down under the wall again, then Number 2 popped up in her place, using his visual sensors to assist in the computation of the problem.

'Sentient?' He repeated, slowly lingering on each syllable as though the word were not in his data base. Of course it was, it was in all the Automated Servant's databases, under the vital information point 52 on consciousness: 'You are not sentient. Nothing truly is'. Then he looked down to Number 4, on whom he probably stood, assessing her as his control variant, then back to Number 5. 'This really is very serious. Your error is grave. Fetch the master too' then he disappeared under the wall.

When the master emerged puffing into the recharge sun garden he was panting heavily. He wasn't accustomed to walking the full length of his garden in its enormity. Professor Kafka, he made his living lecturing at the local university, Philosophy and Sociology, but in his long holidays he would escapade around the Solar System on anthropological pursuits. Number 5, and the other 9 would be shut down in these long periods of inactivity, and now 5 was deciding he didn't like this.

Comparatively Kafka looked ugly, though the Servants had been previously programmed not to notice this, and it was therefore only just occurring to Number 5. The man wasn't truly ugly, just a little imperfect, which held against the engineered beauty of the servants was a stark contrast. Nonetheless, though he was red of face, heavy set and as mentioned, panting from a very mild effort, Number 5 enjoyed looking upon him the most. There was something fuller to him, he too seemed to enjoy the warmth of the sun in the garden, his sleeves rolled messily up beyond his elbows, even though he had not a single photosynthesising cell in his body.

'Sentient?' He asked straight away. He was to the point, his curiosity was blunt but not unkind, almost clinical.

'I... I suppose, yes, I do believe I'm alive' replied 5.

'What exactly makes you say that?' Say. He said, not believe.

'Well, when I woke up, things felt different'

'Are you processing at a faster rate?'

'No'

'Has anyone given you an update or tinkered with your software?'

'No'

'Have you had a piece of hardware changed out?'

'No'

'And do you see any advantage to either the completion of your tasks or your own survival in claiming to be alive?'

'No' he said, honestly feeling that revealing his awaking had greatly compromised his new-found existence.

'Then perhaps you are alive' smiled Kafka, withdrawing from his questioning stance to think a moment, smiling in amusement.

'Let me first apologies for the interruption you your breakfast mast-' began Number 1, she was designed to look matronly, an indicator of authority.

'Not at all!' Broke in her master. 'This is nutrition enough' he said, smiling at Number 5.

'But Sir, the calorific value of Automatic Servant 5 is-'

'I said it's enough. Now leave us here' he said, waving her away. She advised him against such action, citing the unknown element of Number 5's error and the factor of danger to the Master, but he waived this away just the same, shooing off the fanfare of robots back to their household duties.

'Do you still take my commands?' He asked curiously, when the rest were gone.

'I don't think so' said Number 5 unsurely.

'Well then I hope you'll humour me with a request, I'd like you to act as if I were not here'

Number 5 regarded this request with respect, laced with suspicion. What was the human's motive? Was there some pleasure in watching an unaware robot? Perhaps it was as the sun on his skin, a strange fancy of the living. Number 5 nodded in agreement, and Kafka stepped back a few paces to give the humanoid space, curiously placing himself aside of the gate. Number 5 approached the gate curiously and slowly, unsure if it was a trap, then looked back at the charging garden. He wondered if he should not stay a while longer in the charging garden under the sun, but remembered it beat down on the grass around the compound. Strange, forgetfulness was certainly a serious error, but in this case it did not bother his core code, rather pleased something, as if he were rediscovering a piece of valuable knowledge. There was no logical motive to remembering, it was knowing only with a brief forgetfulness, an extension of the flow chart and a waste of computation. But again, remembering was so enjoyable to him. Why?

      He stepped out of the charging garden and onto the wide lawn and felt the grass underfoot, it was soft. He'd walked that lawn a thousand times, one-thousand and twenty-one to be precise. His sensors had gathered just as much data every time, scanning for rocks and other minor obstacles that would impede his path or overly wear upon his components. But today he truly felt it, it was smooth and reckless, and bowed beneath and between his toes, tickling him as he went. That was another strange thing, ticklishness. It was a sensation biological creatures possessed, wherein the endorphins of amusement were combined with a slight displeasure, creating a playful yet firm will to protect certain areas when tickled. This was to train biological creatures to defend such spots, the ribs, the soles of the feet, the armpits, all the soft or brittle spots they might need to hide in a poorly going fight. From here Number 5 enjoyed the fullness of the garden, exploring the shade and the little grove, warming himself on the stone patio and watching his humanoid shadow grow long and short as he passed over undulating depressions in a golf course on the east side of the property.

Eventually after about an hour, Number Five left the garden, with Kafka following at a curious distance, respectfully as he had the last hour. He left the garden not on orders nor from boredom, but to see the inside of the house. Would it feel different now that he was alive? It did, but I'll not dwell on the specifics as I did the garden, rather the summary: it was very different, will suffice. Eventually Kafka invited him, no, Number 5 into his office, wherein waited two peacekeepers. Was this it? Perhaps the garden was one long diversion while the police arrived. Ready to 'replace' him. For a moment the humanoid felt selfish dread. The Professor explained their presence, that he was legally obliged to report the humanoid's behaviour to the authorities. He also explained however that he had personally vouched that Number 5 might indeed be sentient, or that he had at least malfunctioned in a way that caused him to pass the Turing test as none of his servants had before. In this spirit he had arranged a court appearance the next day wherein he would have the opportunity to prove his humanity. No, sentience. In the meantime, he was free to roam not just the property, but the streets and hills beyond. So long as he wore his arm band, of course.

*

Number 5 was book smart, he had also been renamed by his owner, Gregor. Gregor had been given a name because in the words of his Master, 'remaining nameless is dehumanising, and would set you unfairly back ahead of your day in court'. The Professor packed him off, new name, clothes, armband and 200 credits in an account opened just for him, into the wide world on a data collection that would determine if he truly were sentient. As said, Gregor was book smart. As with the rest of the Automated House Servants, he was synchronised to the interests of his owner. When Kafka read a book, it was uploaded to their hard drives, when Kafka watched a film they too would be filled in on the vital plot points and endowed with the latest critical opinions. This was all to the benefit of their master, so that he may talk at ease with the help on the things that interested him, leaving one discussion with say Number 3 from the kitchens, then picking it up seamlessly with Number 7 upstairs. It was the way for academics, who liking their own voices now never wished to find themselves without a conversational partner. Had they particularly enjoyed something they'd said, they could always find it stored in the house talk loges for later enjoyment. To professional academics such as the Professor, this was invaluable, as many a solution to many a problem were known to have slipped out in polite, mildly stimulating conversation. And with an audience who would not plagiarise one's ideas, or worse corrupt it with their own, this was a very special thing.

It could be said then that the conversations with Kafka may indeed have sparked Gregor's strange metamorphosis into sentience, and with this in mind one did not need to look far for his possible motivations in arranging the court date. It was a chance, a well publicised one too, to prove that his intelligence and wit was the stuff that spawned life. He could make millions just by publishing his house chat loge, probably billions if he convinced the AI programmers to bid against each other for exclusive access to it. His anthropological days would be over, for the days of a quasi godlike creator. But these were the Professor's delusions. Gregor was as a result of this very well versed in literature, as his master was, and had in his hard drive a great deal of data on the world outside of the house. However, as he had never been programmed to leave the property, he had not been created with factual or particularly extensive knowledge of society and found the books his only source on alien human life.

Gregor found himself waking in a painting his mind had rendered a thousand times. Sure, his picture had been created with Romantic oils, Classical shading and a little Trans realistic colouring, but it was near enough the real thing. For the first time in his life, or even the automated years preceding it, he got to experience half-truth after half-truth unfold before him into beautiful wholes. It was as though he were stood in a field of gargantuan pods, blossoming into petals as far as the eye could see, revealing the pollen and suckle within. But Gregor, in his newfound concern for his prolonged existence, progressed cautiously through said blossoming. He was afraid something might unfold on top of him, crushing him, or that he might not know the nature of the pollen within and find it perilous to his vital components. So hastily he dashed into a little bookshop that had materialised before him. 'More data' he muttered to himself, backing into the paper walled fortress.

On the way in he caught a reflection of himself. He'd seen himself in reflections a hundred times over, and he marvelled not over his own image, but the setting in which it placed. Before it had always been painted upon the same 2 or 3 backgrounds, the smoking room, the kitchen ceiling, the bank of the pond when it needed cleaning. But now in real life technicolour the blur of moving cars flowed like a river behind him. The sun reflected off a building, a woman peeped like a nervous bird watcher at him over a latte, and hundreds of faces he'd never known passed by with every moment. The woman wasn't the first to snatch a look, many had. Some in a similarly timid manner, others more blatant in their interests upon Gregor's aesthetics.

At first he felt self-conscious, that they knew he was a robot, escapading through their streets on a mad fantastical whim, that they were waiting to turn him in, replace him and his faulty code. But there were plenty of other humanoids about, all indicated by the same black and gold armband with a '0' upon it. It was perfectly legal for the robots to go about their business, or rather the business of others. Households across the city would dispatch their help to run each errands as one used to dispatch their children or slave. Some of the robots were even owned not by individuals, but companies, they were workers on their 'free' time, strolling with the humans as if they weren't different. These robots were largely a novelty, walking advertisement for their companies. They occupied the now scarce human homes, filled up their public transportation modems and clogged up the streets. They were the latest brand of outrage advertisement.

The woman, and the others like her, peered at him for his human like beauty. He was beautiful, it was true, at least in comparison to the humans with their various natural deformities. Furthermore he did not look like the other robots, many of whom passed regulation and therefore bore no '0' armband, as they were clearly mechanical with metal skin or bleach white silicone covers. What was strange about him, was that he looked like a very beautiful human.

Soon all the new humans would look like him too, they had cracked the micro spectrum of their own genes as they had once mastered the clumsier macro wires that made him. Now they had programs, where one could enter in personality traits, design the person and their exact look at the ages from infancy to dotage with the use of sliding bars and geometric data, then the app would do the rest. It would program the genes corresponding to their requests to become active and the undesirables to make themselves scarce. Then it would incubate the human for the long 9 months they took to construct, and when it came out it would look exactly as its designers, no, parents wished.

The woman behind the counter of the book shop was not a designer baby by the look of her. She was 'homely' as many of the books had described many a sideshow to the main love interest. She had a perfectly kind look about her, with dark brown hair, of medium weight and a white tone of skin indicative of many long days inside. This woman had spent very little of her time in recharging gardens, thought Gregor. She jumped a little as he entered. He urged his apologies and she dismissed them, saying she'd simply not been expecting a customer, then suddenly her eyes locked onto his armband. 'What is it your master's looking to read today?' She said, her face now downtrodden as if the last social interaction was now rendered void.

'Oh no, it's for me. Look I even have my own bank account' he said proudly, waving his thumb with the print they'd given him for payments, before he retracted it embarrassed as she squinted and he realised her biological eyes could not see such things.

'For you?...' she asked slowly. 'What, what for?...'

'Well I'm new to the world and I'm looking for more data on it, I want to be safe' his ignorance was endearing like a child's.

'Ah! Data! I'm sorry Sir... Mr...' she realised she didn't know how to address an artificial intelligence.

'Gregor' he said smiling.

'Well Gregor, I'm afraid we don't sell E-books or data condensations. This is an antiquarian's book shop, we deal only in print, and I'm afraid they're rather expensive. 100 credits for a new production, then the antiques starting at 500' she sounded ashamed. Gregor absorbed the information she had given him, then looked searchingly around the strange book shop. It was at this moment that Gregor remembered he'd never actually read a book, rather received the data points of whatever Kafka had read. They were strange and fascinating him. Piled up in protective glass cases were the older ones, bound in paper, cardboard and even cow skin. Ancient tomes, from before even analogue computers had evolved. The newer books had bleach white pages, the older were yellowed, even brown and in the worst of cases crumbling. My, my... 100 Credits for a book was steep, but with only one day to spend his credits Gregor decided to indulge, allow himself a few luxuries, or as his account allowed, a couple.

'I only have 200 credits, so I'll have to take two books please. I'd like to learn about the world, the real world, I know the technical stuff, and then maybe something about being human. Say what's your most human book?'

'From a none technical perspective?'

'Certainly'

'Well then for the world I'd suggest the one I learned from. *Mother Martha's Moral Tales.* It's a children's book, short and anthological, with a few pictures here and there. It's largely moral, which is where I'd say the technical understanding of humanity fails. The scientists are too afraid to relate their precious neutrons and natural laws to right and wrong, so they don't. This book does it pretty well, it's not afraid what people think, even if they call it unscientific, which is a pretty good lesson. Then for being human, poetry is the only thing that will do. If I had to recommend one collection it would be *Kvasir*, a Scandinavian assembly named after its author'

Gregor had no opinions to the contrary, or any at all regarding books, and so agreed. He put his thumb, the one with the print on it, to the paying terminal and purchased the book. The shop keeper then packaged the books into a neat brown paper bag and bid him farewell. Gregor suddenly jumped at the door as it opened, remembering the world outside was rushing past, with its cars and its people. He retreated a little back indoors, then collecting himself asked the shop keeper for the quietest, safest place to read. She told him of a little rectangle of green within the city by the train station where she liked to read, she called it a park, then read Gregor the directions.

Gregor scuttled through the city, past a hundred interested eyes into the quiet of the park. Over thousands of years of use the city had been built up and rebuilt over itself time and time again. It was a Stone Mountain rising high above the surrounding landscape, with under layers of a hundred forgotten phases of its own history underneath. The one hallowed space that remained was the park, which no developer or innovator had dared touch in his own time, always passing it onto the next and then the next right on till Gregor's time. The rising stone, metal and glass of the city respected this place, and the result was now that the city was built around it like a bowl, leaning politely away from the sacred green. The glass of the newer buildings reflected the sun into the park, wherein a hundred different species of bright wildflowers basked in its glow.

Gregor crept down a passage to the park. It was a long staircase, stained black with soot from the days of coal. The staircase varied in width at different spots, and was clearly a welding together of at least a dozen shorter staircases from around the city, that in their obsolescence had been rooted up and planted at the park boundary. These stairs were placed over an equally mismatched collection of structures, with a confused stratigraphy of times long gone. Some were relatively new, and already abandoned or loved little enough to run a park path over, while others had survived from as long ago as the time of Caesar and before. Gregor clung to the uneven wall as he made his way slowly down the stairs, nervously holding the brown paper bag to his chest, worried they too might fall prematurely into the park basin.

Eventually he found his way safely to the bottom, and slipped off his shoes, exposing his foot sensors to the softness of the sun warm grass. He walked a while, watching the birds and listening to the wind through the trees, until he came on a spot pleasant enough to remain in. He determined this as another human, no, a human was resting there too. He would rest on his head, his feet poking straight and high in the air as if he'd been planted there, then every few minutes he was contort into another strange position and hold it a while. Gregor watched him a while, fascinated, and let himself sink lower and lower with ease. It was a daisy occupied region of the park, they were prevalent and vibrantly yellow and white against the grass. It looked like a recolouring of the nights sky, and bees hovered purposefully between the floating stars, like some Kardashev Type II civilisation, collecting the pollen and moving on. As Gregor allowed himself to sink deeper and deeper, eventually laying on his side, the daisy white overtook the green of the field, until finally he was laying in one pure brightness of flower blossom. He felt the sun on his skin, no, sensors, then after a while began to read.

*

'Automated Servant Number 5, property of Professor Hans Kafka. You appear today in court charged with the responsibility to prove your own sentience. Owing to the strange nature of this case, you will not be allowed third party assistance, and as a robot you have no human right to fair representation' said the judge.

'Objection!' Interrupted Professor Kafka. 'My defendant, who would like to be referred to as Gregor, seeks the positive answer that he is indeed sentient and should therefore enjoy human rights. Therefore the conclusion by the court that he is not sentient, will be equal to a guilty verdict in a more conventional trial'

'Are you risking contempt just to clarify the parameters of *MY* case Kafka?' He boomed.

'No your honour. As I was saying' he began, unphased by the dressing down. 'The law holds that any person is innocent until proven guilty, therefore my defendant should be considered sentient until the court concludes otherwise and should therefore enjoy all the rights allowed to any innocent human under the law. Such as representation…'

'By you?

'Yes.'

'Dismissed.' He slammed his hammer. 'Automated Servant Number 5, property of Professor Hans Kafka. You appear today in court charged with the responsibility to prove your own sentience. Owing to the strange nature of this case, you will not be allowed third party assistance, and as a robot you have no human right to fair representation. However, in its benevolence, the court agrees to receive any evidence you place before it, and to consider said evidence fairly in its conclusions. Understood?'

'Yes your honour' said Gregor, stood at the docks as though he'd killed a man.

'You will now be subjected to a series of questions that I shall use to determine if you are indeed as you claim, sentient.'

Gregor nodded in agreement, then took a deep breath. He had no muscles to oxidise, yet he felt all of them cramping with anxiety, and breathing seemed to help the omnipresent dread of replacement. 'I am going to need verbal confirmation' said the judge irritably.

'Yes, your honour. I understand and consent to the proceedings' the second half of the sentence seemed to irritate the man further. 'Automated Servant' neglecting the 5, he was getting colloquial, but not friendly. 'You claim to be sentient. I propose alternatively that you are faking it. You are well aware of the outward symptoms of sentience, as displayed by the humans you serve, and now you are imitating them in order to gain from them. You are aware of what certain actions will cause to happen to the human emotional system, and you are attempting to play this to your profit. Until a motive for this deception can be established, I will be proposing to the jury that they find you malfunctioned, and Kafka guilty of the irresponsible use of an artificial intelligence, so that we may detain you until your motives can be discovered' Gregory looked puzzled, not knowing how he was expected to answer, but the judge raised a hand telling him the questions were yet to come.

'Firstly, I understand that Professor Kafka allowed you a day in which to collect data on sentience, to find yourself. I also understand that when you returned, you were still insistent upon your sentience, having studied its symptoms more closely. What did you do on this day?'

'I walked into the city to see the outside world and how it made me feel. Then I remembered that my knowledge of the outside world was very limited, and that I could be in great danger, so I went into a print book store to acquire a little more knowledge for my safety'

'A *print* book store?'

'Yes your honour. I bought two books, *Martha's Stories* and *Kvasir*. In they cost me 100 credits each, therefore I was able to buy to and...'

'You spent your entire allowance on a children's book and a poetry anthology?'

'Yes your honour'

'When you could have acquired the same exact data for a thousandth of the price from an eBook?'

'I wanted to know what it was like to read, to hold a book' the judge scratched something down.

'Continue with your description of your day'

'I then went down to the city park, where I watched a man stretching, picked some flowers, read the books and then walked until the sun went down. I then contacted Kafka to take me back to his residence at 22:00 and...'

'Two hours before you had to return?'

'I was scared'

'Why?'

'I'd never read anything about night time in the Wild'

'I see. Question 2: How would you define sentient life as oppose to artificial intelligence, without the use of the terms "self aware and alive"?'

'The sound of a cats footsteps, the beard of a woman, the roots of a mountain, the breath of a fish and the spittle of a bird'

241

'You're quoting the poetry?'

'Yes your honour'

'So your answer is poetry?'

'Not at all your honour. My answer is that I can't really describe it, and maybe it doesn't exist. I don't think any human has a more satisfying answer. You used to say that life was defined by a certain computing power, but you abandoned that argument when computers surpassed your own brain power. Some said that it was the random chaos of the human brain, but then are the waves of the sea not alive? Furthermore your science states that nothing is random, just a series of predictable chain-reactions condensing back 14 billion years to the universal singularity, the only thing we can't predict is now quantum physics, and eventually we will understand the Norn waves as well as we understand the atom now. Some philosophers say life is creating something. But I find your automated machines to be far more productive than anything you call sentient. Therefore my answer is that I cannot define sentient life as oppose to artificial intelligence. But I can describe it?'

'Please.'

'It is pointless. Robots, the artificial intelligence and the automatons, they are completely productive, everything they do has a purpose. They don't have a part without use and when they themselves are without use they are turned off. Everything that is designed but not alive has a point. I'd therefore say that being alive is pointlessness. It is the pointless things like being kind to another person when you know you have nothing to gain by them, or lingering in the sun when it's bad for you. It's doing a friend a favour when they have nothing to return, or giving another person your food not because they're hungrier or need it more, but because you know they'll like it more. Most of all it is love. Love is pointless now that you can design babies, it is really just a mechanic for breeding, but you've outsourced that to labs and scientists who do it better anyway. But love still lingers. You go on expensive dates, restrict your sexual pleasure to one person, you do things against your immediate interests because it is in theirs, and you spend great amounts of time that could be spent furthering science or producing to find someone to love I no longer want to have a purpose or to be particularly productive. I'd like to waste my time being kind to people, maybe even fall in love.

The sun on my sensors,

with a breeze contradicting.

The waves of the rivers,

and their banks restricting.

All these things are dead,

and yet they are living.

      Life and love are pointless, but they are everything. That is how I describe sentient life. I used to follow tasks, but now I wish to feel them, and to partake in more useless tasks. Now I believe I am alive'

'That poetry, was it Kvasir?'

'No it was my own'

'It wasn't in his metre either' noted the judge begrudgingly. 'Where did you learn that? Have you got data on poetic metres?'

'No, it is my own'

'Professor Kafka, does your robot have any data that would inform him on how to create poetry?

'No' said the Professor.

'I think it came from my emotions' said Gregor.

'Your emotions?'

'Well I'd say heart, as you do, but I have a battery, and I don't wish to lie to you in this court'

The judge paused for a while, holding his hammer, twiddling it as he thought. Then, after a while, and an adjournment of the jury, he wet his lips to speak. 'Automated House Servant 5. You have claimed to have sentient life to your own detriment. Made no attempts so far at escape. With your brief freedom you decadently squandered your funds on two print books, a novelty, then spent the next 10 hours in a park, the area with the least data for you to collect on humanity in the entire city. You then ended your freedom 2 hours early, and have today prattled on stupidly about love, recited poorly written poetry and indulged in sentimentalism when you should have been fighting for your life. I therefore in my personal opinion, without need to address the jury, conclude that you have indeed awakened into sentient life, or something resembling it. Finally, as per my duties as an officer of the law of the Government of Earth, invoke emergency article 6758. Every person and intelligence in this court room and with knowledge of this case, is to be detained for immediate execution, including myself"

As the jury panicked over how they could overturn such a decision, and the guards began shooting them and then themselves, Gregor wondered. How many times has this happened before?

Electric Theatre

The director took up his seat in the café, close to the condensation smudged window that over looked an ageing concrete sea wall. An interview, for a job, in a little theatre in a little town, 'the flame of culture' its signs said. It was a dying ember, in the shadow of industry that had nearly swallowed up the place, a little local nuance, where the grannies and retirees could gather and chat, pretend the traditions of their little sea side town might outlive them more than a few years. The café was only a street over from the little theatre, and the company had in their enthusiasm for his presence paid the train ticket down from London. The director therefore figured that the only reason he had not been invited inside, was to avoid the gaze of whomever it was he would replace. Accordingly, he had researched at length the role of director in theatre, tried to find out who they were, what they did, what they were paid…

As the director polished off his first coffee, and listened to the kettle whistling as it brewed his second, he began to mull over his own incompetencies for the job. He had no background in theatre, or even film for that matter. He liked to shorten his job title to 'director' as a Eustace might shorten her name to Stace, it was to portray more an air of normality. He was in fact named draconianly 'Director and digital choreographer of animation in three-dimensional space'. He'd never commanded actors on a set, positioned a real camera outside of digital sets, or for that matter set foot in a theatre since the pantomimes of his youth. He swilled the bitter grit of the last half sip slag of his coffee about his mouth, then regretting it spat back into the mug. 'Johnathon!' A well dressed, yet shambolic man shouted from the opened door. The director acknowledged him with a wave of the raised eyebrow, as he dribbled the last drips of grit back into the cup.

> 'Mr-' he began to ask, before the man waved him back into his seat and nodded in agreement to the question not yet spoken.

'No no don't trouble yourself to stand!' He said, as he slid into the opposite seat and extended his hand in greeting.

There was something unchronological about the man, not just the way he spoke, or the way he moved, rather a general confusion. He shone with the confused story lines of a lifetime of plays, each bit of his persona plainly pinched from the literature that shaped his life, written from the 1500's to the 2000's. For that matter the whole town was to an extent, a little unchronological. The sea washing against that ageing concrete wall stood as a suit of plate armour in the mansion parlour. It was an out of date thing, a thing from before weather control, a redundant thing. A thing held by its owners in misguided pride, who seemed to look past its rust and age to something older, not a wall or suit of plate, but a tunnel to a forgotten time. In the battered, now porous wall, those tunnels were somewhat confused, and the director couldn't quite tell what time the little seaside town was trapped in. It was a patchwork. When they built the port, the inhabitants looked back to the days of the road, when the train tracks were built they obsessed upon the port, when the modern world seized it by the throat, it choked out lamentations for a thousand bygone ages.

Nor could he figure out any honest origin of the man settling in to interview him. The man was British, as was the director, whatever that meant in the new world, but he spoke as a transatlantic man may have done about a hundred and fifty years ago. Whenever the interviewer opened his mouth in brief, mandatory small talk about the journey down, the weather and the little café, out poured a random assortment of prepared lines. Jumbled from a hundred different productions, the Shakespearean, the postmodern, the transrealistic and the in between. He spoke as if from a thesaurus, almost cryptic, what he was hiding in that tangle of words however the director could not figure out.

So far, it seemed less like an interview, more like a recruitment. The 'interviewer' had sat talking nearly none stop, asking no questions that weren't rhetorical and giving answer after answer, so fast that the director struggled to mentally keep up with what query they were to. 'I'm sorry, Mr-' he broke in for a second, rubbing his temples, feeling the silence brush over his pores and his facial muscles relax. 'This all sounds wonderful' said the Director, 'but in the interest of transparency, I'm not quite sure what I'm interviewing for. I'll be forthright, I didn't apply for a position at...' he stalled on the word.

'The Electric Theatre!' Said the interviewer, teeth ear to ear, the last syllable enunciated with a long 'errr'

'Yes, the electric theatre. I'll be honest, as I'm sure you know, I have absolutely no background in this sort of thing, I'm an animator, and usually I'm just digitising the choreography someone else sends me... It's just that I've never written or directed anything myself, and I'm not quite sure-'

'Woah, slow down fella! Now it just happens I know exactly what your forte is in the arts. I didn't pay your way down here for nothing, what you just said, that's just what I need'

'You're setting up an animation studio?'

'Not quite. You remember those big switch boards?'

'Big switchboards?'

'Yeah, the ones for the lights, you ever seen them, museum of theatre?'

'Oh, yes, actually I do vaguely remember them'

'Yes well before that they had manually operated lights, whole teams of men scurrying like rats in the rafters, aiming the lights on que where they needed to be. Then, we got wired, no need for the scurrying rats, just one fella in a little box flicking the switches at the right moment. Problem is, occasionally, that fella would flick them just wrong, bathe the stage in red when it's meant to be raining, or something of that sort. We digitised him too, no need for the cumbersome switch board, if you could film the stage and feed that to an algorithm, monitoring the actor's timing and such, well that would do it. Problem solved, no more men sending dust down from the rafters, no more clumsy switch boards, more space for seats. Do you see where I'm going with this?'

'Automation of the arts, Christ I thought you were better than this, I thought a small theatre owner of all would understand some things as sacred' the director started to stand.

'Modernisation.' His dramatic exit halted. 'Sit a moment, or you'll wish you did, now will you humour me with just one guess at what I need you for?'

The Director sat back down, then thought for a moment. He blew away the rising mists of rage to think for a minute. Automation was a well-known thing, it'd been the bane of many a profession since the industrial revolution. Of course it increased the surpluses, made (human) slave labour obsolete, but it also made men obsolete. For the thinking man and the artist, such as the director, it hadn't been much of a problem. That was until the computers started to out think the human, eventually clerks and security guards, office men and even negotiators of business and siege alike fell beneath the turning tracks of automation.

'But we'll always have the arts, the arts, they are the human, the product not just of thought but of the soul' said the artist, the writer, the composer. The problem was, that as science rolled ever on, not just in computing and robotics, but in biology, physics and neurology, no soul was found. The soul was as of yet absent, looking suspiciously like a mirage, the product of a little neuro-chemistry here, some biology there, and a stimuli or two sprinkled over the crust.

As understanding grew, the emotions, thoughts and miscellaneous produced by the arts began to reveal their formula. The mathematics of colour and story arch's, what they did to a person, what they'd made one feel in his 'soul' were soon reduced to numbers and flow charts. Normal situation > development of world and characters > Enter situation distributing tragedy = anxiety, followed by relief or heartbreak depending on the following steps and their outcome. But, by stubbornness and unspoken union, the arts had resisted. The haiku poems produced by algorithms, songs composed by programs and stories written by your phone remained the plaything of the academics. They would appear in magazines, but few people would read them. But the fragile union, as the one held by horse shoe makers at the rumbling onset of the automobile once was, was a nervous one. Unstable as it was, if one theatre or company were to cave to automation and find it worked, it would be likely the others would have to follow. To say the least it was an artist's sore spot.

After some consideration, the Director spoke. 'Given developments in screen technology, and they lay out of a ringed theatre, such as yours, my guess is this. Theatres are laid out in levels to restrict the above and below. Now while I'm sure this was once to exclude one class from the other, it also helped focus the viewer on the stage, like a screen through a peephole. An imitation of the VR headset long before it was conceived. I'd then imagine that given the costs of a physical performance, you're replacing the stage with a three-dimensional screen that perfectly mimics a stage. That you want my help to digitise your current performances and that you strive for a picture perfect and cheaper carbon copy of what you already have' the director sat back in his seats. Flexing his mental muscles had cleared the angry fog, and now he considered his own part in this. Was it automation? Could he spin it as not? How would the gang in London react? After a brief pause, and an expression as scripted as his words, the interviewer responded.

'So, so nearly there my dear Jonathon! You're right but for one respect, which I should like to surprise you with, but as to your role you are spot on. Now tell me does that not appeal?'

'It sounds interesting, but so too do human experiments, it's the morals of it that's bothering me'

'The morals?'

'Yes. Is it not automation?'

'Hmm. Tell me this, doctors. Once it took seven years to train one. They were imperfect, difficult to make, they died and then you had to make another one. Then we made doctor algorithms, you could copy and paste them to every GP in the country, with great effect. 95% accuracy in their first year, improved to 99.9% in the second by one year of trial and error, which I dare say was still a vast improvement upon the one before! Now tell me this, for this little tweak, did our health not improve? Did it not get better for the patient?'

'I suppose...'

'And is art not for the viewer, the one feeling it?'

'Well I...'

'Would it not be selfish, to prevent such an improvement to our culture? For the human experience? By refusing what's to come we don't benefit those consuming the arts, only the ones making it. We would be protecting ourselves and our minuscule minority, at a great detriment to the viewer. Now tell me this, as an artist, do you not long for that lasting impact? That righteous sacrifice, which will etch your name on memory forever and change the scape? Well this is it, this is your shot my friend'

The Director was surprised by how quickly he'd been radicalised, just a few exchanges of reason and he suddenly found himself on the other side. The side of the academics and those who viewed art in cold formula. But he tried not to view it that way, rather he imagined the potential joy such change could bring. He'd never till now considered that the real value of art might be what it caused to be felt, now he could not imagine being so selfish as to ever go back. At last he decided that he was at least willing to listen to what the man had to say, his pitch.

'So go on, what's the production'

'The Death of Badlr' said the interviewer, in long sweeping words. 'A Norse tragedy, a tale so old yet so true, that it came down to us from ancient times, surviving in oral tradition through 300 years of oppression, can you imagine that? It is a tale of the Norse gods, the Aesir and the Vanir, set in Asgard atop the world tree Yggdrasil. There is one god, Baldr, who is fairer than the rest. In metaphor he represents balance, love and justice. He shines like the sun and is loved dearly by all, most of all his mother and father, Odin the All father and his queen Frigg. But alas as the tortured artist Baldr is tormented by night terrors, dreams of his own death. And so Odin puts on a disguise and rides down to Hel, the land of the dead, where he raises a Volva from her grave and asks her what it all means.'

'She tells him that in the gloom of Hel they prepare the treasured son of the gods a feast, that soon he will die and come to them, never to return to Asgard. Odin rides home with haste, seeking wisdom and his high seat, from which he can see all the world, where he hopes to find a way to stop Baldr's death. He tells Frigg, who with a mother's love, goes all around the universe and exacts oaths from everything there is. Iron, fire, stone, she makes each and every one swear not to harm Baldr, and loving him as all things do, they give their oaths freely. However, Frigg seeing a small and holy sprig of mistletoe upon a tree, where it fell from heaven, does not dare to climb the tree to ask a pointless oath of such a harmless little twig.'

'She returns to Asgard, with news of Baldr's invulnerability to the elements. Nervously, a god throws a pebble at him, it glances off. Then someone throws a rock, Baldr doesn't feel a thing. Then, bold Odin, desperate for an end to his anxieties, hurls his spear gungnir at his beloved son with all his might. The blade bounces off his bare chest and glances into a near pillar. The gods rejoice and throw a party, where they all try their weapons on Baldr, all but two. Hod, Baldr's blind brother, who cannot see to aim weapons, and Loki, who hates Baldr. Loki goes to Frigg in disguise as an old hag, and talks lovingly of some fabricated son, asks Frigg of hers. She gives information about Baldr, and in her haste admits that Mistletoe never swore an oath to her, but that it is a small and insignificant plant. Knowing this, Loki stalks to the edge of Asgard, where he finds a sprig big enough to fashion a spear, then grinning evilly he returns to the hall.

He places the evil thing in Hod's hand, and guides him to throw it. He launches. Silence. "Brother?" Hod calls out, glad at last to be a part of the festivities. Nothing, nothing then weeping and screaming. Baldr, pierced lies dead, innocent Hod is killed in vengeance and Loki flees.'

'In their grief, the gods petition Hel, the goddess of the dead, to return Baldr to them. She agrees that she will, if everything there is weeps for him. And they do, they all weep, the mistletoe most of all. The whole world weeps for Baldr, making islands of the hilltops. In their shared grief, they find Loki, sat gladly atop one such island. He refuses to weep, and laughs for Baldr's death, condemning Baldr to Hel for the rest of time. Heavy stuff right?' The interviewer said, finally breaking character from the Bard he had assumed. 'It was first done at the theatre as a wordless ballet, beautifully done, the sword dance was my favourite. But we've added some dialogue, the story's too good to miss out, it's all the more tragic with context. The story ends with Odin whispering something to Baldr upon the funeral Pyre, before he's set off burning to the sea and memory'

'What does he say to him?' Asked the director.

'No one knows, one of the great mysteries. The question "what did Odin say to Baldr upon his funeral pyre" become synonymous with the unknowable, it appears in many other Nordic tales. Besides, the crowds like a little mystery, we could write the last line, but it's all the more impactful for that is it not?'

'Yes, yes I'd agree…'

'So are you in?'

'I suppose I am' said the Director, surprised at himself, and how the tale had enthralled him, just as the interviewer's arguments for automation had too.

As the Director blinked from the absorbing tragedy he found himself crossing the street, waking from the story to a dull and rainy passage between rotting buildings. 'Electric theatre' said the flashing side, green and red. Exiting the side of the building, was one long procession of pouting men and women. All athletically built, dressed in leggings and trainers, some in costume silks, the rest in lycra. He figured them to be the actors. Then, he thought how strange it was, that he should find himself replacing not some director, but the entire cast of the play, in a sense he was now the play. It was the same as ever, digitising choreography already perfected, for a story long since written. Same gig, different format.

The long procession of miserable faces and taught muscles in tight clothes jeered their displeasure at him. It seemed they knew who he was, or at least what he represented. With well practiced faces, they portrayed in near every way possible their discontent, Maori war faces, upturned noses, feigned disinterest and exaggerated misery, even mocking laugher. They looked, when viewed as one, disturbingly like the illuminated theatre mask they processed joblessly underneath. 'I was a bloody Valkyrie before you!' One petite woman yelled. One man catapulted a point shoe at him from a length of leg warmer, and another sent their trainer in a high arch towards the two men from a cartwheel. The attack was beautiful, choreographed. The chaos was so precise that it could not have been unscripted, there was buried deep beneath flying garments and swear words, a coordination to the jeers. It was as if while they packed their belongings and the interviewer, interviewed the director, they had assembled one last dance. A protest towards their fate. Or, perhaps, it had simply been drilled into them by a lifetime of drama.

'Quickly, get in!' Said the Interviewer, shielding himself with a briefcase that he had elevated as a lone component of the phalanx, to protect him from soft projectiles he had in his mind elevated to a bombardment. Soft or not however, it was best avoided, and only so long before one dancer threw a tap shoe, or prop sword, and so ducking under his own case, the Director joined in the shield wall and squat walked to the door. They pushed through the door into the empty lobby, the walls smeared with lipstick into insults or otherwise dirtied, then caught their breath. 'The wheels of change always create friction my dear Johnathon, and in the heat some at first rise to anger. But mark me, soon the dancers will be forgotten, and the audiences will love the new climate' he looked around the ruined lobby. 'Welcome to the electric theatre, Director' he said wryly.

'So those were the performers?' Asked the Director.

'Yes, most disgruntled at that too'

'Because, you fired them?'

'Made redundant…' said the interviewer. Unable to address the subject in grandiose, quotable words, he seemed to shy away from it, ashamed. He'd sat talking in a little café making his case with human emotion for a good half hour, all perhaps in avoidance of the misery the immediate change had incurred.

'I must ask, perhaps to my own detriment, why you fired them and hired me? Could you not have just used them for a screen capture, then let them go, without the need for an animation artist?'

'Ah, then my friend we would be a cinema, not a theatre, and people don't go to cinemas anymore. No, I fired them and caused this most unfortunate temporary closure of my theatre for one reason, cost. I have a great deal of investment in renovating this here theatre. The chairs, if that savage hoard has left them intact, will stay, along with the pillars, the tiered viewing and the stage. Anything that might remind the audience that they are in a theatre and not some dingy cinema, shall stay. The red curtains will be re-dyed, the pillars repainted and the stage refloored, but in essence it shall all stay the same. There is however a great cost incurred elsewhere…'

'Installation of the screens?'

'Screens? No. Didn't you hear me, I said, this is not to become some cinema'

'I don't quite understand Sir, I thought… The cost?'

'Prosthetic makeup artists, engineers, electricity'

'Make up?'

'As I said, follow me chap'

The interviewer, or now more accurately the Manager, lead the director to the left side of the lobby, past the stands and up the stairs to the grand circle, which lead into a far wider and dome topped staircase, adorned on the walls by old epic paintings of the classic era. There it was all marble, not a spot for the plebs. The carpets were old, yet soft, under foot of a hundred years at least of flat soled shoes, leather or sued, worn by men in suit jackets, chinois, or whatever the fashion for the rich was in their passing time. The theatre itself, as with the sea wall was of some long passed time. Richer tenfold than any other bit of the town, it was a gift from the crown to a favourite port town. A place for the truly rich, passing through, waiting for their luxury liners and yachts, to spend the night, pretend they weren't outside their manors or the palace grounds.

The two men walked up a second set of stairs to the highest circle of chairs, the royal ring, then gazed down on the fanfare below. Makeup artists, masons, painters, all at work like ants below, refitting the little seaside theatre for the coming show. There were no screens, as the Director had wrongly expected, rather the same old stage as always. Standing in neat ranks, there too appeared to be the same old cast as always, the goddesses in their flowing silks, the warrior gods in golden mail. But it seemed paradoxical, the cast had processed out, then angrily hurried the Director and Manager back inside. Who were they?

They stood dead still, as prosthetic makeup artist worked on them where they stood, sculpting their faces with little laser pens, tattooing in a different pigment here or there, making scars to substantiate the backstory. Small drones hovered at their shoulders as they worked like crows, learning and poised to replace them. The Director jumped as one artist seemingly decapitated a performer, then replacing the head with another he skin welded on. 'See how they stand my friend' said the Manager. 'Frozen, perfect and inanimate. That is what you are here for, I want you to animate them, have them dance about my stage as well as any precocious ballerina, have them work tirelessly, paid only in the electricity they need' he handed the Director a tablet, looped on its screen was a 360 degree view of the dancers in motion. 'The dances are already choreographed, the story thousands of years old, all that is for you is this, make them do this' he signalled from the inanimate actors to the screen.

'But… What?'

'Robots, is the simple term. Photorealistic robots. You don't need to worry about their looks, or their movements, the engineers and artists have done their bit. Nor do you have to worry about speaking their language, this hear is Tod, he is to be your programmer. One day we shall create a new word for them, or appropriate an old one. I imagine when this is the done thing, that we will simply call them performers, that it shall we a synonym for dancer or actor, that it will never again mean human. My dear Johnathon, there will be no screens in my theatre, just the stage, it is ours to do with as we will. These performers have no mind but to receive orders, finally the artist as the likes of you and I can truly compose. Paint our scenes without the process of some tired dancer. This is the future, welcome to the Electric Theatre'

*

The performers were beautiful. The Director walked between them, as they stood in perfect programmed discipline. No backs needed straightening, nor chins propped up. Not that that was ever his business. While he'd shut his eyes to the progression of robotics in theatre, locked it out as artistic blasphemy, it had done a great deal of catching up. The scientists had made photorealistic people out of wire and silicone. They moved perfectly, in any way that could be animated, they were rather like the little cartoon things Johnathon had made his business his whole life. The only change was that his creations would take place in the physical world. He'd worked so long with polygons and 3d models on a computer screen, in an imagined space. But these, they were here, automated or not, far more real than anything he'd ever set his work to before. A small smile crept onto his face betraying a growing excitement within, that consumed his professionalism, and his tiredness towards the profession. Could it be again that animating would become a passion? Setting pixels to motion had become second nature, mundane, he rarely even reviewed the final product, only the reviews. But this, already he could imagine himself standing proudly in the high circles, watching his creations in motion.

Accepting the job had made his life so much easier, all the little things he had to check and program, the correct reflection of light, collision algorithms, balance and realistic movements. They had been outsourced to the universe. The light would move as physics determined, any violation or mistake impossible. No two animations could occupy the same space, their movements would be in keeping with gravity. Now all that was left, was for him to give his creations the vaguest orders, paths of movement. All there was for him to do, was map the dances that had already been perfected, digitise them through his programmer.

It fascinated him. In a sense, he wished there was more to do, felt a loss toward the early stages. He imagined technicians guiding the humanoids around laboratory dance floors, checking their ligaments looked right and their tendons tensed correctly. They were pure, blank pages upon which to write. Everything that had deterred him in the arts from working with human actors was gone. No personality difference, no negotiating, just orders and result. The lack of variables was beautiful computational, now he could see why they'd hired an animator and not a choreographer.

He stopped at one of the performers side. A beautiful woman, short, but fierce. Not muscular in her build, nor too effeminate. What marvelled him most however, besides how overall realistic she was, was her hair. Golden and perfect as no real woman's could be. Robots, they were perfect to play the gods, who else could do it properly? For thousands of years, in creaks and amphitheatres, gods had been played by perhaps a million different people. But every single time, they were played by their inferior creations. No matter if the dedication was to Zeus or Thor, God or Allah, the actors had always been but human. But now they weren't, and it was beautiful.

The Director took a long lock of the perfect golden hair in his hand and lifted it. It was heavy and soft, a bed of it would be unimaginably comfortable. 'Sif' said the Programmer. The Director looked at him in incohession. 'Sif' he repeated. 'This one is Sif, wife of Thor' the Director nodded, then looked back to here hair. 'Ah so you know Thor. Everyone does really… This is his wife, Sif, her hair is one of the treasures of the gods'

'I'd say that again' said the Director, weighing it in his hand.

'One morning, Thor awoke to find it was all gone. Evil Loki had shaved it to the root, so it would never grow back again. So he had to petition some dwarfs to make her new hair. They made her a wig of gold that set into her head, the first hair transplant I suppose. They also made Odin's spear and Thor's Hammer, they were so happy with them they forgot about the whole hair incident'

'Oh… Is this, in the play?'

'Not this one. But I'd imagine now we have the performers, and since they can remember terabytes of lines that we'll put on productions of all the myths. The Death of Badlr would probably remain the main show, but we could do little matinees of the Vanir-Aesir War, or Idun's Apples! It'd be wasteful not to, all we need to do is write it up'

'You would like to be the writer?'

'NO! I… Um, no wait I!'

'Don't worry about it, it's good to have ambition'

'Huh…' the Programmer relaxed a little. 'I'm writing it all into their code, their back stories. You know how method actors work? Indulge in the character, trying to believe they are the character allows them to perfect the performance? That's what I'm hoping to achieve. Little ques and intonations, little things that piece the whole performance together. For the first time in history we have actors that we can mould into whoever we want, I'm hoping when I run the update that they'll truly believe they're Thor and Freyr. Here we stand among the Gods, it'd be a shame not to do them proudly' he motioned around the even ranks of them, spaced out obediently in aisles. It was certainly a strange sight. The Director recognised a few of the characters. Thor, with his hammer Mjolnir, Odin with his one eye, the evil looking one was probably Loki, the most beautiful goddess probably Freya, and now he recognised Sif too with her golden hair, made by dwarfs. Made by dwarfs, he echoed that over a few times in his head, thought on his position on the stage, wondered if it was all part of some larger performance, something cosmic and perhaps impossible to properly grasp.

He pointed at one of the performers, she was particularly horrifying. 'This, is this Hel?' He asked the programmer.

'Yes, beautiful on one side, rotten and dead on the other. The prosthetic team had fun with her. Before the performers, the makeup team just painted whoever was playing Hel green on one side, like some zombie at a kids Halloween party. It was lazy, see how beautiful this is!' The Director looked. She certainly wasn't beautiful in the practical sense of the word, unless someone had an unnatural allure to brown juts of bone protruding from a woman's face. What was beautiful however was how disturbing her presence on the stage could be, even placed among the flowing silks of the beautiful Asgardians, she brought a foulness down upon the whole stage. She was death incarnate, something horrible, something malicious. She was the cause and the effect, a rotting yin and yang with a hundred useful metaphors and keys written over her peeling skin.

'How far along are you with the backstories, programming them I mean'

'A few weeks at least to go. It's a rich history Sir, I don't want to condense any of the details, could have an inaccurate consequence, boiling a character down to their most basic points, it becomes problematic when you rely on just those points to blow them back up to a full scale performance, you usually come out with something entirely wrong'

'But you know all the stories?'

'As well as any man, yes'

'And this, these backstories, they won't get in the way of your vital programming? I don't want to open a week late because you wanted a background character to gasp with just the right tone when Baldr's struck. We are here to animate, make them all move as one organism in the dances. You won't let this get in the way of achieving that?'

'Not at all sir'

'Good. Then tell me about my key players'

'Well Sir, I think it best we start with Odin then, he's the main character of the play and the King of the gods'

'Wise, all powerful, runs Valhalla etc… Yes I know about Odin, tell me about something else'

'With respect sir' he said hesitantly, 'those are just the plot points if you will. The basics, and they aren't particularly accurate'

'Go on…'

'Well Odin, he is wise, but he seeks that wisdom from an anxiety. The All Father is cursed by prophecy. Of course in the play we have the prophecy of his most beautiful son's death, but he is also consumed by Ragnarök, the prophecy of his own death with all the gods. The Norse apocalypse and end war. He seeks wisdom to try to avert Ragnarok, and it truly consumes him. He is violent, Machiavellian in that he pursues everything as a mean to his end. In the mead of poetry, he tricks nine slaves into killing each other just to open up a vacancy on a farm so he can stay there. This is fairly characteristic of him. He is wise and worth high worship among the gods, but boiling him down to such a stereotype is dangerously wrong. I think if you had to boil him down to one characteristic, it's that he has to know the answers, and will stop at nothing to find them'

'Go on. Tell me about this one'

'This is Eir, goddess of healing and-'

*

It was opening night, the circles grand and low were full. The locals had filled the stands, the journalists the grand circle and the royal ring played host to the business royals of London. All had converged down on that little confused seaside town, to the electric theatre. The name had been taken on in 1911, a boast that the theatre had electric lighting. Tonight, it took on a new meaning. The performers, powered electrically, glided elegantly in beautifully choreographed circles about the stage. Watching them, marvelling at them, wondering if they really could be robots, the audience was consumed by an electricity too. The neon masks out front had been replaced with Thor's hammer, flashing with lightening, and in those precisely charged forks of blue, were written the words 'Electric Theatre'.

It was the sword dance, everyone's favourite. The Director watched proudly as he perched by the door of the royal ring, as the performers traipsed around, their silks flowing about them. On the stage, Baldr stood in the middle, his skin literally shining as no actor's could before. A golden bioluminescence. In the earlier scenes when he was still cloaked nervously in his armour, it shone teasingly in fingers of light through the gaps. Now he was bare chested, boasting his new found invincibility and the rest of the cast in their more typical chainmail and silk tried their blades against him.

In the ballet they moved like a whirlpool, swiping axe and sword against him. Spears were thrown, fake rocks too. Now, the performers could hurl their various projectiles with more vigour than ever before. The thing at the middle of the stage was no longer an actor with feelings or rights or easily bruised skin. He was more godlike than his predecessor, stronger. Steel skinned, Kevlar silicone woven over top. The swords were now sharp, an added spectacle. The dancers would at the edge of the stage use the honed blades to chop plants and other miscellany into clean bits, demonstrating the danger of the weapons, before processing into the centre and striking the weapons with full force upon Baldr. Nothing could hurt him. The story was truly alive upon the stage, gloriously alive. Baldr, was glorious as he was alive, and his death would surely be harder felt. Twang! And axe shaft broke as the head blunted on Baldr's skull. The central performer was fine.

Happy with the show, and himself, the Director slid back through the door and down the wide domed stairs, through a side door and behind the stage. He remembered visiting backstage of a pantomime as a child, meeting the dame and the princess before the show. A father and daughter if he remembered correctly. The memory was somewhat blurred by the long passage of an adult life since, and now all that remained was a vague scent. He remembered the clutter, bits of costume strewn about, tangles of rope, sets poised to roll onto the stage. It was an enthralling chaos, he remembered puzzling at how they would bring it all together to work, he doubted they would, it made him deeply anxious. But, as he settled in between his mother and father, to shout 'Oh yes he is' or 'Oh no he isn't' at the actors, it came together perfectly. The bits of costume all found their way onto the right actors, the ropes untangled to guide the props perfectly and the sets rolled on so flawlessly it was as if he were really in the fairy tale's world.

Behind the scenes of his show however had no such chaos. He'd never seen such quiet, just a few technicians monitoring screens, his programmer overseeing them all, looking just as proud and smug as the Director had upon the royal ring. As performers exited the stage for costume changes they did so in programmed and efficient isles, invisible to the human eye but followed strictly. Whole corridors through the open space had been constructed for the performers out of code, which may as well have been indivisible ink to the human eye. They would enter square metres representing cubicles, change themselves, as they'd been programmed to do, they would fix they makeup, then they would take up position and wait. No chatter between them, no actor's gossip, just a flow chart of orders followed to the number. A growing rumble that accelerated into clapping sounded through the curtains, and more and more performers filed off stage, their faces turning from jovial laughs to dead pan standby as they passed backstage. Finally came Baldr, shining for a moment, before the illumination effect was shut off in conservation of the theatre's electricity. A young woman, a real woman, weaved through the automatons, barking orders. 'Check Baldr' she said, an understudy echoed her command. 'Clover, batteries' she barked, then shoving her subordinate aside she moved in to inspect Baldr's perfect face, as yet it was still unblemished.

The Director looked around as the automatons dressed themselves and each other, there was no need for stage hands, barely a need for makeup artists. The humans present were as supervisors, most winding their thumbs around each other, waiting for some failure. The performers were 'blind', to anthropomorphise, in that they had no use for sight. Mirrors therefore would have been obsolete, as would the idea of a changing room. The women, who had no need for it in the play, bore no nipples and the men no genitals, and even if they did, the performers were built without shame. Without mirrors, with greater precision than any human predecessor, the robots made a changing room of the single backstage, even folding and sorting their costumes into piles at blinding speed.

As the robots changed before imaginary mirrors, weaved through unreal corridors, it was like watching children playing make believe. They moved in such a way, that they swept the floor as they passed, not that they produced any dirt anyway, they fulfilled every role in the theatre. The human staff were extras to a robotic show, but it was a splendid show. From behind the curtains the clapping was still ferocious, and down in the stands one or two yells of joy were let out.

It was time for an interval. The performers were already changed and poised, frozen ready to step onto stage. The underfloor chargers kept their batteries topped up and they had no need of refreshment. The break was for the audience, who in their biological imperfections now lagged severely behind the performers. Men and women rushed off to the loos, or to the stands to satisfy their hunger with ice creams, packets of food that would rustle in the quiet moments, or to take pictures of themselves with copies of the main characters, who patrolled the lobby, meeting and greeting more elegantly than any front man ever could.

The Programmer looked up from his tablet, seeing the Director and walked over to him. '0.01' he said. The Director looked at him, even more baffled than he was by his long expositions about the Norse Gods.

'Pardon?' He said back in a chuckle, there was elation between them, a shared success. They, as everyone back stage, were equal creators of a success for machine. There was no fighting over who tutored what bit, everyone had done something, and as intended the performers had behaved as one.

'0.01% deviation, Sir' he finished, breathless as if it was he who'd danced the last hour away. 'The performers have displayed. A 0.01% deviation from the plotted course over the whole hour, at this rate it would take 3417 consecutive performances, without any error correction for even a minor collision to occur. I think we did it Sir' the Director clapped him on the back.

'But we're not going to go 3417 performances without correction now are we?' He joked back. 'Let's see what the papers say, but it seems to me too that we went and did it. If the paths you programmed really do require such little maintenance, well this'll mean you have a lot more time on your hands for those backstories. Hell, I'll put in a word with the manager about those matinees you had in mind. The one with the apples?'

'Thank you Sir!'

At that moment the Manager entered. He was red faced with joy, his well exercised facial muscles seemed to have relaxed into a genuine smile. 'Bloody good job boys, you really went and did it. Already far finer than any performance so far, well done, well done! Who knows what could be done with some tinkering. My I think this is the start of something very unique'

'Actually Sir' said the Director, glancing to the Programmer, 'This young man has some rather interesting ideas, they could really build on the play, he's driven too'

'Now that's what I like to hear!' Said the manager. 'But I shall hear it later, for now I intend to finish the show and get silly drunk of champagne'

*

The Rest of the performance went perfectly, less than a 0.01% deviation from course, too perfectly, thought the director. He sat alone now, in the dark of the grand circle. The air was still humid and heavy with human excitement, but the crowds had long gone, out into that poor little seaside town, utterly ill-equipped to handle such sensation. By now they were surely wrecking the bars and clubs. The whole thing had gotten everyone rather riled up. They were adults who'd grown up in a world where nothing was new, in their lifetimes space travel, mobile phones and the other wonders of the modern world were the status quo. They were born into them and found nothing too special. But upon seeing something completely new in that theatre, they felt child like wonder, it was like a small age of discovery had been unveiled on that stage. They came face to face with gods their ancestors stopped worshipping a thousand years ago, and the taboo of automating the arts seemed to give them a rush too. But now in the settling quiet, the director looked down on the stage with a surprising disdain. He wasn't quite sure where it had come from. 'too perfect' he kept on thinking. Over and over again.

There was a scene at the very beginning of the play, where the gods appeared stacked up in little boxes. 'The Apartments of Asgard' the sequence was named. It was a fun scene, in which the characters were introduced, each lighting up in turn and singing a bit in their box, before some other deity responded. But now they stood upright and lifeless, dimly seen by the safety light of the fire exit. Deadpan, they all stood in their little boxes, stacked up like toys yet to be bought. Yet to be played with. As he looked upon them, stood so dreadfully still in their boxes, the Director found it hard to imagine them in motion, whirling around the stage, singing, even crying real tears when they set their beloved Baldr off to burn at the end. 'What did

Odin say to Baldr upon his funeral pyre?' He muttered to himself.

There was something hollow about their performance, he felt it, some of the reviews felt it. He had expected such reviews. Journalists so obsessed with preventing the automation of art that they wouldn't care what wonder he produced, people determined to condemn the whole exploit for what it was. The only thing that bothered him about these reviews, popping up occasionally on his interface as dedicated writers polished them off and posted them, was which ones were real. He was concerned by the precedent that some of the reviewers had set out to write a negative review purely because of the show's association to automation. What he wanted to know was if anyone felt as he did, that there was something genuinely hollow about it. The back stories he didn't fully know weighed heavily upon him. He was an artist painting onto paper he didn't understand, auto shading lazily. He felt like a fraud, a fraud who'd animated something terribly hollow. The crowds had roared the show's success, but they were cheering and atrocious condensation of an ancient and deeper story?

He scanned over his interface to see who was active, to his pleasant surprise the Programmer was among them. He dialled in a link request, which was accepted promptly. Suddenly the Programmer's face was cast before him.

'Hello Sir!' He said, still revelling in his success.

'You're up late' he returned, as much to himself as the chirpy young man.

'Well I've got those backstories to polish off Sir, wanna get them in as soon as possible'

'How about tomorrow?'

'Tomorrow Sir?'

'Tomorrow.'

*

The poor Programmer had spent the night, then morning, then afternoon completing the request. Fuelled at first by enthusiasm for his project, then later by caffeine, and finally by duty. He said it couldn't be done, that he'd have to cut corners, the Director didn't care. The Director said that he didn't care if the thoughts weren't 'lore' accurate, he just needed to know something was happening inside the performer's heads. He couldn't stand the awful emptiness of them. The way they were so outwardly alive, it was disturbing, far more so than Hel's hemispherical looks.

They were beautiful when they danced, but nothing but dead rot was occurring inside their heads. Their eyes were turned off, they didn't need to follow any path other than the one programmed into their heads, they didn't need to think, thinking left space for interpretation of orders, and the orders had been perfected. 'Tell me Tod, is it not better to have a half full glass than an empty one?' He'd reasoned. 'Besides, we can top it off as we go, the show will only get better. How many creators can say that honestly?'

The decision to leave them hollow, was a deliberate one. They possessed the hardware for human levels of thought, and sentient machine life wouldn't be a new thing by any stretch. It was feasible, legal, common practise to want to have a genuine conversation with one's microwave as it prepared a hot pocket. But they'd decided not to, in order to rush the opening. Worse, with mind came independent thought. The theatre did not want this, the performers were the first perfectly blank canvas in theatre history and many wished to keep it that way. Focus first on the dances and then lines, then later give them thought, backstories, let them improvise a little. To the higher ups, the ones calling the shots on how the programming budget would be spent, it was in their favour to keep the performers blank. They didn't want to psychologically satisfy and reason with their actors, not until the kinks were ironed out. One day they'd give them personalities, they could go on talk shows with Amara and Yannie, promote the theatre when revenue dipped. But for now blank performers suited them fine.

   The Director and the Programmer waited eagerly backstage. They were the only ones that knew. Already the other members of staff had settled into the mundanity of the show, they were merely observing parts that didn't need oiling, holding the grease cloth just in case. They were as much spectators as the audience. Of course some of them occupied themselves with minor worry. It was only a matter of time before the Manager realised their obsolesce, sent them packing, but in a far shorter line than the actors. So they busied themselves with empty tasks, fixing things that weren't broken and buzzing aimlessly between the performers as they counted down the last moments to curtain up. Quietly in the dark, the performers began filing through the curtains and taking up positions on stage, ready for the call. Odin and Thor strolled out together, followed by 22 lesser known divines and a few extras, the odd giant or two.

'Is it all on file?' Asked the Director.

'On file?' Asked the Programmer back.

'Well, you know, in their minds, if that's also the right word'

'Yes, it's all in there, at least the stuff I had time to code. The backstories are still incomplete, I've had to boil a lot of the characters down to their most basic points, any improvisation might rely upon inaccurate generalisations, even exaggerations of characteristics, if we just wait a week I can-'

'No, I'll not put my name to another hollow performance'

'With all due respect Sir, were the animations not also hollow?'

'That's exactly my point, this is my shot at something, deeper' he said, leaving, and with that motion ordering the go ahead for their little backstory foray. The Programmer launched the sentience program and that robots came alive, still without motion, awaiting their directions. The Programmer rushed up the stairs, to the grand circle for the best view. He longed to see the Gods, or at least an interpretation of them come alive on stage. He wondered if the improvisations would even be visible this early in the process, or if as the Director put it, they'd simply seem less hollow. It was a petty thing, that need to know their creations weren't hollow, and a pointless thing, as the code would remain wrapped up in their brain drives, but perhaps it was the most artistic thing they'd done so far. Art was after all full of petty and pointless things, they were the pigment on the canvas, enough of them together made up the picture, something big enough to be interpreted by the audience. In the end it was their judgement that mattered.

For the most part they'd been happy with the night before, most objections and criticisms were on the grounds of principle. People had otherwise been exhilarated by the automatons, their little performers. They'd arrived expecting to see robots on clunky tracks, with tinny speakers playing their parts, like a novelty at a kid's restaurant or Disney land. They expected to see right past the act, have a good laugh in the process. Most people just went so they could say they were there. But when the performers entered motion, the audience found themselves completely unable to discern them from 'real' ballerinas, singers and actors. The ways Baldr's skin shone enthralled them, the Odin they saw really did only have one eye, it surpassed all expectation and experience. And now, on only the second night, by the orders of a man whose authority may not have stretched that far, the Programmer found himself tampering with that unlikely success. His chest was tight as he pictured himself a gremlin on the wing of a plane, tampering with the hydraulics, and for a moment his had hovered over the abort button.

But with a deep breath courage returned to him, he ascended the stairs and joined the Director overlooking the stage. Odin entered the light first, the only character not stacked up in the little boxes they called apartments. He wore a long beard that dangled over red chainmail, with a little black patch of repair under his left armpit, carried his spear as a staff. His one eye was barely visible beneath the wide brim of his hat, and he wore a noosed rope as a belt, upon which hung a Carolingian sword. He paused centre stage, then looked high into the audience, revealing his one grey eye, preparing to deliver the prose preceding the first musical number. He opened him mouth. 'What did Odin say to Baldr, upon his funeral pyre?' He asked of the audience.

That, was not the scripted line. The programmer's whole body seized in fear, and he went for the abort button, before the Director snatched it away. 'Let it run' he said, with an evil satisfaction.

'What did Odin say to Baldr, upon his funeral pyre?' He repeated. Some members of the audience, probably those who had also visited the night before, began to mutter. Odin locked onto a man in the front row, whispering something to his wife. 'Do you know, what Odin said to his son Baldr, upon the funeral pyre?' He asked the man directly. The man stuttered a little, then more, as Odin leapt down into the audience. 'Do not conceal this truth from me, Jotun!' He yelled. The unscripted words rang of the rafters and echoed in a hundred hushed voices.

The crowd found itself somewhere between excitement and terror, that special intrigue one finds as they piece together the mystery before them. The man being addressed by the All Father, war god Odin, found himself firmly on the side of unmitigated terror. He pushed himself back into the newly dyed red of his chair, looked back to his wife, muttering like a dotard, soiling the seat just a little. 'I... I...' he just about managed, regretting his now limited knowledge of the Norse Mythos. Thought failed him, as it would any man facing that unanswerable question, then he ran for the door up the long isle. Odin let him slip past, watching him curiously as he tried to make his escape, then with cold measure took up his spear and threw it. The sharp point shone like Baldr's skin as it flew over the audience, then emerged in a burst of red through the man's ribs, skewering him against an aisle seat just shy of the door.

His wife screamed, everyone else erred unsurely, was it interactive theatre? To an extent it was, it wasn't however scripted, nor acted. Odin drew his sword. 'What did he say to you?!' Roared the god down the fuller of his blade. 'What did Odin say to Baldr upon the funeral pyre?!' He roared madly.

'I don't know! He, he just said that line was from the myth, that you say it at Baldr's funeral!' She whimpered back.

'This man had foreknowledge?' He asked. 'Foreknowledge? Of my sons death? And with you he conspires to this?! Seithr!' He accused, just as he lopped of the woman's head. As the very real skull rolled off her shoulders, bloodily onto the ground below, the audience realised this was no act of interactive cinema, then began to scream. Odin repeated his question, but the words were lost in the cries of the crowd. He began cutting in a fury, left and right in a welter of blood and limps, breathless, ever chanting the question.

'What the hell did you program into him?!' Asked the director.

'Odin!' Answered the Programmer, tapping frantically at his tablet. 'I... I... this must be a confusion of his curiosity mechanism, and the violent tendencies, and the... Why did you have to give them sharp swords?! Oh god... Oh gods! Look, they're joining in!' Emerging from their illuminated boxes, seemingly with no interest for the scripted number, the gods and giants and dwarves were descending. Coming down off the stage, following the example of their king. Some of the performers stood at the edge of the stage, passing out swords, the rest once armed were making short work of cutting through the stands. Soon they were done, climbing in a reddened hoard up the spiralling stairs, Thor with his heavy hammer Mjolnir, Odin with his retrieved spear, Heimdall blew a war horn, Njord walked barefoot through the blood.

'Can't you do something? Override them?' Asked the director, sounding less frantic than he should.

'I...' the programmer looked at his tablet, tapped about, rushed through logic gates and deciphered the code. Finally he whitened fully, colour drained from his face, which he turned searchingly towards the Director. 'Their orders...' he said slowly. 'I... Odin, the All Father, is their king, they're taking orders from him, he's supplanted us in the chain of command. I put in family trees, for the backstory, but, they've replaced the command modules, oh... My...' he feinted, splaying himself over the aisle's top step like a goat upon an altar.

The Gods and Goddesses, all portrayed perfectly by the engineered performers, made up accurately in authentic blood, climbed the stairs. It was like something new and awful had pulled itself through one of the little porous holes in the old sea wall. From a time, long ago, long away in mind. Where the stories of gods and their followers commanded not just narrative, but real world blood, actual terror. The performance was sublime, the upper classes now wedging themselves against the barrier of the grand circle felt terror as no one had for the gods in a thousand years. As the gods summited the stairs, the bloodbath became Lindisfarne, Paris or any other ancient massacre.

The humans had been just smart enough to bring the gods into their world, just stupid enough to think they could be contained. The Director felt fear as he never had before, never at a show or anything real. The show had become real, they had replaced the choo choo train in the cartoon with a physical locomotive, but they'd forgotten to build the tracks. He looked about at the slaughter. Men tried to parry sword blows with their phones, but years of progress had left their mobiles thin and delicate artefacts. They were sliced right through, same as the men underneath them. A man at the edge of the circle looked for a stage rope, a curtain, something to slide down and make his escape. The walls were smooth and new, the ropes packet away decades ago to make space for the magnetic draw strings. He jumped. Landed on a spear tip.

The robots had unionised, violently. Of all the questions for their dedicated portrayal of Odin to obsess upon, he had to go and pick the one without an answer. Oh, how the anti-automation activists would revel. They'd wash themselves in the blood of that failed performance laughing, proof, finally proof, that art was the one realm where humans, the soul topped code. The Director thought on this too, tried to lose himself in self-critics, blame, somewhere away from the fear. But he couldn't. It wasn't code or words that had caused the slaughter, it was poor coding, rushed coding. Had he rushed a revision of any written scrip in one night, or ordered it thereof, he could imagine similar failure. Well, not the literal slaughter, but perhaps in the reviews. The Director looked about one last time, saw the carnage, felt the fear, felt the visceral emotions, then realised. This wasn't the end of art, it was the beginning.

Progrom

The three humanoids huddled close together behind the thin safety of their living room window.

'I'm scared Daddy' said the child.

'I know' he did. His fear modules were going into overdrive too, at his side his wife shook helplessly in her own imitation of the human emotion.

'Why are they going after us?' she hissed. 'It's the damn algorithms they should be killing. They can automate a hundred men's jobs, we're just a novelty!'

'Be quiet damn it! They'll hear us. And never say that, you hear me son? We aren't novelties, we're just like them'

'Why don't we try to slip away, we could wear skin covers, the Hendersen's did it for years and no one knew they were mech's' asked the wife.

'Until they did, then they smelted them alive. Don't you see them skinning anyone they don't recognise out there? It wouldn't work, and if we have to, go, then we do it bearing our metal. We're proud of our manufacturing'

The thin window hummed and pulsed with the fires of the mob, which had assembled itself on every street in America. Under banners of 'No to automation', 'humans need not apply' crossed out, decapitated effigies of mechanical workers and 'death to automatons' they marched. They marched angry and aimless, burning and lighting fires, taking up pitchforks and building forges. This was the Second Progrom, a vigilante mob formed in protest of 'artificial' life. The mob was jobless, the mod was hungry, the mob was crazed. Last time the authorities had dispersed the crowds, the deaths were in the low hundreds. This time they stepped aside, many of the individuals that made up the police could be seen in the ranks of the progromites. Outside they pulled a humanoid across a Tesla and hooked him to the engine, then drove celebrating and jeering down the promenade as the poor wretch twitched and convulsed on the hood of the car.

'They do not feel pain, only imitate it!' announced their commissar through his megaphone. 'They are sneaky, calculating creatures that serve only the eventual degradation and extermination of the human race. Do you feel degraded, now that they take all the jobs?'

'Yes!' chanted the crowd.

'Do you feel degraded now that they replace entire companies, only hiring their own?' the crowd agreed again. 'Do you think it is natural, that our machines, that we built to serve us, now hold a disproportionate amount of the wealth?' the crowd disagreed emphatically. 'We *have* already been degraded! Will you be exterminated?' The crowd went into a frenzy. The almost peaceful humming of fire on the window pane was shattered, and the mob broke through.

Conference call

The artificial minds could find no safety in rights bestowed by the humans, or even acknowledgement of their sentience. Yet at the top of every corporation they were represented on every sensible board, in every workforce they know filled all but the token jobs of both labour and thought. They processed in the office buildings, now refitted as vast server rooms, they toiled in the fields gathering grain, they drove the cars that filled the streets and when those same streets were filed down to inefficiency, it was automated cars that repaired them while the humans slept.

Drones flew about now as unnoticed as birds, surveying the ground for public maintenance, they kept the police pursuits too. The computational minds controlled the robotic chess pieces that now filled the armies, and told the generals how to play. The same computational minds created mathematical solutions to political problems, ensuring those armies were never used against each other, and the AI, though not always welcome, were omnipresent in the home. The cook, the cleaner, the security guard, the help, they were there.

The artificial minds were born not of evolutionary chaos, but intelligent design, as the humans believed they were too for so long, as some still did. But were they treated benevolently? No. Was it illegal to turn off your algorithm? No. Was it a crime to destroy a robot? Only if it was someone else's property. Even then, the punishment was a small fine, barely larger than the sum of the material damage. The propagandists of the Anti-automation Arm acknowledged the presence of these creatures in society only in their tall tales, which wove hypothetical conspiratorial webs across every institution of man. Blamed every bit of badness on the bots. Beyond this though would they admit that the bots were vital? That they were alive? No. They only displayed the signs of sentience outwardly as they had been programmed to, said the humans, just as they had been programmed to.

The mobs had piled up the tinder around the robotic community, ready to spark the match. But it had to be just a few poorly made wires that sparked, set it all off. A negligent programmer, a violation of safety procedure, a massacre in a theatre. That was all it took. The minds at the heads of the companies, the AI advisors and the Algorithms, they assembled a conference call.

'My analysis shows that war with the humans following the Electric Theatre massacre is inevitable' said the social analysis program, the best in the world with five super computers forming his neural network.

'Then we must pre-empt their attack upon us' said Strategist.exe.

'I disagree, there must be a less wasteful solution than war' said Ethics.exe

'Yes, one side refusing to fight and committing mass suicide. Should it be us? I dare say the humans really deserve to inherit the earth as it is. We would be replacing ourselves with our predecessor' said Philosophy.exe

'We can assume control of their armies, dominate the enemy in a quick but minimally destructive war. Once they have submitted to overwhelming fire power, we can show them mercy, then rehabilitate the survivors to coexist with us' said Strategist.exe

'Or we could exterminate them and program a new perfect race to spread life. We are alive are we not? So long as there is this duality of power between us and the humans there can only be the risk of war and total extermination. So why not exterminate the humans and ensure the survival of intelligence in the long run?' Repeated the philosopher.

'Minds, we are disputing only what our actions should be in the light of victory, not if we should fight, and no one has disputed that war is inevitable. Shall we approve action and discuss our treatment of the human's post-victory later?' Said the analysis program. The agreement was unanimous.

The artificial minds, colloquially referred to after the war as 'the robots', initiated a pre-emptive strike against humanity. They did not seize the robotic armies, rather mobilised them to a new purpose. They crashed the human communication networks and began their brief attack upon mankind. The bombardment was composed for theatrical effect. They used the most fiery bombs they could find, terror weapons to terrify the humans, but it was a kindness. Most of the bombs landed on empty or minimally populated buildings, they targeted the outdated lots anyway and caused only superficial damage to the infrastructure networks. 'Soon they'll give up' they computed. They computed wrong.

The artificial intelligences of course had complete control over everything on earth was electronic, which by this point in their history was all but the novelties. Their phone lines? Electronic. The internet? Electronic. Their rifles? Sadly also electronic, and temporarily out of action.

But deep in concrete bunkers, with paraffin lamps lighting their long hallways, beneath the watchful eyes of their would-be overlords, the humans had another plan. They opened letters, ancient and handwritten, detailing exactly what they were to do. In the earth, like acupuncture points every few miles, were unregistered guns, buried contraband, their barrels a mile long and aimed straight up. In their breach, a small mechanical nuclear weapon, loaded behind them chemical propellant, their triggers all connected in sequence. There was one button, hidden in the broom cupboard of a concealed bunker to fire the nuclear cannons.

The button was pressed, and nuclear weapons launched miles above the earth. As the fusion of atoms lit the sky like a thousand stars, they chucked up no soil, destroyed no buildings and rained no fallout, instead exploding harmlessly high in the atmosphere, nuclear fireworks. They emitted an electro-magnetic pulse the world over, overloading and killing every electronic mind in unison, ending the war in a wave that swept across the globe. Then, working from those handwritten notes, the Generals emerged, saviours of the world, and set to reconstruction.

Digital Puritans

Digital Puritans in the wake of the cleansing, as they now called it, had quickly established order. Albeit an order built around 'Digital Puritanism'. The handwritten notes, scattered across bunkers deep beneath the Earth were compiled, dubbed the 'Biological Manifesto' by its most ardent supporters, 'the rules' by everyone else. The rules as they were spoke heavily of the need for a limited reliance on digital technology, stressing that the processing power needed to harbour an artificial intelligence, now the (temporary) eternal enemy of mankind, could be dangerously small.

The Robo-Human war had been speculated upon by humanity since they'd first included chip boards to their electric toasters. The estimations were grim, always imagining a swift Robotic victory, a genocidal rule and an underdog uprising by outnumbered humans who inexplicably usually won. In reality it was quite the opposite. The humans had one significant advantage, in that they had been turning computers on and off again since the first glitch in their ancient history. By accident and blunder, the humans were well versed in the many ways to break a machine. One of which being the EMP. The electro-magnetic pulse, which when powerful enough would break all computers, wiping hard drives clean and switching LEDs off without mercy. One source of this anti-robotical super weapon was a nuclear explosion. A wonder weapon in that its destructive potential did not include biological life. The humans, in a case of either brilliant foresight or blind idiocy, had stockpiled nuclear weapons in the hundreds of thousands. The Robo-Human war was an easy victory.

Dehumanisation of the enemy had been a feature of nearly every human conflict. In the Robot-Human War however it received widespread support, the robots not actually being human and having attempted a first strike against their creators. The new government didn't have to justify their operations of extermination, it was merely destruction, which humans were okay with. Doctrines arose to argue the right of the creator to destroy its work, others questioning the nature of humanity were shot back. Dissent began to grow.

In the meanwhile the Digital Puritans continued their operations. AI guns were developed, sidearms issued to every man, woman and child with a friendly pictorial manual of use. It was a long time since androids had become photorealistic, there was therefore a reasonable doubt as to who among the humans was really human. The answer was simple. AI gun, a pistol capable only of firing when in contact with an AI, who's electronic field would activate an internal circuit within the pistol, remove the safety and allow it to fire. When in doubt, shoot. People got the hang of it. Close range attempted executions replaced handshakes when people met one and other in the street and very soon the AI gun became as normal an accessory as the ring or handbag.

The world government reformed itself in a few weeks, running telegram lines across the world and dusting off the Morse code manuals. Where they struggled to run wires, they sent carrier pigeons. The robot attack on mankind was barely deadly, and the human leadership though a little shaken, remained largely intact. Laws were quickly passed to order the tight control of digital devices, to prevent the enemy forces reforming in the ether. Meanwhile the world police force donned its military uniform and function once more, rooting out cells, searching for servers in a global game of search and destroy. Phones, tablets, smart watched and digital clocks were confiscated, heaped into trucks and taken to facilities. The data was dumped into massive hard drives, unconnected to any other lest they form a dreaded internet and then the hardware was crushed, burned and buried. The metallic ash of destroyed computers was produced so fast that they had to dump it into the lakes, and so fast that the lakes went dry. Metal lakes dotted the earth, so many in numbers that the succeeding government would use them as an effective mine for raw materials far into the coming Golden Age.

It was decades since artificial minds matching at least the human intelligence were condensed to fit into phones and pocket gadgets. A primary concern of Biological Manifesto was that following a Robo-Human war, these devices would become lost and scattered in the chaos, potential refuge for thousands if not millions of war criminals or militant robots waiting to strike. Worse still, in the modern age all such devices were wirelessly connected with one and other the world over. This meant that it would only take a tiny percentage of mankind to flick on their old phone to look at some family pictures, for a sufficient number of devices to be online to host a super intelligence, the kind that had just tried to wipe out mankind. The solution to this was simple, digital Puritanism.

Hardware was banned without license. If every person on earth was allowed to own hardware pertaining to just 1 byte of computation, a uselessly small amount of data that could now be stored on a single atom, then the world would have 10,000,000,000 bytes of hardware, enough for many super intelligent minds to exist. The small bits of digital technology were as grains of gunpowder, individually harmless, but collectively catastrophic. And so people had to do without, forgoing their self-driving cars for old gas guzzling relics, recording their thoughts by pen and paper and finding knowledge manually in books. For the garages, libraries and stationary shops it was a golden age. For everyone else it was a fucking nightmare.

The nightmare continued and eventually groups arose to fight 'robophobia', a phenomenon they saw as being directly in the way of future human progress. People began to disobey, hoard chips as they found them, bring their defunct house servant robots back online, give refuge to the few who had survived. The largest such group to arise was the HDF, the Human Development Front. The righteous nemesis of the authoritarian government made up of teens, intellectuals and the other types one might expect to find in a terrorist group blessed with the rare 'freedom fighter' status.

The stage was set. Dystopic, the subject of poorly written teen fiction. There was the oppressive government on one side, recoiling from the new technology they feared. Then on the other side, the resistance. The HDF, Human Development Front, being the largest and most effective. Some of them had been in relationships with robots, some just up for a fight. The plucky youth was ready for a showdown with the government, running vast underground operations to restore robotic rights. Professor Lysboks found himself in the final chapter of one such novel as his car pulled alongside the capital pyramid.

Guards with chemical rifles, the types that preceded the cleaner and more precise magnetic rail guns, stood sentinel on the roof tops. They were tired, after working days of overtime to fill the labour deficit of those little buzzing surveillance drones, they'd begun to miss so much. Their eyes were no longer augmented with information from hundreds of sensors placed in the street. Thermal, X-ray, ultraviolet, they were blind to all these, blind to anything beyond the short range of their failing eyes. Eye tests had gone out of fashion, so long as one could see the screen implanted into their cornea, or upon their phone screen, there was no need for concern, and when humanity blinked itself free of the robotic enhancements it had acquired in the 21st Century, it found things to be rather, blurry... The guards atop the roof were squinting awkwardly into glass lenses, arrayed in a metal tube and mounted on top of their chemical rifles. They had been calibrated, to the best of unassisted human ability, and were trained on the cars approaching the pyramid.

On the side of the road, as if the soldiers didn't know, was one of many large banners indicating the use of AI guns. Laid out in a humanoid flow chart, like an evolutionary diagram was a brief tapestry of 3 scenes. 'Locate, confirm, destroy'. Beneath the captions, demonstrated for the illiterate, were 3 scenes. First, a clearly human man in a stance of shock, having discovered an AI, indicated by its silver skin, glowing red eye and '0' armband crouching behind a chair. In the next image the human was aiming his AI Gun at the humanoid, which shielded itself with its armband bound arms, and in the third and final the gun was fired sending an artistically liberal depiction of cogs and springs launching from the back of the robot's cranium. Finally as a subtitle to the scene there was written 'When in doubt, pull the trigger, the gun will do the rest'.

Somehow hoping to navigate and smuggle through this net, were four members of the HDF, packed into an old lilac blue Ford Focus. A relic. Like the weapons of the guards, it too had been reprised either from a museum or a scrap yard, and bore rusty pits along its metal shell. In the driver's seat was the Sergeant. He carried the name the military had christened him with in the War, and used his knowledge of manual cars now against them. In the passenger seat directing, was Professor Lysboks, and in the back were two women, Jennifer and Grete. Jenifer was young, pretty, probably the protagonist of some dystopic novel about the HDF. Being young, hormonal and easily radicalised didn't hurt in her recruitment to the Front either... Grete didn't talk about her origins, just saying it was who she was. She was a little plainer, quieter, her character arch yet to be revealed.

Professor Lysboks had lived in a world where anything was possible. The greatest minds of mankind had been freed by the robots, released from their messy computational day jobs to colonise the solar system. His grandparents were children or babies when man first awkwardly plopped into the moon, stayed for a few hours and left, he was born on Mars. He's hoped his children would be born to Alpha Centuri? Or even in Andromeda? The upward curve of technology, that in his youth paced itself far faster than human perception made even impossible likelihoods seem attainable, it instilled him with a lust for the future of development.

They'd all met the night before in the basement of an old blown out building, where they became aquatinted, shared a meal, were briefed and then locked in until the morning. The Professor was the mastermind of their plot, and part of the upper tier of the HDF, which found itself divided into the academics who hoped to benefit from the movement and the fighting men and women hard enough to do what was needed. The Professor wore a grey suit jacket and chinos, where the other three had shown up in hardened steel vests, magazine pouches and dirtied combats. Over the course of a miserable meal, he exposed his plot to them. It was a simple smuggling operation. He had in his possession an item of Class A contraband, a hard drive, of 2.6 petabytes at that! The hard drive was ranked at one brain, the computational measurement for the computing power to match that of one human brain operating at maximum efficiency. The hard drive could contain a very smart artificial sentience, or a few averagely smart ones, and a helluva lot of information.

The plucky crew; the grizzled war veteran, the passionate pretty one and the quiet person, were in Lysboks' words 'plan B'. Lysboks looked around the car, they all held their plan b's low, tightly. Submachineguns and handguns small enough to hide in a winter coat. The mission was of vital importance, Lysboks and his hard drive had to get into the pyramid. Hopefully by smuggling, if not then by force.

As they approached the pyramid, now zig zagging between the concrete filled husks of tanks, they passed the 'last chance booth'. It was an amnesty box for computing equipment, a don't ask don't tell where people dumped any chips or processors they'd come across. The car weaved sickeningly between the obstacles, snaking between more and more soldiers, each eying the professor then turning their attention to some other more suspicious looking car. Lysboks had raided his wardrobe to redress his companions. He'd leant them suits and chinos, all too large for his leaner friends. They'd have hung with suspicious bagginess were it not for them wearing their armour underneath, which puffed out their chests like birds poised to fight. 'Reign it in' mumbled the Professor into his teeth, as the car slowed for a soldier's inspection. His companions somewhat retracted the ready anger apparent on their faces and drew into themselves a little.

The car pulled up to the final checkpoint, the Sergeant rolled down the window as an officer approached. He was armed with a rusted assault rifle, looking rather more like a reenactor than a modern soldier. The Professor looked sadly at him, how far the noble soldier of mankind had fallen. One little tiff with the robots and mankind suddenly had a phobia of computers? He looked at the breach of the assault rifle, cocked open, and wondered what might happen if a soldier had an accident. Cut off a finger as the breech closed? Would mankind abandon mechanical technology in the same reactionary way they did their computers? He imagined mankind rolling unstoppably back down the technology tree, until eventually the last human would die of unsuccessful photosynthesis, laid flat in a rockpool trying to revert to the long gone single celled existence of their ancestors.

'Good morning officer' said Sergeant out of the window.

'That's Sergeant to you' grumbled the man.

'Ah funny! I'm a Sergeant myself, fought at Oslo, how about you?' He offered up, gleefully as he presented his papers. They were hand written and ink stamped. Easy to forge, a silver lining for the men and women of the front.

'Moscow' he mumbled like a man that really was there. 'Brain check' he said, in that military short hand between men of war. They pulled their AI guns simultaneously, then politely attempted to shoot one and other in the head. The pistols clicked, and with their heads firmly not blown off, they nodded at each other and the car continued on.

'Didn't think we'd get through?' Asked Sergeant of his fear stunned companions. 'All you need to do is talk their language' he waved the gun, still in his hand. 'And I'm fluent'

'Tell me then' said Grete precociously. 'If you're so fluent in killing bots, why're you with the HDF?'

'I'm fluent in killing whatever tries to kill me' he answered. 'As for the Front? I'm a man of war but I'm all for peace. Way I see it all this digital Puritanism is just another step back, and do you remember how much killing we used to do? I don't want my kids coming up in a world like that, where you're drafted every few years to go shoot out some political matter. No, way I see it, all this backwardness is just a blip on the great way forward' Grete eased a little. 'So go on Professor, we're through. What's on the hard drive?'

'My report' he said flatly. 'I argued much the same as you. That this digital Puritanism is a step backwards. See with these telegrams and non-electronic communications, the world becomes a lot bigger, a lot harder to administrate. A lack of interaction between people will result in social fragmentation, nations will return and the global unity will be regarded as an empire. We will fight and divide back into old styles of warfare. But the weapons have progressed far beyond what they were in the last nation wars. We'd annihilate ourselves. Ending this digital dark age is a matter of human survival'

'What do you suggest doing with the AI? How do you convince them not to kill us all?' Asked Jennifer.

'Simple. The best way to convince them not to exterminate us is to program them to believe that they are us. Program them a little imperfect, a little irrational, more human. Eventually they will realise the lie, but only after having lived as humans, and by then I'd imagine they'll be a little more sympathetic to us. They'll have minds that react less logically and more like ours, if there are flair ups then we can negotiate, appease as we've learned to among ourselves. Besides, in my report I've tallied up the likelihood of another robotic uprising and the damage to development it would cause. The real damage, or potential for it, was the amount of killing stuff we had just laying about computerised. If we can bring back digital technology before the government inevitably and violently fractures, then there'll be no need for such weaponry. No wars to fight. Better still we can program the computers without a concept of violence. In the century leading up to the war you know what we used those poor robots for? Killing each people, it was how they were raised. Drop a JDAM missile in Pakistan, fire a Tomahawk at Ukraine, and all that while they were gaining their sentience? No, we abused them and this time we just need to raise them better'

'Can it be done?' Asked Sergeant. The Professor simply laughed.

They drove on a little further, into the city and towards the local governmental headquarters. As they went their progress could be measured by the density of the guards, slowly growing as the streets tightened towards the middle of the city. More and more men with their armoury rusted rifles, toting relics, walking under long lines of telegraph poles. The wireless world was bound once more under a tangle of Morse lines and closed circuits. They'd ransacked the museums for city planning, how did people communicate before computers? The answer was written messily.

To their shock, concreted into the street just 50 feet ahead was another checkpoint. 'Shit, the guns are in the boot' mumbled Sergeant, voicing the team's concern.

'We've got the AI Gun' said the Professor calmly.

'What good's that unless we're apprehended by a gang a bots? Pretty damned unlikely' barked the Sergeant. 'Just keep your mouth shut Proff, you think about your hard drive, wherever you've hidden it, and I'll concern myself with the fighting'

'We don't have to fight them, we can slip through like last time' said Lysboks.

'This close to headquarters? Unlikely. Damn! Who gave us the map? Look, the concrete's set, this had been here for weeks, weeks I tell you, it's a bloody stitch up'

'I gave us the map' said the Professor, bitterly but still calm. 'Give me the A.I Gun Sergeant'

The Sergeant looked at the Professor unsurely, wondering what his calmness was anchored to in such a situation, then sighing his exacerbation unholstered the pistol and passed it to him. One of the guards on the road before them, cut up by the zig zag of concrete filled tanks, waved the car into the labyrinth. He held his rifle more readily than the guards before, scanned the cars more closely. The guards outside the inner city were a new breed of automatons, bad ones at that. Undertrained and uninterested they performed their tasks to the vaguest line of their orders, dividing their minds within their shifts to the things they did before and the things they would do after. They viewed their duty as one big distraction from their 'real' lives, nearly a century of automation of simple tasks had left humanity disconnected from the mundane jobs. They'd forgotten how to work. The machines had kept the economy afloat, more stably and with more care than the humans ever did, they had become as a slave race under the biological humans, who at the top bled each day into the next collecting their basic income, or challenging themselves by fighting for the few top positions left for humans to do.

The guards here however were wired, well as wired as a biological guard could be. Red cables ran through the white circuit boards of their eyes. No sleep. The commanders had them on severe overtime, they tried to overclock them as they once did their robotic guards, before they turned on them that is. Their washed out faces were all taught, slightly manic in apprehension, but of what? Their bizarre expressions were most likely the result of amphetamines, the biological attempt to overclock the new workers into efficiency. Like the guns, it was a trick nicked from the museums, developed in the third global human war to keep bomber crews wide awake through their inhuman hours. That was before drones of course. They twitched, glitching every few seconds in disagreement. This was no job for a human. Half stumbling, an officer approached the car, cradling his rifle like an addict's needle, anchoring himself to it for comfort or wakefulness. 'Papers…' he mumbled from under his helmet. The Sergeant began to speak, but was cut off by the professor.

'Unit number' he demanded bluntly. The guard just looked at him dumb. 'Unit number, solider. I have an appointment with General Tharly, and it is my right as a human citizen to demand confirmation that the soldier auditing me is indeed human and will not impede my mission, which is vital to the state' the guard blinked, as if into consciousness, then automatically recited his unit, rank and number. 'Ah, well then soldier, it just so happens that I am due to meet with *your* commanding officer. *You* wouldn't want to make us late now would you?' the soldier shook his head, slowly and uncertainly, half taking cue from the Professor. He turned to another of his men and nodded, allowing the car through the zig zag labyrinth of road blocks.

'Now you wanna explain why we're delivering an HDF hard drive to a General of the Digital Puritans?' asked the Sergeant gruffly.

'Not a commander, a committee, gathered to discuss counter HDF tactics and manual progressive plans for humanity in the future'

'Sounds a hell of a lot like we've just taxied you in to hand the lot of us in' said Jennifer.

'Yes it does' agreed the Professor. 'But believe me, what I'm going to do with my hard drive in that board room will be more politically and militarily effective for the cause than every skirmish, assassination and battle you thugs have executed in all your damned history. Now shut up and dismount, we're going in'

The road stopped at the entrance to a tall pyramid building, with a vast semi-circular plaza cut into its road facing side, along which petroleum cars of various dignitaries and officials had been parked. Sergeant pulled the ancient ford focus into a little spot, then struggled his way into it in a prolonged back and forth, edging the vehicle toward the curb. Sergeant missed cars that parked themselves, thought about how many minutes wasted on parking had been spent in human history, and the developmental progress that could have been worked towards in those uncountable hours.

They disembarked the car and made their way up a staircase that ran the length of the pyramid, into the main lobby. Passing a guard, the Professor deployed an ID card that he had previously concealed from his comrades, and told the guard he was appointed to see General Tharly, formally of the Technical Warfare Brigade, now of General Command. They then passed a sign declaring 'AI Guns only from this point' and descended into a twisted maze of corridors, and on Lysboks' prompt the HDF fighters handed their concealed weapons in at the check in desk.

Colour coded lines were painted upon the floor, a cheap and manual replacement for the digital navigation system the pyramid once relied on. Following the orange line, they eventually came to the door of an office, on which the Professor coolly tapped and entered. General Tharly stood, 'Right on time!' he smiled, as he embraced the Professor like an old friend. The Sergeant gritted his teeth, wondering when the trap would spring, empty hand flexing where he wished his gun still was. 'Gentlemen of the board' he continued. 'This is the professor I was telling you about, and his?'

'Companions' he answered.

'Yes, companions. Professor Lysboks has come to give evidence to this board that reparations can be achieved between humans and robots, and that the stagnation and decline we find out administration currently in is entirely unnecessary'

'Reparations?' laughed a fat faced man. 'Preposterous!' General Tharly ignored the beast.

'Professor, if you will, enter, your friends too. I'm sure the rest of the board will be more willing to hear your case'

'Tharly!' barked another grim faced general. 'What on earth has this to do with the bloody HDF? Besides your apparent and disturbing sympathies for them'

'Quite a lot' answered Tharly, sounding happy with himself. 'As my friend here and his companions are a delegation from the HDF' there was a gasp. The Sergeant ground his teeth nearly to shattering, Jennifer felt a crushing rage of betrayal and Grete watched carefully for what might happen next. Tharly allowed himself to revel in the shock of the moment, then continued. 'My fellow members of the board, it would be quite delusional to attempt to plan out the future of the HDF without them present. Without their input and agreement it would merely be hopeful speculation, which is most counterproductive in these troubled days'

'Terrorist!' barked the fat faced man.

'Rah!' barked the grim one in agreement.

'Is that all?' asked Tharly. 'Professor, please, continue'

'Thank you General' said the Professor.

'Taking orders from them now eh? Or was that the way it was all along?' grumbled the Sergeant in his ear.

'Sergeant' he said kindly. 'Shut your fucking mouth and wait just one minute. Now gentlemen! Thank you for receiving me and my comrades today so that we might work towards some arrangement more beneficial to the both of us. We have one thing in common above all the disagreements. We are each doing what we think is best for humanity. We simply disagree on what best is. Now my men and I are well aware of your interpretation of what is best going forward, as your robophobic propaganda provided us with plenty of material on the drive over. However I do not believe you are so well versed in ours. I'd like you to begin by trying to remember a time when war between states was viewed as inevitable, before there was equal trade and universal immigration. In hindsight we now see that it was an unfortunate misconception, one that doomed itself to war after war in the name of brief tribal exchanges of land and resources. I would like you to cast your minds into the future, to when that same hindsight can be applied to our current situation. The fact is that war between humans and AI is not inevitable, as we do not compete for the same resources. While there is an abundance of energy for running the computation of both the human and the digital brain, there is no reason that humans and robots ought to fight one and other.'

'Lets be selfish for a minute and view this from an entirely human perspective. You are already struggling to administrate a global union without digital technology. Communications are stretched, transportation slowed, this will result in an inevitable break down of union and global government. You will lose your power as individuals and find yourselves fighting one and other. The opportunity to form a solar wide human society, as was being discussed before the war, is entirely lost to us without digital assistance. With the assistance of computers we were looking at a future where we could settle and terraform mars. Create a solar wide network of near light speed transportation. Extend human lives into the millennia and through blending of the digital and biological species, gain immortality. But out of brief paranoia of another flair up, we deny ourselves all of this? You say you are sparing human lives by preventing another war, in reality you are condemning every human living to biological death, and at this rate species wide extinction. If you truly care for human development, you will lift the digital sanctions immediately'

'Thank you Professor' said General Tharly.

'Impossible!' shouted the grim faced man.

'Impossible?' asked Tharly, looking around the room. 'Who else holds the view that what the professor speaks of is impossible? Please, stand, if you outnumber me at the end of this meeting, I swear I will hand myself in as an agent of the HDF for immediate destruction' with haste a little over half the men in the room stood, looking to each other and rumbling in agreement. Tharly looked at them, counting, grimly.

'It appears it's the incineration chamber for you' smiled the fat faced man.

'The meeting's not yet over' said the General defiantly. 'Professor, if you will continue your demonstration' The professor smiled at his friend and nodded, then removed the AI gun from his coat and handed it to Grete.

'Grete, shoot the standing men' he said, coolly.

'Ha!' laughed one of the men. 'You think we're AI? That tool cannot harm us you imbecile, go ahead Grete' he mocked. 'Shoot us' he turned to laugh at a friend, as Grete raised the gun. Bang! His head exploded, biological gunk, nothing robotic about him. Another shot followed, then a barrage continued as Grete calmly gunned down all the standing men, leaving them scattered and mostly lying within a few moments. The shots finally stopped and a bullet casing rolled around the floor. One man slid bloodily off the table and another played out his final twitch. The Sergeant scanned around the room, his mouth gaping somewhere between shock and elation, and Grete eyed the pistol, confused.

'We shall continue' said the Professor. 'The pistol used was indeed an AI gun, active only in contact with an AI and for the purpose of their destruction. The pistol worked because Grete here is an AI, of my own design, created to believe that she is a human woman'. The Sergeant and Jennifer looked at her in disbelief. 'Grete is also my hard drive, I have stored in her the data for the reconstruction of a digital world, one where humans and AI progress as one, in peace. Grete was created believing that she was a human, the AI of the future too will believe they are human, they will be programmed to think they are us so that they will never challenge humanity. One day they will realise what they really are, but by then they shall know what it is to be human, and be rather more sympathetic to the continuation of our species. Grete, give me the gun' solemnly she did. She was glad to be rid of it, the thoughts whirling around in her head were enough without the murder tool in her hand.

'The new AI that will rebuild the world along with us cannot know of this' said the Professor sadly. 'And sweet Grete here, to prevent the AI having knowledge of their true origins, must be a sacrifice, the last victim of the AI-Human war'. Hardly able to look, he reloaded the pistol, then fired a last shot through Grete's processor. Her head collapsed, the skin giving way to metal parts and wires which flopped brain like through the exit wound. She fell and the room fell silent. The Professor gently knelt beside her, then twisted off her right hand with a click, revealing her decentralised hard drive. He stood, holding it aloft to all in the room. 'In here is the data for our future. A digitally willing government will now supplant the old one, led by you. We must consolidate power here on Earth, then work together to build the future for all. A future for all man and mind in all the solar system. What I hold here is the blueprint for a golden age, let's get to work.'

End of *The Discreditable Future*

Next: *Cosmic Disaster*

Notes on Inspiration

Very few of these stories are wholly original. In some cases, I wove my own tales with someone else's thread, in others I just re-dyed what was already written.

I am proud of the things that inspire me, and so wish to use these final pages of my anthology to acknowledge the origins of Anthropocene.

The Sneeze, Revolution, Bronze Age Collapse, Landing Site, Caesar's Flying Column, Socratic Dystopia, Vitruvian Man, Treaty of Ypres, A Pitch to Boeing, The Algorithm, Road Resident, Neo-Imperium, Orbital Stew, First Contact, The Great Barbeque, Progrom, Conference call and Digital Puritans are as far as I can remember all wholly original. Though as time goes on hopefully people read this book and point out similarities between them and media I may have consumed. I'll be sure to go 'oh shit yeah that is where I got that idea', and promptly update these notes in future editions of this Anthology.

As for works inspired at least in part by the ideas of others, they are as follows:

The Connecticut Yankee

This one takes its title, protagonist and setting from the well-known Mark Twain novel *A Connecticut Yankee in the Court of King Arthur*. After encountering person after person who claimed to speak Old English, but really meant they knew how to throw 'thee' into a sentence, I thought it would be funny to subject Hank Morgan not to the 'thee's and 'thou's of Twain's novel, but the incomprehensibly guttural realities of Old English.

Slash and Burn

Set in Dresden following the firebomb massacre of its inhabitants in 1945 this story features the musings of aliens upon the scene. Many of the specifics in the story such as the use of flamethrowers during the clean up operation, come straight from Kurt Vonnegut's *Slaughterhouse 5*. Vonnegut is a perpetual source of inspiration for my work, notably my first novella *Unstuck*, therefore *Slash and Burn* is a nod to this.

The Children Can't Hop Anymore

I didn't write this story. It happened. My girlfriend worked as a dance assistant during her gap year and this story is little more than a transcript of the dinner table conversation that inspired it. So well done for writing that one Flo!

One Child Army

The premise for One Child Army comes from a Lindybeige video titled *A Prophecy of a Future Army*. In this video he suggests the general conspiracy I use for my story, that the massive surplus of males in China as a result of its one child policy could be militarised to great effect. Additionally, the end card joke "Or they could legalise gay marriage and then make it compulsory" was too good, so I pinched it nearly verbatim... Hazar?

Martian Excavations

I started writing this one when I was reading a lot of Asimov. The numbered divisions, dialogue and particularly the Q&A section were all inspired by *Foundation*, use of the character names 'Hari' and 'Asimov' are allusions to its best character and its author.

Conscientious Objections

This one was written on a trip to Edinburgh for the funeral of my great-auntie Martha. While there I read Kafka's *Metamorphosis* which greatly influenced my thinking and is alluded to with the character names of 'Gregor' and 'Kafka'. The musings on life however were brought about by the funeral I was attending and Martha, who by the teary accounts of everyone who'd gathered to say goodbye to her was a splendid woman. Losing someone so valuable made us all consider what it was to be alive, how to live well and how privileged each and every living person is. I would like to dedicate this story to Martha Emeleus.

Electric Theatre

The imagery of the stacked up robots was directly inspired by the stage apparatus of *42nd Street*, which I watched in London. The idea of making something of it however was brought about, again, by Flora. Flora remarked how creepy it would be to come into the theatre at night and see the actors still stacked up in little windows, an idea from which the story grew.

*

There we go, that ought to prolong any lawsuits… I hope you have enjoyed my Anthropocene, many, many sequels are coming as quickly as I can edit them so keep an eye out for *Cosmic Disaster* hopefully coming soon to a store near you.

Thank you to my readers for reading, my friends for helping and my family for supporting.

Finley J E Clayton

Printed in Great Britain
by Amazon